Wood's Relic:
An Early Mac Travis Adventure

STEVEN BECKER

* * *

Join my mailing list
and get a free copy of Wood's Ledge
http://mactravisbooks.com

Chapter 1

The only thing separating the two men was two feet of water. Wood struggled with the wheel and throttle, fighting the wind to keep the barge as close to the seawall as possible. If he could have reached Eli Braken, he would have strangled him. As it was, he could only hold the piece of hydraulic hose in his hand.

"Somebody cut this. It didn't just blow."

"You're drunk again, Wood. Hell, it's barely past noon!" Braken yelled into the wind. "I need you to get this job back on track, or I'm pulling the plug on your contract and cutting you loose."

Wood put his head down. He was standing at the helm of the fifty-foot steel barge, shirtless, his overalls covered in grease. *What the hell did a few drinks matter?* He was working his butt off to get the bridge section rebuilt. Desperate to pay his bills after his insurance company had cancelled his policy, he was forced to take smaller less profitable jobs, instead of bidding the larger projects that required bonding. The deepwater span he was working on between Big Pine and No Name Key had been damaged by a wayward boat blown loose from its mooring. A casualty of Hurricane Andrew. The insurance company had blamed the failure of the span on his construction, further infuriating him. "I'll get 'er done, Braken. You know I always do."

"You always *did* you mean," Braken said. "I get that you can't get bonded, and you're mad at the world, but I'm giving you work here. The insurance companies are screwing everyone, not just you, to try and recover their losses from the storm. I'm sorry this came down on you." Braken leaned into the wind, hands on hips, wanting to end the conversation. "You know if it was just me I would cut you some slack, but I've got investors on this project that are busting my balls."

Wood was not placated. "This wind's killing me. No way I can work in these conditions. How 'bout we meet at your office, and I can get that draw you owe me." Losing his insurance in the wake of the storm had been bad luck. Damned adjustors, blaming his work when a stray boat had crashed into the bridge pile. Every other project he'd built in the last twenty years had survived the storm unscathed. This one bridge section was the only failure, and that had been due to a boat, not the construction. Now without the ability to bid the larger projects he was known for, his equipment sat idle, and so did the payment books stacked on his desk at home. He thought about the money now past due to the IRS — for withholding taxes on his employees prior to the storm — and clenched his fists. Of course, to make matters worse, the bank had been notified by the insurance company and cancelled his line of credit.

Without waiting for an answer, he pulled back on the throttle and the two engines went into reverse, pulling him away from the seawall. The barge coasted back to the deeper water, where he found a section large enough to turn the twenty foot beam and headed south toward Bogie Channel which led to his mooring in Spanish Harbor. Braken stood on the seawall, hands on hips, glaring at him.

Water crashed over the low freeboard as the barge moved slowly through the building chop. The rig was dangerous in this kind of water; a John Deere excavator sat on the bow and a shipping container on the stern. The twenty-by-fifty steel hull floated on two pontoons, with a Mercury 115hp engine mounted on each one. Two cylindrical steel spuds, used to anchor the barge, projected twenty feet into the air. A big wave over any quarter could upset the top-heavy craft causing it to capsize.

Wood entered Spanish Harbor and approached the mooring ball. He judged the current wrong on the first pass, and had to circle around, his small aluminum john boat swinging from a line tied to the large white ball. He lined up again and moved forward on the ball, this time setting the engines in neutral earlier, allowing the barge to coast to a stop at the buoy. He grabbed the free line with a fishing gaff and threaded the thicker line from the barge through its eye. Once secure, the barge drifted around the buoy and stopped, bobbing in the swells.

He shut down the engines, drank the last quarter from the beer in the cup holder, and headed for the john boat. As he secured the barge and hopped into the skiff he hoped he could get enough money out of Braken to get his bond reinstated and go back to bidding real work.

* * *

"Whada ya mean you're not going to pay me?" Wood slurred.

"You better listen to my words. I'll pay you when you catch up to the schedule. You're three weeks behind now. This is costing me money. I can't show the properties on No Name until you finish the bridge."

"What's the rush? There's no power on that hump of coral. How you gonna sell that crap? Anyone around here knows it's about as worthless as tits on a boar."

Braken didn't answer, and the smile on his face was enough to push Wood to the edge. He stood and closed the space to the desk trying to force the response he sought. The small deposit Braken had given him when he started was barely enough to cover the materials he had bought.

After losing the line of credit his cash flow was non existent. Braken had been around construction long enough to know that you had to grease the wheels to get things done. If he wanted the job finished he needed to write a check. With some cash he could hire help and finish the job. As it was there were few skilled workers left, most having gone to Miami where the storm's damage had created a shortage of workers and raised wages. He was left with what he could find and they often insisted on being paid every day. The only help he had was old Ned, who was good company, but too old to do much work.

Wood stared him down. "This is *your* schedule. It's not in my contract, and I didn't sign off on it. There's no weather allowance in here either." He slammed his hand down on the desk. "Never done a job down here without a weather allowance. Look at it out there." He shifted his gaze from the desk, past Braken, and to the window at the bent over palm trees. "It's blowing more than twenty knots, and there's no work when the winds are that high. Been like that for as long as I've been in this game."

"Maybe," Braken said, "but my investors write the checks, and they don't give two shits about the weather. Just get it done."

Wood snarled. "I got problems here, and you're one of them. And remember, I gave you some slack on the change orders last time you started crying about your investors. Now, that old pier holding the bridge strut has got to be replaced down to bedrock. That's going to take some blasting and excavation. Then I'm gonna have to find somewhere to dump the debris. Can't leave it there." Now he regretted not being more proactive documenting changes. Some contractors made their living bidding work at cost and counting on the inevitable change orders for their profit. That wasn't his style, and he had given Braken a rock bottom price just to get the work.

Braken leaned back, as if he was deep in thought. "OK. I'll go to my investors with that. I can get you something if it'll get you moving. But you gotta get it done."

"You give me ten grand and I'll have it done in a week,"

Wood boasted, unsure whether he could really finish it without finding a diver and some equipment. The weather report didn't look favorable either, but he'd do whatever it took to get his hands on some cash; whatever promises he had to make, he would. He cursed his pride for getting in the way of his sense.

"Done." Braken went for his checkbook, and started writing slowly. "If this isn't done, there are going to be repercussions. Do you understand me?"

Wood didn't answer. He grabbed the check from Braken's hand, turned, and went out the door. A glance at his watch showed 4:45; he would have to move to get to the bank and cash the check. A list formed in his head as he allocated the money, hoping nothing else would go wrong. With any luck this draw would get the job finished and pay some of the bills growing dust on his desk.

Rain lashed at him as he made his way to the beat up Datsun pickup. The door squealed on its hinges as it opened. He jumped in and slammed it. The motor started, he rubbed the foggy windshield with an old rag sitting on the dash board, cracked the windows, turned on the wipers, and started out of the parking lot. Traffic was slow, the rain decreasing visibility to barely a car length. When he finally reached the bank, he got out and ran for the entry.

Once inside he waited impatiently while the single teller worked slowly through a transaction. Finally it was his turn and he approached the window. The teller looked at the damp check, as if waiting for the ink to disappear. "Give me a minute. I have to get Mr. Bailey."

"What for? I've known you since you were knee high to a tire."

"It's a lot of cash. More than my limit." She locked her cash drawer and went toward the back office.

Wood waited impatiently until she returned with the manager.

"What's up, Bill?"

"Mr. Woodson. Can you come back to my office?"

"What's this Mr. Woodson crap?"

"Come on, Wood." They moved toward the back of the bank and entered the sparse office, then sat opposite of each other. Bailey put his hands on the desk. "Look, Wood. I've got to hold this against your line of credit. You know the bank called it in." He stayed stoic, waiting for the outburst.

"Goddamn bankers and insurance men will see me to my grave. Look, Bill, you know the deal — I'm never going to be able to pay that back if I can't work. This here check is working capital."

Bailey looked at the check. "It's drawn on the bank across the street." He handed the check back to Wood. "Take it over there and cash it. They'll have to honor it. I never saw it." He winked.

"'Preciate that, Bill," Wood got up and went for the door. "I owe you one for this."

He walked toward the door with his head low, as if he had done something wrong. Ignoring the rain, he walked across the street and several minutes later, he emerged from the other bank with a wad of cash in his pocket. Back in the truck, he reached under the seat for the bottle stashed there. He leaned over and took a long draw off the bourbon before putting the cap on and starting the engine. The gears ground as he released the clutch.

The truck weaved down US1, passing the airport on his right as he headed south. Rain banged on the hood of the truck, the wipers running full out but not making a dent in the increasing torrent. With no visibility, he was forced to slow down and pull off onto the shoulder to wait out the storm joining the other cars that had already taken refuge off the same embankment. Reaching under the seat for the bottle, he drained it while he waited. He had just ducked below the dashboard to stash the empty bottle when a knock on the windshield startled him.

"Hey, man. Can I get a ride up the road?"

"I ain't your man, and I'm going down the road not up."

"Sorry. Just looking for a ride to Key West," the stranger

said as he stooped slightly to show his face.

Wood was about to tell him to get lost when he spied the Scuba Pro dive fins sticking out of his backpack. "You ever do any commercial diving?"

"Yeah, man. I'm actually down here looking for work. Got certified in Galveston, and worked on some oil rigs out there. My girlfriend got tired of it and—"

"I didn't ask for your resume. Get on out of the rain." He waited while the stranger tossed his bag in the back of the truck and came around to the passenger door.

When the guy got in the truck, he stuck out his hand. "Mac Travis."

"Well, Mac, whatever, you work for me now." Black smoke erupted from the tailpipe as the truck coughed and died. Finally, on the third try, the engine kicked to life, and Wood accelerated onto the wet pavement. He hit the gas, seeming not to notice as a truck swerved out of the right lane to avoid contact.

"Think maybe I should drive?" Mac asked.

"I want you to do something, I'll ask." The slip stream from a passing semi pushed the smaller truck onto the shoulder, and Wood overcorrected, hitting the curb. He stopped the truck and slumped forward. "In fact, it's been a long day. You can take it from here."

Wood got out of the truck, leaving the door open as he went to the passenger side and waited for Mac to get out. They drove in silence, Wood giving directions to his house, and after a couple minutes, Mac pulled into a driveway, which sat between a stilt house off to one side and a larger garage on the other. Beyond the buildings he could see a seawall and dock.

Wood looked over at Mac. "Bring your stuff. You can stay here with my daughter and me for a bit. Don't look like you have too many options."

"Thank you, sir," Mac said as he got out of the truck, grabbed his bag from the back and slung it over his shoulder.

"Ever call me sir again, I'll clock you upside the head." Wood led the way up the stairs, Mac following behind with the large bag over his shoulder. He waited patiently, watching Wood stumble several times before he reached the front door, which opened just as he reached out his hand.

"Dad, not again," the teenage girl said.

Wood rose. "Melanie, don't give me no lip. It's been a bad day."

"And who's this you dragged home?"

"Huh, oh... Name's Travis or something. He's going to be staying with us until he can get situated."

"Well hello, whoever you are, and thanks for getting him home, but I think you need to find somewhere else to camp out." She yanked Wood into the house.

Wood turned toward the open door. "Sit tight for a minute. I'll at least offer you a beer." He turned and went inside, Mel following behind. In the kitchen, he opened the refrigerator door and took out two beers. "Listen, don't take me for no fool. Just 'cause you're seventeen and all, doesn't mean you know everything." He popped one of the tops. "Did you see the dive fins sticking out of his pack?" He didn't wait for an answer. "No, because you were too busy criticizing me. Now, turns out he's a commercial diver. Think that might come in handy to have close by?"

"It scares me to have a stranger living here. You don't even know his name."

"Point is, girl, there won't be a *here* to live in if we can't get this job done, and that old boy there could be exactly what we need." He went back to the door without waiting for an answer, turning toward her before he opened it. "Set him up in the guest room." He yanked open the door and handed Mac the beer. "Welcome home."

Chapter 2

"Cody, come in here. Did you hear a damn word I said?" Bracken sat behind his desk, waiting for him to enter. He cringed when the door slammed behind him and waited for him to approach. "All I asked you to do was to keep an eye on them. That's it. I know you cut that hose on his excavator and shut him down yesterday." His son stood in front of him, head down, taking the scolding like he always did. Sooner or later Braken hoped the boy would grow up. Hell, he was already in his twenties and had a kid. He just couldn't get his head out of his ass. What was he thinking, sabotaging Wood's equipment? How was that helping to get the bridge done? The opening of lobster season, just days away, would bring hordes of tourists to the area, a prime time to start showing his new development and sell some lots. After the next few weeks he would have to wait for the snowbird migration in December to sell anything. Looking at his son he shook his head. Sometimes the boy just did things for spite without thinking and this was one of those times.

"What do you mean keep an eye on them? I thought you said we were going to put that old man out of business once and for all."

"Son, you need to think." He must have said something offhand about putting Wood out of business and Cody had misinterpreted it. "Unfortunately, we need him. And watch the old man line. He's the same as me, forty-eight, just rode hard and put up wet. There's nobody south of Miami we can get to fix that bridge in a week besides Wood. If I could find somebody else, trust me, I would. I just need to know he's getting the job done."

Cody turned to go. "All right. If that's what you want."

Braken turned to his phone. "Nicole!" he yelled.

"She's not here," Cody said on his way out.

"What do you mean?" He looked at his fake Rolex, frowning. "It's almost ten."

"Yeah, she's probably still asleep. Had to work late at the bar last night."

Braken looked at him. "We need to talk about that. There's no need for her to work two jobs to support your sorry ass."

"Well, set me up with some more charters, then." Cody stormed out.

Braken left his office and went to the Rolodex on the reception desk. Finding the number he wanted, he retreated back to his office and closed the door behind him. Grateful that Cody was gone, he paused for a minute before dialing. Already a month behind schedule, and now a pier had to be replaced before he could use the bridge. He was going to need all his wits to satisfy his investors.

If he could just get the bridge open, he could start selling lots. Treasure Cove was almost through the rigorous approval process. The for sale signs for the fourteen lots were ready to be stuck in the ground, he just needed the bridge repaired to start showing the new development. Then the money would start rolling in. His investors had bigger plans to put a Casino on the island and he sat back thinking that if they could actually pull it off, he would be set for life. If not, he would be happy with the development he had planned.

He just needed Wood to do his damn job.

He dialed, sat back, and waited. Relieved when the

answering machine picked up, he left a message and sank deep into his chair.

* * *

Mac was getting anxious. He liked to start early. It was only ten o'clock, and he could see several thunderheads forming. The weather here was the same as on the Texas coast with thunderstorms prevalent on early summer afternoons, and from the look of the sky, today would be no different. They had just left the dock fifteen minutes ago.

Mac studied the route as Wood steered, trying to remember the turns through the canals, but quickly became disoriented. Finally, the skiff pulled up to a large barge. Mac reached for the nylon line floating from the mooring buoy, tied off the small boat, then tossed his bag onto the steel platform and stepped onto the barge. Wood struggled with the balance of the smaller craft as he handed two steel SCUBA cylinders over to Mac and joined him aboard the floating work platform.

Wood went forward to the helm. "Untie us and let's get it on. See if you can dive or not."

The engines fired, and the barge moved out of Spanish Harbor and into Bogie Channel. They coasted up to the old pier. "Yo, boyo, drop the hook."

Mac went forward and tossed the anchor over the bow, the line slipping between his hands until he felt the steel grab coral.

"Get suited up. I'd wear a three mil wetsuit if I was you. No telling what kind of stuff you'll find down there that'll cut you to shreds."

Minutes later, Mac was in the water struggling as the current pulled him away from the pier. Hoping it would be calmer on the sea floor, he released the air from his BC and descended to the bottom. Visibility was low, maybe five feet, thanks to the current stirring up the sand. Carefully he inflated the BC with enough air to hang two feet over the bottom, checked his compass, and followed the bearing toward the invisible pier. It came into view, and he swam to it. With a gloved hand, he released the line clipped to his weight belt and worked it around the concrete base. Holding the line would allow him to observe the pier without having to waste energy fighting the current.

The pier showed every bit of its age. From the brief history lesson Wood had given him on the way out, the original bridge connecting Big Pine Key and No Name Key was built in 1928. Although the bridge was rebuilt in 1967, after being wiped out by a hurricane in 1948, this pier looked to be from the original construction. He could see the coral shells embedded in the decaying concrete — a sure sign of its age. The concrete was probably mixed by hand with local sand and coral; not brought in by truck from a plant.

Rusted steel was visible, clearly not the epoxy coated ribbed rebar the construction companies used now. This was smoother, probably coming from discarded railroad ties. In some areas, water was flowing freely into the crevices around the embedded steel, advancing the decay. This condition, known as spalling was in an advanced state and he could tell the pier was failing.

He left the line in place and surfaced, allowing the current to slide him back toward the barge. Wood grabbed the tank valve and helped pull him aboard. He was surprised by the strength of the older man. If he hadn't needed the protection of the wetsuit below, he was thankful for it now as he was pulled against the rough metal hull.

"Well. Assess the situation."

"Bad. Concrete's old, really old. Probably from the original bridge. Steel's rusted and exposed — not rebar, maybe railroad ties."

"Good work." Wood sniffed the air. "Beer thirty," he said as he went for the cooler. "Have to think on this."

Mac stripped out of the wetsuit and let the sun warm his body as he watched Wood sip on the beer.

"Reckon we could excavate around the old one, build a cofferdam and pour a new pier around it? Have to take out some material to get to bedrock." He paused as if running some calculations in his head. "Won't hurt to encase the old pier. As long as we can drop a steel cage around it. It'll be faster and easier than having to shore up the whole bridge, demo the old pier, and pour a new one." Satisfied with his solution, he drained the beer and went for the excavator.

Mac looked over at the old man sitting in the chair at the helm, sipping a beer, and wondered if he really had the balls to do this on the fly. He had always had professionals spec out the work. "Don't we need to get an engineer …"

"Son, I *am* an engineer. Don't look like one, I know; no pocket protector or calculator. Got a degree after my Naval service."

Mac was shocked. Maybe he did have the qualifications, but the beer couldn't be doing much for his math. "Maybe we should put this on paper. Get a second opinion."

Wood reached for another beer. "This here's bridge building, not rocket science. You build a foundation on bedrock, weld a steel cage, and pour concrete. Only options are how the size of the footings, steel size and spacing. I've built enough bridges around here to know the safety factor. Hell, they all made it through the storm except this one, and damn if it wasn't struck by a boat."

Mac felt slightly better. His training as a commercial diver had certified him to weld steel cages underwater. If that was all they needed to do, perhaps it would work out after all. "What's our next step?"

"What's got your panties in a wad? Let me finish my beer, then we'll move onto phase two."

Mac sat in silence, slowly eating a gas station sub sandwich and sipping a Coke. He finished, glanced over at Wood, and checked the pressure gauge on the tank. With 2,000 PSI left, he felt comfortable going back into the seventeen-foot-deep water. The barge was close enough that he could easily make it back if he ran low. He was about to suit up again when Wood interrupted.

"No need for that yet. I'm gonna dig some, and then let you have a look at what's going on below the silt." He crushed the empty can and tossed it aside, then glared at a boat in the distance. "Damn if that ain't Cody Braken out there, acting like he's fishing. Ain't no fish in that hole. Old man must have sent him to keep an eye on us." He reached into the cooler.

"I'll run the excavator, if you want. You can direct me where you want me to dig." Mac said, not wanting a confrontation, but was pretty sure Wood was through the better part of a six pack.

"Damn, boy, you're becoming useful. Where'd you learn how to run equipment?"

"My dad had a road building outfit in Galveston. Used to work for him after school." Mac went to the excavator sitting on the bow of the barge and climbed into the cab, but Wood put a hand up.

"Hold on, son. I've got to drop the spuds, or we'll capsize." He went toward the stern and released the safety pins from the steel cylinders suspended in casings on each side of the barge. Back at the helm, he flipped a switch, and a winch started to lower the starboard spud. The barge shook as the weight hit the bottom. He repeated the same procedure on the port side, and gave Mac a thumbs up.

Mac started tentatively, getting a feel for the old machine. Once sure of the controls, he looked to Wood for guidance before lowering the bucket into the water. Wood pointed to the spot he wanted and made a digging motion with his hands. The water splashed as the bucket entered, and Mac extended the boom until he could feel resistance. He manipulated the controls, coaxing the bucket to make a scooping motion, and returned it to the surface. Water drained from the holes bored through the bucket, and Mac looked at Wood, who motioned him to dump the rocky load on the center of the deck. Mac repeated the process around all four sides of the pier, then climbed down from the machine.

"Want me to go have a look?"

"Yeah, but you might want to wait a few and let the silt settle. It's pretty close to slack tide now."

Mac went over to check his equipment, watching Wood as he grabbed another beer and started kicking around the pile of rubble on the deck. He watched as he went to the wheelhouse and started uncoiling a hose looped on a peg. "Don't just sit there with your jaw hangin'," the old man muttered. "Give me a hand."

Wood directed Mac to the hookup, while he screwed a high-pressure nozzle onto the one inch thick hose. Once the hose was secured at both ends, he went to the helm and turned on the pump. Seawater gurgled off the stern as the pump sucked in the raw water and pushed it out the nozzle. He started hosing the top first, and working his way down toward the deck, the silt flying from the coral. "Look here, boy, maybe you'll learn something. See this here?" He picked up a chunk of coral near the bottom of the pile. "It's had water running over it for years; looks like a river rock." He picked up a piece from the top. "This here, you just broke off. You can see how clean it is where it just fractured."

"What's that sticking out of it?" Mac asked.

"If you'd just let me finish." Wood held the piece out. "Hmm, looks like wood and a piece of metal — maybe copper. But it's embedded in the rock, like the rock grew around it. Must be older than old, 'cause it was undisturbed when they dug back in '28."

Mac wanted a better look, but Wood pulled it back. "Should be clear down there now. I can have another look."

"Not alone, you're not. I'm going with you." Wood went toward the container on the stern and returned with dive gear and a light.

Minutes later, they were both in the water. Mac swam toward the old pier first. He used his hands and flapped them back and forth to mimic fins, trying to tell Wood to be careful, and not allow his fins too close to the bottom, as it would stir the silt that had just settled. Wood flipped his middle finger back. They moved closer to the pier. Barnacles and other growth reached down to where the bottom had been before they excavated, like a tide line on a piling. Mac had to remove several large rocks to totally uncover the old pier. The original builders had built a buttressed concrete column, dug into the coral sea bed. A steel I beam projected toward the surface, surrounded by newer concrete. Mac thought back on the history of the bridge and guessed the rebuild in 1967 had reinforced the existing piers and beams, instead of replacing them. After years in the saltwater, the steel was in questionable condition. The footing was completely uncovered, showing what looked to be jackhammered coral encasing the concrete.

Wood waved the light toward their excavation, moving it to indicate which rocks needed to be moved. He examined them as they were tossed aside. After moving several boulders, Mac realized his heart was pounding and instinctively checked his air. The needle was well into the red, somewhere around two hundred PSI. Signaling that his air was low, he inflated his BC and surfaced.

Back on the boat, he waited for Wood, one eye on the light shining below the surface and the other on the thunderhead closing in on them. The storm was moving closer and he realized Wood was unaware of the pending danger. He looked around the deck, found a piece of steel pipe, and took it forward where he started banging on the hull.

A long minute later, Wood's head appeared. He spat the regulator from his mouth. "What the hell? I got plenty of air."

Mac pointed to the sky just as the first drops of rain steamed off the sunbaked deck, then helped Wood back on board and took the tank from his back.

The old man grunted. "I'll give you that one. Probably a good call on the weather. Got someone I need to talk to, anyway."

Chapter 3

Wood sat in the corner seat at the bar, a glass of bourbon, neat, in front of him. Mac stood by him, drinking a beer.

He turned to an older man next to him. "Ned, this here's Travis. Found him by the side of the road, but he can dive and run equipment, so I may keep him around."

The two men acknowledged each other. All three were huddled in the corner, studying the lump of coral sitting on the scarred wooden bar top.

"That's it? Piece of driftwood sticking out of coral. Ain't the first time I've seen that," Ned said.

"Put your glasses on," Wood scolded him.

Ned took the reading glasses from his pocket and buffed them clean with the tail of his shirt. He placed them on his nose and took the coral in his hand. "Hmm. Now this is interesting," he said as he rotated the piece.

"Like I said. That ain't natural, and it's damned old." Wood recounted the excavation in as much detail as he could. "Didn't really get a good look at it until we got back. Big 'ol storm drove us in early."

"Can't figure what kind of wood it is. Doesn't look native. That looks like a piece of roughly worked copper, or maybe bronze. Lucky the corral grew around it before the seawater got to it. Unusual." Ned handed it back to Wood.

"That's it? You're supposed to be the expert on wrecks around here."

"It's pre Columbian, not Spanish, I can tell you that. The only wood not rotted out from those wrecks is the oak they used to lay their keels and sections of the larger pine masts, but I can tell you this isn't pine or oak. And the copper … No, not Spanish, or even European."

"Well, got any ideas?" Wood asked pulling the relic towards him as the barmaid came down the bar.

* * *

"What are those two old men doing down there?" Cody whispered.

"I don't know. They've got a lump of coral they're looking at." Nicole leaned over the bar top.

"Why don't you swing your sweet ass down there and see what they're up to. Dad told me to keep an eye on them. I'm pretty sure they brought that up from the old bridge pier today." He looked her over and gestured to her top. "Think you can cover up some of that? You know, we *are* married, kid and all."

"It's just for tips." She dismissed his concern and moved toward the other end of the bar, where the three men were still huddled around the rock. "Wood, you boys need anything else?" She wiggled flirtatiously.

"Another round, sweetheart."

"Sure thing." She quickly returned with a beer for Mac, another refills for Wood and Ned. "What'cha got there?" She eyed the rock.

"Oh, it's nothing," Ned replied.

Her twenty-two-year-old eyes had seen the glint of metal, though. Having been raised here she had heard all the stories of the Keys being a graveyard for Spanish ships running treasure back to Europe. Most was just talk, but once in a while someone actually recovered something valuable enough to keep the legends alive. Any mention of treasure got on the residents' radar quickly and she wondered if this was something to take note of. "It's pretty. Can I have a look?" She pushed her breasts towards them.

Wood started to pull it away from her, but she was faster. She handled it gingerly, taking it to the back bar, where the light was better. The men were staring at her, anxious for her return. "Here you go. Guess you're right — kind of cool looking, but not treasure."

Cody was waiting impatiently when she returned. "Nothing but a piece of wood. There was a small piece of metal, though. Didn't look like much to me."

"And you're the freakin' expert? Go back down there and see what they're up to."

"I got work to do. I don't have time for super secret Cody spy missions." A group of jovial fishermen came in and she adjusted her top down to reveal a little more skin, just to piss him off.

* * *

"Cody's down at the other end of the bar. Bet he sent her down here to see what we're looking at. Besides, she knows you're a cheap son of a bitch. Flashing those boobs at you like she was going to get a tip. Don't be so naive, man," Ned said.

"Probably showing off for the boy here." Wood glanced back at Mac.

"Well, whatever. Now Cody knows you found something, and you know he's already been watching you. Boy's an ass, but he's not an idiot. He knows where that came from."

"So, what about it?"

"You think there's something else there, you better get out now and go look. Tonight, he'll sit on that bar stool, drink, and watch that woman of his flirt all night. No one will be watching if you go now. He's sure to be shadowing you in the morning. "

Wood gulped his drink, downing it in one swallow. "Maybe that's not such a bad idea." He turned around. "Travis, you got any night diving experience?" He got up slowly and staggered toward the door. "Ned, pay the bill, and leave the girl's tip."

Mac followed warily, and turned to Ned before he left. "Can he really function like this? I've been with him all day, and there's at least a twelve pack in him plus the shots."

Ned shook his head, "Sad to see. That was once a strong, proud man. Built half the bridges in Monroe County. Now, 'cause he's got no insurance, he can't even bid jobs anymore."

Mac let the two men walk in front of him through the bar. As they headed toward the pickup he quickened his pace to reach the driver's door before Wood could attempt it. "We need air if you want to dive. There were two tanks; mine's empty, and the other can't have much left, either."

"Son, I don't suck air like a rookie. I guarantee there's enough in my tank for another dive."

Mac reached the truck first and climbed into the driver's seat, watching Wood as he reluctantly went for the passenger door. On the drive back to the house, he thought about the dive. Looking over at Wood, he saw he had his head on the window, maybe passed out.

The last day had been interesting. Wood's drinking alarmed him, but the work suited him and the allure of their find had him intrigued. With the better part of a tank left he thought about going down tonight and having a look without Wood. Working on oil rigs required him to dive regardless of visibility. It would be dangerous, but he was comfortable diving at night.

Ned sat between them in the crowded cab, and leaned toward Mac. "You know we can probably get Mel to put him to bed, and he'll have forgotten about this whole deal by morning."

Mac thought for a minute. "No, we said we were going to do it. Let's just make it quick." He pulled into the driveway. "See if you can get him moving. I'll get my gear and meet you at the skiff." The door opened as he turned to head up the stairs.

"What are you all up to? Ned, is that you? And where's Dad?" Mel asked as she walked onto the deck.

"It's all good," Ned responded. "We're going to head out to the bridge and do a quick dive. Seems like they found something out there today that might need to stay quiet. Better to have a look around at night, if you catch my drift."

She turned to go back inside, and Mac followed her up the stairs. "He's drunk again, isn't he." It was a statement, not a question.

"I don't want to get into family business, but yeah, he's had a few."

"Then I'm going with you. Give me a minute to change."

Not sure what to do, Mac grabbed his bag and went downstairs. He told Ned about Mel's intentions, and he just nodded.

"Girl's a good diver," he said. "May be useful having her along. I'll go check on Wood."

After the gear was stowed on the boat Ned went back to the truck to get Wood. "He's out cold. Maybe we ought to just leave him there."

"I heard. Leave him there. He'll find his bed if he wakes up."Mel stood next to them, a gear bag slung over her shoulder.

"We only have one tank," Mac warned her.

"Come with me." She led him toward the storage building, opened the door, and turned on the light.

Mac was stunned to see the assortment of equipment and gear. He followed her to a small compressor with several hoses coming from it, with regulators on their ends. "Hookah rig might be dangerous down there. That's a lot of hose to get snagged on something," he said.

"You said you were diving on the bridge. It's less than twenty feet at its deepest point. I'd free dive that if it was daylight.

If something happens, just spit the regulator out and head for the surface. Besides, without a tank, it's easier to move around down there, and that shallow we don't have a time limit."

Mac was impressed with her knowledge, but distressed by her cockiness. Over confidence was one of the biggest causes of dive accidents. "Fine. But we're just going to go check it out. Ten, fifteen minutes tops." He went for the compressor and carried it to the boat. She followed with the rest of the gear.

The water was glassy calm, the wind dying with the earlier storms. They cast off the lines and Ned steered the twenty-four-foot center. They had decided to take the larger boat for its array of lights; the barge would be cumbersome at night, and the skiff was too small. Once they were out of the canal, the green and red markers reflected the spotlights guiding them to the deep water channel parallel to Howe Key. Making a hard right at the point, he reversed course into the well-marked channel between Annette and Big Pine Keys.

"Tide's running out now. I'm going to nose up to the pier, and you throw the anchor as close as you can. If the visibility is bad, you can use the anchor line and follow it down."

Mac tossed the anchor against the pier. Ned waited for it to sink before he reversed the engine. Mac let fifty feet of line slip through his hands before he tied it around a cleat, and waited for the backwards momentum of the boat to set the hook. When he saw the bow swerve, a sure sign that the anchor had caught, he signaled Ned with a closed fist. Instead of shutting down the engines as he expected, though, Ned shifted back into forward and moved slowly toward the bridge.

"Take in some of the anchor line. She's hooked and I want to get right on top of it." He went to the port side and set out two fenders. "Swing the line to port and pull us as close as you can."

Mac did as he was told, wondering what the old man was up to. He was about to question him when the water below them lit up. Lights mounted under the hull shone all the way to the bottom.

Small bait fish schooled toward them, and several larger fish started to retreat into the darkness.

"Works good for lobstering," Ned said as he shut the engines down. "Now, let's get you guys in the water before someone sees us."

Mac and Mel put on mask and booties, but went sans fins to keep the silt down. Weight belts were strapped to their waists to compensate for the three-millimeter-thick wetsuits they had decided on, more for protection than warmth. Each grabbed a regulator and slid off the back of the boat. The boat lights illuminated the scene, the colors of the coral and sponges vibrant in the artificial light. Mac landed in the sand five feet from the pier, and gingerly walked to the structure, being careful not to stir up the sandy bottom. Mel met him at the pier. They went down on their bellies and started wafting sand away from the pier. Mac wondered if Wood had a dredge in his shed. A suction line would make short work of uncovering the remaining concrete. He put that in the back of his mind and continued.

Suddenly Mel grabbed his arm and motioned for the backup light he had clipped to his belt. He released it and handed it to her. The added light cut through the fine particles suspended in the water, revealing a longer piece of wood. Mac swam around to her side, motioning for her to hold the light while he tried to move the loose rocks away. With every rock he moved, the silt cloud became thicker and larger, finally causing them to lose all visibility. He touched her shoulder and signaled for them to surface.

"I can see that silt cloud from here. What are you two doing down there?"

Mac grabbed the transom to keep from sinking back to the bottom. "Something's there, all right. We're going to need some equipment to get at it, though." He moved back to allow Mel to board first, then grabbed the handle mounted on the transom, climbed the three steps of the dive ladder, and stepped onto the deck.

Chapter 4

Cody barged through the door, slamming it behind him, causing Braken's coffee cup to jump in his hand. He was barely agile enough to keep it from splashing his nylon shirt. "What the hell? The reason there's a door there is so you knock."

"Those guys are up to something," Cody blurted out. "They were in the bar last night — Wood, that new diver, and old Ned." He sat down in the chair next to the desk. "I saw them passing around something, so I sent Nicole down to check it out. She says it looked like a piece of coral with wood and a small piece of metal embedded in it."

"Slow down there." Braken sipped what remained of his coffee. "You were supposed to be watching them yesterday. What did you see?"

Cody told him about the dive and then the excavation. "Looked pretty much like what they should have been doing. Ended up with a pile of rock on the barge. My guess is they found it on the deck."

"Why don't you go out there and cover for your wife 'til she shows up. You can start by making some coffee. I've got to call some folks." Cody went toward the lobby, head down. "And close that door behind you."

Braken sat back and thought about what Cody had just told

him. An old hunk of wood with a piece of metal sticking out of it was hardly enough to call in Mel Fisher. Finally he picked up the phone, then deciding that unless the treasure hunt delayed the project, he didn't need to involve his partners, and set the phone down. Things were complicated enough satisfying the greed of the Jersey mob. "Cody, did you check the messages?"

"Huh?"

"Call that wife of yours and wake her up. I swear without a fishing rod in your hand, you're worthless. Once she gets her butt in here, why don't you go see what those guys are up to."

Cody walked back into the office. "You know, she works at night. Why do you have to be such a ball buster?"

"Why don't you find a job so she doesn't have to? I set all the charters I can up for you. But you've got a reputation. Half your customers love you, and the other half wouldn't set foot on a boat with you again if you paid them. Guess we know which half are the sober ones. Now go."

"You know it would be a lot easier for me to tell you what's going on if you got me one of those." Cody pointed to the cell phone standing upright on the desk.

"I said go."

Cody turned and left. Braken exhaled, feeling exhausted by the conversation, and picked up the phone again. He held it to his ear for a long minute. Finally a voice came on the line and he paused, listening to the response. "Yeah, I got him out there working. Had to pay a ten-thousand dollar advance yesterday for the new pier he had to pour." He listened again. "I know, but there's no way out of it." He held the phone away from his ear, but could still hear the man shouting. Finally, it stopped. "Yes, sir. I'll keep them on schedule. I'll let you know if there are any further delays."

He heard glass break as he set down the phone. "Cody! What the hell?"

"Sorry, I was on the way out the door when I forgot the

coffee. It just slipped."

"Never mind that." Braken got up and walked past the broken glass. "Nicole can clean up when she gets here. Serves her right for being so late. Get out there and give me a progress report. Come back and get me at noon. I want to check it out myself."

* * *

The color of the water was indescribable — the darkest indigo he could imagine, fading to black at some undisclosed depth. Mac looked over the side of the barge as Wood watched the Loran and depth finder.

"Now. Throw that sucker."

Mac tossed the buoy and watched it rotate on the surface, spinning as the lead weight took line wrapped around it to the bottom. He looked back at Wood, amazed that he didn't look hung over. Thankfully, he had showered. They had left at dawn, wanting to beat the wind and storms that were sure to brew later in the day.

The Spanish Harbor Bridge was behind them when the sun rose, and an hour later they arrived off the deep side of the reef. They were anchored in eighty feet of water, and Wood was in the excavator, dumping the rocks and rubble they had loaded from the pier over the side while Mac used the high pressure hose to wash the deck.

"If you make the cut and I decide you're worth keeping around, I'll take you diving down there. My own reef. Been dumping rubble on this spot for years. Now get up there and pull the anchor."

The seas were still down and they made the five-mile run back to the bridge in forty-five minutes, going the maximum speed the barge could safely travel, the boat lighter without the rubble. Once under the bridge, Wood turned before the channel and went steered toward the boat ramp just west of Scout Key. As they coasted up to the ramp, Mac saw a ten-wheel flatbed truck standing by, loaded with lumber and steel. Wood inched the barge closer as the truck backed down.

"Good timing, old boy!" Wood yelled as Ned got out of the cab. He reversed the engines and turned the boat so it was stern in. "Drop those spuds!" Then he went for the excavator. "There's some choke rigs in the container. Go get what we need and get the first load ready."

Mac went to the container on the bow of the barge and pulled out two straps, each about twelve feet long, with a loop sewn into each end. He went forward, but hesitated as he looked down at the three feet of water he would need to cross to get to the ramp. He slid off the barge, unsure of the footing. The knee-deep water embraced him as he waded toward shore. Fortunately, Wood had set the barge even with the end of the concrete ramp allowing him a solid footing; any deeper and he would have been sucked into the mud. Once clear of the water, he hopped onto the bed of the truck and started to work the chokers around the steel beams. A mental picture in his head showed where each strap should go — about a third of the way in. Once in place, he slid one end of the choker through the loop on the other and slid the strap so that the loop was on top. He repeated the procedure on the other end, then signaled to Wood that he was ready.

The bucket came toward him. When it was just within reach, Wood curled it up, allowing Mac to slip the free end's loop onto one of the steel teeth projecting from the bucket. Then he moved out of the way as Wood lifted the load and swung the materials over the barge. Hopping out of the cab, Wood set a couple of two by fours on the deck, impressing Mac with his agility. Then he ran back to the cab and lowered the materials into place. They repeated the process twice more before Mac returned to the barge.

"Lash 'em down. I'm going to talk to Ned." Wood lifted the spuds and went forward, turning so the bow faced the ramp. Ned had parked the truck and was waiting on the dock as the barge kissed the dock. Ned slid onto the barge and Wood backed away, swinging the boat toward Spanish Harbor, where they picked up the skiff bobbing in the swells by the mooring buoy, and secured it to a cleat.

* * *

Braken pulled the Cadillac into the marina lot and brushed his hand against the warm metal of the polished hood as he walked past it. Cody was already in the boat waiting with engine idling, when Braken finally made it out to the dock. Without a word, he bent over with a grunt and untied the dock lines, then half hopped and half rolled his bulk onto the boat. Without a word, Cody put the boat in forward and started a wide turn. A small wake pushed against the other boats as they motored out of the canal, ignoring the angry screams of "no wake" followed after them during the short run to the bridge. Braken directed Cody to pull up next to the barge.

"What in the hell did I do to see your ugly face twice in two days?" Wood yelled as the boat coasted toward them. Braken was at the bow, a line in his hand, ready to heave it to Wood. "No way are you tying up and boarding this vessel."

Braken hadn't expected a warm welcome. "Ease up, Wood, I'm just wanting to see what you've got going on." He scanned the deck of the boat. The rock pile Cody had told him they excavated yesterday was gone. In its place were several piles of sheet metal. They were cut in what looked to be six-foot lengths. Toward the centerline of the barge were what looked like a dozen steel I-beams.

"I see you're lookin' at what your money bought. Well, set your mind at ease. I got all the stuff to build a cofferdam. Should start getting it set today and start pumping."

Braken rubbed his balding head. "That should have you pouring concrete tomorrow. We can work with that."

"Not so fast. Gotta pump her dry and then weld a steel cage

31

around that old mess of a pier down there. Then we need an inspection from the city boys. I figure we can pour it in three days."

"No. It's going to have to be done sooner than that. I need this bridge open for the weekend." Braken thought about the influx of tourists due on Friday for the start of the sportsman's lobster season. This was one of the busiest weekends of the year, and he intended to be able to show some real estate.

"Ain't gonna happen. We gotta follow procedures, or you're going to be suing me in a few years when it fails."

"I'll give you a release. If it's not done, there's no more money. I'll hang whatever is left of you out to dry."

Wood turned away.

"Look at me when I'm talking to you." Braken made a move to board the barge, but Wood came at him.

"Now look here. You want this done right, I'm your man. If not, I'll pull off this sucker. I don't need —"

Ned grabbed Wood and whispered something in his ear, causing him to back away. "We'll get it done," Ned said, and turned to follow Wood.

Satisfied he'd done all he could to push the schedule, Braken signaled for Cody to pull away. There were not a whole lot of choices to get this done. Most of the contractors that would work with him had made a beeline up US1 as soon as the hurricane winds had died down last fall. And now with the mass of tourists soon to descend on the Keys for lobster season, his investors were anxious for some quick sales. He left the site reassured that Wood was on the job and not after some mythical treasure.

Chapter 5

Mac watched the wake of the boat disappear as Braken pulled away. Then he went to the storage container, dragging the two spent air tanks with him. Inside the door was a large gas compressor mounted to the floor. He primed the gas line, opened the choke, and pulled the cord. The engine coughed and released a white cloud of smoke, so he set the choke to half and pulled again. The motor started and sputtered. Before it could die, he closed the choke and waited as the carburetor gulped air and the engine warmed up. Two hoses were attached to the air tank mounted below the motor. He took each hose, screwed the first stages attached to them onto the tanks, and opened the air valves. Watching the gauges, he thought while he waited for them to fill. *What was the dynamic between Braken and Wood? Who was wrong, who was right?* His thoughts were interrupted by yelling from the excavator, and he ran toward the voices on the bow.

"We need to slow down and see what's there." Ned was in Wood's face.

"Hell we do. Ain't no treasure down there — it's all out on the reef, where the Spanish fleet went down."

"Damn, Wood, maybe it's not treasure, but it's old and important. Aren't you the least bit curious about what's there?"

"The only thing I'm curious about is when I'm getting my

next check, and if we go prying around down there, it might be never. You heard Braken."

"He's just grandstanding. There's no one else in a hundred miles right now that can fix this bridge for him. And like you said, it's gotta be done right."

"I'm the only one within a hundred miles because the rest of them are up North, scamming insurance money off that storm. I need a couple of finished jobs to put enough money in the bank so I can get a new insurance policy and start bidding real work again."

"Why not start to set up the cofferdam? That'll keep Braken happy, and we can come back again tonight with a dredge, see what we can find before we put the steel plates in and pump it out."

"What do you mean again? Y'all came out here last night?" He looked over at Mac, who was trying to be invisible. "Truth, boy. You work for me, not this old coot."

Mac hesitated, but realized that the truth was going to come out sooner or later. "We did come out and dive it last night. We need a dredge if you want to see anything, though. It silted up pretty quickly."

"And you dove this alone?"

Ned jumped in and saved him. "Mel wouldn't let us out of your place without taking her."

"So now you're dragging my daughter into this?"

"Wood. We've been friends way too long for this. You know she's as headstrong as you, and dammed independent for her age." He paused. "And that's a lot of your doing. Why don't you climb out of that beer can and start seeing doing right by her?"

"Ain't had a beer today, and you still look ugly to me. Guess I'm seeing things right," he laughed, breaking the tension.

"Hey. Where do you think you're going? We've got plans to make." Wood sat on a steel bollard. "Now that Mel knows there's something here, and this old boy is preaching to her, there is no chance of walking away from it. Got to admit I'm a bit curious too, but I can't risk what's left of my business on a treasure hunt. We work today and then dive tonight, but that's it. If we don't find anything, I'm going back to my schedule with Braken, see if I can still salvage a paycheck out of this."

"We're going to need a dredge. And someone that can handle hoses down there." Mac hoped his message was clear — he wasn't comfortable with Mel diving with him again. The weight of the dredge and hose management required an experienced hand - especially at night.

"If you can manage the dredge, I'll handle the hoses. Ned and my girl can stay topside." Wood rubbed the stubble on his chin. "I'm thinking we leave the barge out here. Moving this thing is just too slow. It's a little dangerous leaving it unattended if a storm comes up, but it looks like we might as well stay out here all night. Mel can bring the center console and come and go as she needs to get to school."

Mac quickly unhooked the full tanks and turned off the compressor. Before closing the steel container door, he did a quick inventory of the tools and equipment available, and started making a mental checklist of what they would need for later. Then he closed the door and hopped in the skiff with Wood and Ned.

They rode in silence back to the boat ramp, where Ned gingerly hopped out and went for the flatbed truck. Wood watched him pull out of the lot before turning the small boat and heading back to his dock. They reached the house twenty minutes later where Mac hopped out, tied up the boat, and waited for Wood.

"Hold on." Wood grabbed two beers from the cooler.

Mac looked at him, but held his tongue. He checked his dive watch and realized there was too much drinking time between now and dark. Wood remained a mystery to him; but then he had never understood the allure of alcohol. It was clear that at least when sober, the old man was competent.

He declined the outstretched beer, and followed Wood into

the garage. There they uncovered a dredge, buried deep in a pile of hoses and equipment. The metal cylinder was about six feet long and eight inches in diameter, with a long section of flexible hose attached. When hooked up to a pump, it would pull the small rocks, sand, and silt off the bottom without destroying the visibility.

"We need to check it out?" Mac examined the dents and dings, wondering if the dredge would function at all, or if it was too old.

"Nah, it works."

Mac shook his head. "If it's all the same to you ... if we only have one shot at this, I'd just as soon at least make sure that there's no damage to the hose. A leak, and it'll destroy the suction." Mac eyed a small pump and went to it.

"Suit yourself. Only got this one hose."

Mac carried the pump out to the dock and went back for the dredge and hose while Wood stood to the side, sipping his beer and watching, a vague smile on his face. Mac ignored him as he dropped the dredge into the water and attached the hose to the pump.

"Got a discharge hose?"

"Yeah, I'll go get it."

"Just tell me where. I'll get it." Mac started toward the garage, but Wood stopped him.

"No. I don't mean to make you do all this yourself. Just wanting to see what you're made of; if you knew what you were doing."

Mac watched Wood disappear into the garage and wondered if *he* weren't being evaluated for his competence. Wood returned, dragging an old hose, and hooked it to the pump's outlet. The motor started quickly, the impeller sucking air until it caught water. The vibration deepened as it started to spit water out of the outlet.

"Satisfied?" Wood asked, and disappeared into the house.

Mac ignored the jibe and went back to work, loading the skiff with the rest of the equipment they would need. Once satisfied that everything was in place, he went to a lawn chair set in the shade of a palm tree, dropped into it, and was soon asleep.

* * *

Wood had not been interested in food, favoring beer instead, but Mac had scrounged through the pantry and found enough ingredients to make a quick spaghetti meal. There was a freezer full of fish and lobster, but he had settled on the meal he was comfortable making. They sat around the table, finishing dinner, and watching the sun set through the sliding glass door. Afterward, they made short work of the dishes, leaving them in the sink, and gathered around the table to make a plan.

"Mel, you want to go, take the center console. We'll be out all night so we can get an early start in the morning and make up some lost time before Braken shows up again. You can take it back and get to school."

She turned toward Mac. "Coming? You can ride with me. I'd like to get to know the guy my dad just gave a key to the house to."

Mac glanced over at Wood, who nodded and got on the loaded skiff with Ned. Mel was first off the dock, and Wood followed her out of the canal.

"So what's with you and my dad?"

"What do you mean? He picked me up hitchhiking yesterday, and pretty much offered me a job on the spot, as soon as he found out I had some commercial diving experience. I've just been rolling with it since then."

She looked straight ahead. "He's looking at you like his long-lost son."

He caught the look on her face. "I'm just looking for work. My girlfriend and I got in a fight in Galveston where I was working. She couldn't deal with all the time I had to spend out on the oil rigs — or at least that's what she said." His story rolled out of his mouth. "Thought I might find some work in Miami after the storm, but I got curious about what the Keys were like, so I kept heading south. Miami was a little too crazy for me."

"Just watch him. He hasn't been himself since my mom's passed away." She paused. "Then the insurance thing, and he's just bitter. I've been around. I know he's drinking too much, but all I can do is try and keep him going until he snaps out of it."

"Seems like he's a good man," Mac said.

They continued in silence, both watching the water for obstacles; an excuse not to talk. They passed around a bend and the bridge appeared. She put the boat in neutral, waiting for Wood to catch up as the dark night enveloped them.

"If he dives with you, keep an eye on him," she said quietly as the skiff coasted up to them.

"Anchor up on the pier like last night," Ned called to Mac. "We'll need the lights again."

Several minutes later, the boat was securely anchored and the lights illuminated the scene. Wood pulled alongside, and Ned held the boats together as Mac and Mel went over the side and joined them in the skiff. They tied off the barge and immediately got to work. Mac fit right into the flow, setting up the dredge and tossing the end into the water. He suited up and did a giant stride entry into the water. Wood was suited up as well, but grabbed for the beer set next to him, quickly finishing it before joining Mac in the water.

Chapter 6

The spoon tapped the crystal glass and silence quickly enveloped the gathering. Mike Mesculine stood at the head of the table in the dimly lit dining room, allowing for a pregnant pause before he began. Instantly all eyes were on him; as head of the Jersey syndicate, he had the respect of the group. Joey Pagliano looked around at the others. He feared the coming moments with everything in him. It was not unlike Mesculine to stage a 'last supper' before he exiled someone to a distant outpost of the group's control. Permanent disappearance was also possible, but Joey didn't think it was going to come to that. He straightened his silk tie against the tailored shirt and sat upright in the chair. Any sign of weakness would only further lower his standing. The problems with the job were not his fault, but that was not how the establishment worked. If it happened on your watch, you were guilty.

"Thank you all for coming," Mesculine started. "As you know, we have some money at risk in a venture down south."

Joey knew the reckoning was coming. Mesculine was also famous for getting right to the point.

"It was presented to me by Joey Pagliano here. You all know Joey? Come on, stand up."

He had no choice but to comply.

"Treasure Cove on paper is a beautiful island resort in the Florida Keys." He paused, "with Indian rights." The men murmured, knowing that Indian rights meant gambling. "It all sounded good, so I let him run with it. Turns out Treasure Cove has a not-so-glamorous name of No Name Key. What the fuck is that!" He slammed the table. "No Name fucking Key! Turns out the Indian rights are sketchy, and the bridge to the hump of shit is out." He looked down the table at Pagliano.

Joey knew it was his turn to talk. He had been rehearsing the speech for two days, ever since the meeting was called. "Mr. Mesculine, please. It was unknown to me at the time that the bridge was out. It is my understanding that it will be repaired in several days. Regarding the casino, our man down there, Eli Braken, is dealing with the Chontal Mayan tribe. I believe we will overcome the minor obstacles and establish their provenance for the site."

All eyes shifted to the head of the table. "You're so sure, then. It's your deal. Pack your shit and get out of here. You'll be based out of Miami. Fix this. I want to be down there throwing dice by winter."

Joey sat. It could have been worse, much worse. He thought about his exile to Miami; warm winters, women— he could live with that. A little geographic space, like two thousand miles, would also be a nice buffer. Give him some time to fix things. The real estate deal would make money, but as Mescaline had pointed out, it was the chance for a casino that made this a home run. Just out of Key West, the island was a steal because of some obscure zoning deal that meant it had no electricity provided to it. Money wasn't an object when a casino was involved and he had read up on solar and wind power. He thought he could handle that problem.

He needed to use the restroom, but knew that would be seen as a sign of weakness. Instead, he sat and made small talk until the meeting broke up.

* * *

Mac sunk quickly into the dark murky water, the extra weight he had added to compensate for the thrust the dredge would exert on him taking him quickly to the bottom. He walked along the sea floor in his dive booties, having decided against fins to give him better control of the dredge. Wood stood next to him and pointed the beam of his light to the spot where he wanted to start. They each had tanks on, not wanting the long hoses of the Hookah rig to interfere with the equipment. Once in place, Mac opened the lever, allowing full suction to the nozzle, and started to move the loose debris from the concrete base. Working alongside him, Wood moved the rocks too large to fit the intake of the dredge. They quickly fell into a rhythm, and Mac's worries about Wood's sobriety abated the longer they were down.

Time passed quickly and Mac was surprised when a glance at his dive watch revealed an hour had passed. Normally he would check his bottom time more frequently - almost obsessively, but in only twenty feet of water they were not in danger of decompression sickness. The pressure gauge on his console read five hundred psi - enough for another ten or fifteen minutes.

As the hole deepened, its bottom fell into shadow. Wood touched Mac on the shoulder and indicated that he was going to surface and would be right back. Mac gave him the OK sign, hoping he was after a better light and continued to work. He was prodding in the dark with the dredge, unable to see where he was working, when it suddenly kicked back with enough force to throw him on his back. The dredge fell from his hands. Before he could get back on his feet, a dark shadow obscured his vision.

Wood must have seen the panic in his eyes, because he put his face mask right in front of Mac's and grabbed his shoulders. Mac quickly snapped out of it and reached for the dredge whipping dangerously around them. He worked his way along the hose until his hands found the lever and closed the suction valve. The cylinder went limp, and he was able to check the nozzle for the inevitable obstruction. A rock was lodged in the intake. It took all of their strength to unscrew the nozzle and allow the coral to fall free.

Wood shone the light into the hole, using the beam to direct the dredge. They could see the bottom of the concrete footing sitting on loose material, with rust spots visible where saltwater had started eroding the old steel reinforcement. Mac saw Wood slice his neck — the signal to stop the dredge. The suction died, and he looked over at Wood, who held up a single finger, telling Mac to wait.

He watched as Wood walked around the pier, shining the light here and there. Finally he completed his survey of the foundation and gave a thumbs up signal, indicating that he was ready to surface. Mac nodded in the affirmative and dropped the dredge. Both men inflated their BC's and ascended. Mel and Ned leaned over the side and helped them back aboard the barge, anxious looks on their faces.

"Why stop? We were getting to where we need to be," Mac said. They had removed their gear and were all by the compressor, waiting for the tanks to refill.

Wood kept them waiting while he finished another beer.

"Didn't you see what's going on there? That old pier is sitting on sand and rusting out from the inside. We remove any more material from it and it could collapse. Too dangerous."

Mac didn't see the danger. They hadn't undermined it enough to disturb the stability. He felt that Wood had seen what he was interested in, and called off the dive. "We have to get to bedrock, anyway. Let's just work in around it and leave a good base."

"Shit's scary enough during the day. Now you want to go do a fool's errand at night," Wood said.

"Why not? I've worked on plenty of rigs at night. At least we're not being watched now - if we do find something."

"Y'all are focussed on finding something that may or may not be down there. Believe me, I've chased my share of dreams and I'm standing here telling you to give it up. This treasure hunt is over. It's time to make some money the old-fashioned way. We need to set up the cofferdam, pump it out and get to work," Wood said as he drank.

Mel broke in now. "How can you even think of covering up something that may be historic? Could be enough gold down there to —"

Wood cut her off. "I don't want to hear about no treasure that may or may not be there. Might as well go up to Miami and play the JaiLai. Odds are better."

Mac was torn between mollifying Wood and pursing the curiosity of Ned and Mel. He was also deeply interested in what may be there. "While we have the dredge down there, why don't we excavate the holes for the beams? Be a lot easier than pounding them with the excavator's bucket."

Wood scratched his head. "May have a point. Alright, I'll give you an hour down there. But I'll be watching your bubbles and lights. Stay away from the pier."

Mel stepped forward. "I'll go down with him."

"The hell you will." He pointed a finger at her and she backed away. "If I was here last night, your butt would've been on the boat too - or better yet at home. Damn it to hell." He went for another beer.

Mac unscrewed the first stages that led from the compressor to the tanks. He quickly reattached the regulators and squirmed back into his wetsuit. Wood suited up and followed him to the stern of the boat where both men held their masks and regulators while they took giant strides into the water.

They used the hose to guide them to the hole. Mac went for the dredge and turned the valve, while Wood pointed out a spot with his light about four feet from the pier, indicating that he should start excavating there. Mac stuck the nozzle into the sand

and wiggled it around as a hole started to form in the bottom. Wood had explained that they wanted a hole about twenty-four inches in diameter, and as deep as they could get it, to set the steel beams. Gradually the hole enlarged, satisfying Wood enough for him to move to the next spot.

Finally, three holes finished, they moved to the fourth and final hole.

Mac was tiring from the constant push and pull of the machine, but he continued, not wanting to show Wood that he was almost spent. This final hole gradually enlarged, when they heard the buzz. They looked at each other, both knowing the sound a boat's motor made underwater. Although it was impossible to tell direction underwater, he could tell by the pitch of the sound that it was running full out and coming towards them.

Mac looked at Wood as the sound got louder. The dredge was yanked from his hands, pulled by what he suspected was the boat above. The steel cylinder suddenly swung wildly in the water, nearly missing him and smashed Wood in the head. He recovered the dredge and jammed it into the hole to prevent further damage, then crawled toward Wood's light, barely visible in the cloudy water. Mac could see the beam was shining straight up as he approached. Worried, he moved faster. Wood was prone on the bottom, a dark liquid floating up from his head; no bubbles coming from his regulator.

Mac wasted no time grabbing the tank valve and hauling the man to his feet. He unclipped both of their weight belts and tried to push for the surface. Without fins, though, he couldn't get the momentum he needed, and fell back to the bottom. The suction line was floating above him. Gathering his strength, he lifted Wood again, made for the end of the hose and pulled them to the surface.

Their heads popped through the water, he spit out his regulator and yelled for help, gulping seawater as the weight took him back under. The silhouette of two heads were visible in the deck's lights. Mac used the hose to inch closer to the barge and their outstretched hands. They took Wood from him, allowing him to take a couple of deep breaths before he made his way to the ladder.

Wood was lying on the deck when he got there. His tank was off, and he was breathing now.

"Looks like you saved the old bastard," Ned said. "Had to give him mouth to mouth before he came to, but he's alive."

Mac leaned back against a bollard, trying to slow his heart. "What happened?"

"Some fool came tearing through here in an outboard, music blasting, cut right through the hose. They're probably up on some sand bar by now."

Mel was hovering over Wood, trying to get his head up to drink some water. He took a sip and spat it out. "Give me a goddamn beer. That'll fix me."

She ignored him and turned to Mac. "You OK?"

He nodded and rose to inspect the damage. "I think we should head back. That was close. Maybe you're right and we should do this during the day." He looked over at Wood for approval.

The old man nodded. "Go get the dredge, and we can go in. Can't leave that thing down there with the tide change. It'll be twenty miles into the Gulf by sunrise."

Mac knew he was right. Slowly, he put the tank back on his back. This time deciding to use fins, he grabbed them and the dive light, knowing he would have to find the weight belts as well. He was quickly back in the water, finning for the bottom. The light cut through the settling silt, and he quickly found the weights. He put one belt around his waist, and dragged the other to the anchor line where he fastened it around the rode, to be retrieved later. The dredge was still in the hole where he had left it, and resisted him as he tried to pull it free. Tired and frustrated, he yanked on it several times, finally tearing it loose. Spent, he swam it to the surface, where Ned's waiting hands took it from him.

He had just climbed back on the boat, and was ready to collapse from exhaustion, when Ned called out, "Where'd you get this?" He held up a chunk of wood. A glint of metal and the burnished marks of a carving were visible in the beam of his flashlight.

Chapter 7

Braken held the phone away from his ear.

"You do know what the fuck you're doing," the voice shouted.

Pagliano could have been sitting across from him, from the way his voice carried through the receiver. He held the receiver at arm's length for several seconds, to see if the rant was over, then put it back to his ear.

"I've got this," he replied, trying to sound more sure of himself than he actually was. "It's all documented, with the *I*s dotted and the *T*s crossed. The bridge should be finished by early next week. I really put the screws to the contractor."

"It better be handled, or I'll put more than the screws to you," Pagliano said. "I've been transferred to Miami. Going to fly in tonight. So we'll be seeing a lot more of each other."

Braken did not like this development. "It's all under control. I'll let you know when the application is approved and the bridge is open for traffic. I'll be showing properties next weekend."

"Get the casino deal done; that's the money maker. Sell the lots on your own time." He paused, "and make sure I get my skim. After that contractor of yours finishes the bridge get him to dredge out that canal on the other side of the island so we can bring the riverboat in."

"Sure thing, Mr. Pagliano," Braken winced. He wanted to build a casino on the island, not park a Mississippi riverboat next to it. With the new Rate of Growth Ordinance instituted by Monroe County making it almost impossible to build anything, a comprehensive project was more likely to get approved - and be more profitable. They had a permit application in, but he would have to get lucky to secure it any time soon. Pagliano, in his shortsightedness, had vetoed the plan to donate five lots to the County as a ROGO exchange. Those lots, the worst of the development, would have been titled to the county and left as green space. These were the rules now and you had to play by them, but Pagliano had a hard time with rules. Donating the lots would reduce some profit, yet allow the project to move forward.

Pagliano interrupted his thoughts. "You should call me Joey, since we're going to be spending so much time together now that I'm in the neighborhood."

Braken cringed. "OK, Joey." He breathed out and set the phone down. The picture in his mind of a riverboat moored right on the eastern side of the Key, visible from US1 and Bahia Honda, was unthinkable. Braken knew from experience that it would meet resistance here. This wasn't New Orleans; people here liked to get in that *Keys-ian* kind of mood. He looked up at the master plan for Treasure Cove pinned to his office wall. It showed the properties he proposed to be granted to the county. The worst lots on the Key, they were pretty much swampland — too close to the mangroves for anyone to buy. The casino and club would be right across the bridge as you entered the Key, with a gate giving privacy to the lots just past it. It didn't need to stand out like a billboard. The closest casino was on Highway 41 in the everglades outside of Miami.

"Nicole!" he yelled, not expecting an answer.

"Yeah, I'm here."

He looked at his watch, shocked that she was here this early. "How about a cup of coffee, and bring the Treasure Cove file in here." He sat back and waited for her. *Lucky boy, my son Cody is, to have a piece of ass like that,* he thought. She swayed into the room, a cup of coffee in one hand and the file in the other.

"We've got a couple of things to get done here." He opened the file, and flipped through the pages. "Number one, we gotta get the name of that Key changed to Treasure Cove. No Name Key — what the hell were they thinking? Second, we gotta get that Indian to get her butt in here and document the tribe's claim."

"Sure, I'll get right on it." She got up and walked away.

He savored the moment — possibly the high point of his day — watching her walk out of the room. As she left, his thoughts returned to Pagliano. He didn't understand that the Keys worked to their own rhythm; you could massage it, but it wasn't Jersey. You couldn't jam your agenda down the throats of the politicians here, even if you lined their pockets. A lot of them were idealists, just wanting to keep their little piece of paradise. Treasure Cove was far from the rubber stamp Pagliano thought it was.

"I've got the Indian on the phone!" Nicole yelled suddenly from her desk.

He sat erect and reached for the phone. "Cheqea, or is it Chief?" He listened while the woman spoke, becoming impatient as the dialogue continued to be rambling and one sided. He knew she tended to babble and did his best to exercise his patience. Finally, the diatribe paused. "I understand. We will take all precautions with the burial ground of your people. I have the entire area designated as a green area." He listened again. "Right. Now I need you to come in and sign some papers. I've got to get this filed."

Braken hung up the phone, wondering what he could do to motivate her. Cheqea was the matriarch of the last remaining Tequesta Indians — a tribe that had inhabited the area before the Spanish came. All he needed was the chief's affidavit notarized and then he would produce some old bones he had bought from a museum and buried on the property. Instant Indian burial ground.

The government would have no choice but to deed the land back to the tribe. Then a lease back for 99 years to his company and Pagliano would have his casino.

Unfortunately, the woman was not motivated by money and it was holding up the entire process.

* * *

Wood was still asleep when Ned knocked on the door. Mac had been up since Mel started making enough noise to disturb his peace on the couch, finally asking for a ride to school.

"Don't you drive?" Mac asked, slowly waking up.

"I have my permit, but you know my dad…" she answered.

He dropped her off, then filled the empty gas cans from the barge, and was now back at Wood's. He looked out the door as Ned walked in, and saw the sun already high in the sky. Several large clouds were starting to form into thunderheads.

"We want to get something done today, we better get a move on," Ned said, following Mac's gaze to the building clouds.

"He's still asleep. I checked a couple of times to make sure he's still breathing. It would have been the right thing to take him to the hospital last night and get him checked out."

"For anyone else, I'd agree," Ned said. "But that old boy's got more lives than a slew of cats, and enough beer in him to make him bulletproof."

"I guess once we patched up the cut on his head, he seemed all right," Mac said.

Ned went to the bedroom and entered. Mac heard a muted conversation, and Ned came back out. "He's moving. A little slow, but he's moving." He looked around the living room. "Where's that piece you pulled out of the dredge?"

Mac went to the kitchen sink and retrieved the piece. He went to the sliding glass door and opened the blinds, allowing light to stream into the room. "First time this has seen daylight in a few years." The piece was very smooth and had a carving of a canoe with four men paddling. It was actually two pieces joined together with a curve and burnished end. Mac looked at the carving and back at the piece realizing that it resembled the bow of a canoe.

"From the look of it, I'd say more than five hundred. I've been looking at artifacts all my life, and this is definitely pre-Columbian. That puts it at least that old, and it's not from around here, either. That's oak, if I'm not mistaken. You don't see big oak trees this far south. The oaks around here are more like bushes than trees. You could never build a canoe out of them." He took the piece from Mac and ran his finger along the straight grain. "We'd call that quarter sawn, now. Look how that grain runs."

Mac took the piece back. "Where do you think it's from?"

"My guess, and it's a big one right now, is that it's Mayan. See that joint there?" He pointed to a seam in the wood. "Looks like this is from the bow or stern. It's not a dugout canoe. This was joined together not burnt out of a log. No natives around here used any kind of composite construction. And the copper looks like it's got a partial engraving on it. Have to clean it off to get a better look."

"What's all this?" Wood asked as he emerged from the bedroom. "I thought we were bridge building, not treasure hunting."

"This came up, stuck in the dredge. Didn't want to bother you with it last night."

"Y'all can stop right now. Somebody make some food, and let's get out of here. We've got to build that cofferdam and start pumping it out."

Ned looked at his disheveled friend. "Think you could slow down a minute and let me check that cut on your head?"

"Hell no. All I want you to do is make some food." He looked over at Mac. "And you, don't stand there with your jaw open. Round here mosquitoes'll fill it up. Get the boat loaded."

Ned moved to the kitchen. "You know, we've found

something important. I've dated it as pre-Columbian. It's not like anything I've seen from around here." He summarized his findings, but Wood had left the room.

"How do you know so much about this?" Mac asked.

"I've been retired down here for some years, but in my previous life I was a professor of archeology at the University of Florida. This is ringing every bell I've got."

"I'm going to ring the last bell you've got if you don't get some food going." Wood was already dressed and ready to go, standing in the doorway once again. "Oh, hell with the food." He went to the refrigerator and grabbed two beers.

Mac set the piece on the table and went to load the boat.

* * *

Kellie woke when the first bead of sweat sprung from her forehead. The sun had just started to bake the car, which sat alone in the K-mart parking lot. Her head pounded from the drinks at the bar, but it would have been much worse, if she hadn't decided to leave early and stay on course — a decision that was often difficult for her. The lure of a later night and a bigger party was not one she easily denied herself. But she had, and all for the sake of finding him. She checked herself in the rear view mirror, adjusted her hair, and left the car.

She walked over to the McDonald's across the lot, and ordered breakfast and coffee, alarmed at the short supply of funds still available when she opened her purse to pay. Sitting at a table, she ate and evaluated her options. The drive from Texas had depleted her cash reserves. Knowing she was only an hour from Key West reassured her that a paycheck was only a couple dances away, but she wanted to find Mac. Letting him walk away had been a mistake. She knew it when it had happened, and she knew it now. He was the first stable guy to ever show any interest in her unstable behavior. But his absences, working on oil rigs or whatever he did, got her paranoid. It didn't mean she couldn't deal with it. But the invisible band would start tightening around her head, and bad things soon happened. There were the traditional options: using prescription drugs and going to counseling, but the drugs weirded her out more than her natural state, and the clinic was full of losers.

In the bathroom, she tried to clean up in the sink. She leaned over, tilting her head toward the mirror, checking the black streak running down her scalp. That could use some work, and she wondered if Key West was totally nude or just topless, and if she needed to do some touch up down under as well, before she could work.

Back in the car, she thought about Mac, and wondered how to find him. He had walked out after she went into another tirade. Fortunately, he had muttered something about the Florida Keys as he went out the door. She had cried for an hour, regretting her life, and then started packing. After dancing her ass off all night, and trading a handful of cash for a vial of coke, she left Galveston at dawn. Now with the coke long gone, she had gotten her first sleep in days, though it had been in the car.

She watched the heat mirages come off the pavement outside the window, wondering where he was and how she was going to find him.

Chapter 8

Braken's sandwich collapsed, the contents falling on his lap when the door slammed. He was at his desk, eating from a styrofoam container, when Pagliano barged in.

"Where's that gate keeper of yours? That's the best part of visiting your sorry ass."

"She's not here," he muttered.

"Whatever. That can wait. Where do we stand with the casino? The bridge? The lots?" He rattled off the questions in a staccato fashion, like bullets from a gun.

Braken set down what was left of his sandwich and wiped his hands on his ruined pant's legs. He stammered: "Talked to the chief this morning, and the bridge should be done in a couple of days."

Pagliano stared down at him. "Talk is cheap. We need some action. I've been exiled to Miami because of you, and I don't mean to stay in this steam bath any longer than I have to. We need to go see this Injun woman and make sure she's going to cooperate. Then maybe that boy of yours can take me out shark fishing."

"Whatever you say, Mr. Pagliano."

"I told you already to call me Joey. We're going to be spending way too much time together." He walked over to the rendering pinned on the wall. "Treasure Cove. That'll get me some respect up North." He went to the door and looked back. "Let's go."

* * *

Braken's Cadillac plowed down US 1 and crossed the bridge to Big Pine Key. He turned right at the lone traffic light and followed the road past the Key Deer Refuge. Where it turned to gravel, he swerved to avoid the potholes deepened by the daily rain. What a waste to have had the car washed yesterday he thought, as dirty rainwater splashed from the holes onto the shiny white finish.

"Where the hell you taking me?" Pagliano was staring out the window as Braken turned left onto a small, unmarked street.

"You want to see the chief, this is where to find her." They drove past the shell of a decrepit boat hull, broken lobster traps piled around it, and stopped in front of an old bungalow.

Braken got out first, checking for the clearest path to keep his shoes clean. Pagliano got out and followed him toward the partially open door.

"Let me do the talking," Braken said. "She's a little eccentric." He knocked, then called out: "Cheqea."

"Looks like no ones's here," Pagliano said as he moved around toward the back of the house.

"Be careful, you don't want to sneak up on her. Let me go first." Braken took the lead. He pushed an overgrown hibiscus out of his way and went toward the back of the house. Pieces of siding, nails sprung loose from rust, brushed against his nylon shirt as he made his way around the corner and into a clearing. A small stream of smoke rose from a pile of dead palm fronds in a rock fire pit. Around the pit was an array of broken lawn chairs and crab traps. Jet black hair with a thin streak of grey from someone sitting in a chair facing away from them was the only life he saw.

Braken went toward the figure, jumping back when his name was called.

"Kraken, I knew it was you. Only a white man can make that much noise. And who's your friend?"

Pagliano shrugged his shoulders, palms up. "How'd she know we were here and it was you?"

Braken ignored him and went around the fire pit to look at the woman. "Cheqea. This is Joey Pagliano. He's from New Jersey."

"New Jersey?" she spat. Smoke rose from a pipe clamped in her jaw.

"Better looking than I would have guessed, and knows how to party." He sniffed the air. "And that's some kind of weed she's smoking." Pagliano swatted at the mosquitos swarming around his head and stared at the exotic looking woman.

"It's seaweed and it keeps the bugs away." She breathed out a ring of smoke.

"Cheqea here is the chief of the Tequestas," Braken said, trying to placate Pagliano. "She is ready to sign the papers for the casino project, on behalf of her people."

"Sure she's got any authority? A woman chief —go figure."

"True, Mr. Jersey. But here you are, and here I am. You have the papers and my cash?"

"What cash is she talking about, Braken?" Pagliano turned away from Cheqea and faced Braken. "All expenses were to be authorized by me."

"Just a small fee for her cooperation. Comes off the back end of the tribe's first payment."

"Twenty-five grand, or I don't sign." She waved a hand at them. "Need to get some more medicine."

"Fuck this. It's extortion," Pagliano said. He went toward the chair, fists balling at his sides. Suddenly Cheqea popped up as if weightless, grabbed Pagliano's leading hand, and spun the larger man, locking his arm behind his back.

"Didn't expect that, did you, Jersey?"

Braken went to intervene. "Now, guys. This is a business deal. There's no reason to get personal."

Pagliano used Braken's body to screen him as he went to his

ankle and pulled a gun from the holster strapped there.

"Nothing personal," he said, pointing the gun at Cheqea. "Now sit back down in that chair, and let's have us a little chat."

* * *

Mel got up from the table, where she was doing her homework, and went to the sink. She filled a water glass and looked out the window as she drank. Finished, she set the glass down, returned to the table, and looked again at the piece of wood. Curious, she picked it up, opened the sliding glass door, and took it outside. Ned and her dad had been bringing stuff back from their jobs for years, but nothing that looked like this. It was usually stuff from the 1800s, when the Keys were first homesteaded. Occasionally they would have some old Spanish artifact, and start getting all excited, talking about treasure and adventures that usually resulted in disappointment.

This looked different, though. Much older. She turned it in the light, focusing on the copper fitted to the end. It looked to be engraved, and she wondered how it had even survived in the salt water.

Back at the kitchen sink, she took a knife and started scraping the green corrosion away. Then, fearing the knife would gouge the soft copper, she took a toothbrush from the bathroom and started working the metal with the softer bristles. Slowly, the engraving revealed itself, but the intricate lines looked to be a part of something bigger.

Curious now, she wrapped the relic in a dishtowel and left the house. Her bicycle the only means of transportation, she set the wrapped piece in the basket and headed out of the driveway. She thought about the find and her dad's behavior while she rode down the bike trail adjacent to US 1. She didn't understand all the financial stuff he talked about, but this was real and he didn't seem to care. Reaching the crosswalk, she waited for traffic and turned into the parking lot of the library, leaving the bicycle in the rack to the side of the door.

It was cool and quiet inside as she made her way toward a table and went for the card catalogue. The source of the piece unknown, she started by looking for a general history of the Keys. Two books seemed helpful, and she wrote down the index numbers. One book was available, so she took it back to the table and started scanning the pages. Keys history was vague before the Spanish explorer Ponce De Leon cruised by without stopping in 1513 officially discovering the chain of islands. References were made to both the Calusa and Tequesta Indians occupying the area, though, so she went back to the card catalogue. She returned with several books, and was surprised to see a woman handling the relic.

"Can I help you?" She held out her hand to take it back.

The woman handed the piece back to her. "Looks pretty old."

Mel noticed her looking at the books under her arm, and turned her body slightly, trying to hide the titles. "Yeah, it is."

"Aren't you Melanie Woodson? I've seen you around. I have a nephew in your grade."

Mel cursed the everybody-knows-everybody culture of the Keys. "That's right, and you look familiar."

"Nicole Braken. I think your dad's doing some work for us right now."

Mel ignored her, not sure if it was a question or a statement. She sat at the table, hoping the woman would leave. Instead, Nicole sat across from her and started reading from the pile of books under her arm, a notepad at her side.

"Hey, we both have books on Indians," Nicole said.

Mel looked over at the stack of books in front of her. She was about to respond when they both heard a scene at the counter. They turned to see a sleazy-looking woman with bleached blond hair arguing with the librarian.

"Y'all ought to be more helpful. I was just lookin' for some information, is all. I didn't mean to take your book."

"That is a library reference. Please set it down."

"Sweetheart, don't get your panties in a wad." The woman suddenly approached the table Mel and Nicole sat at. "Can I borrow a piece of paper off your pad there?"

Nicole tore off a page and handed it to the woman. "Suppose you need a pen too?"

"Thanks, hon." The woman sat. She had a business directory in front of her. "Y'all know any salvage or dive businesses here?" she asked. "My boyfriend's working down here, and I don't know how to find him."

Mel and Nicole glanced at each other and made a silent agreement to ignore the woman. She mashed her gums as she wrote names down on the paper, then rose to leave.

"Hey, my pen." Nicole rose to go after her, but saw that the woman was on her way out, and quickly realized that it was not worth the effort.

* * *

"Travis, get up on that hoe and lower the bucket to the deck." Wood motioned to where he wanted the bucket. He finished the beer and tossed the can aside. The bucket hovered over the deck, slowly coming toward it until Wood raised a fist to signal that it was where he wanted it.

He hopped into the bucket, taking a section of pipe with a hose attached to it with him. Braced against the steel, he gave Mac the signal to lift, and clung to the teeth protruding from the scoop for balance. Slowly it rose off the deck and when it was about six feet off the ground, raised his fist again. The height allowed him to slide the piece of pipe into brackets welded to the bucket and tightened down the bolts he had set there to keep the tubing in place. At the edge of the bucket, he jumped over the side with both hands grabbing a steel tooth, then lowered himself until his feet were a few inches from the ground, where he released his grip and landed easily on the deck. He motioned Mac out of the excavator.

Despite the disapproving looks from Mac and Ned, he grabbed another beer from the cooler. "So, this is how it goes. You go down with a tank and release a buoy on each of the holes. Then I'll pop this bad boy down and start shooting high-pressure water until the hole is large enough to set a pier in. Should blast those suckers fast, and we won't need that pain-in-the-ass dredge again."

Mac nodded and started to suit up.

He looked at Ned. "I suppose you want to talk about that piece of wood you found," Wood said not waiting for an answer. "I've been thinking about it, and I'll compromise with you so I don't have to keep hearing you bitch. I'm going to go wide of the last hole we did last night. It'll cost me some money, but we can make the dam bigger if it'll get you and my daughter off my back." He had to admit he was interested, but getting the bill collectors off his back and getting his insurance reinstated were his top priorities right now.

Ned smiled. "Glad you came to your senses. Now lay off the beer a little before something bad happens." He paused. "Then we can set this up, pump it out, and see what's there. It'll be much easier to work in a dry hole than having to dive."

"Never worked inside a cofferdam with the tide running, have you? Scary piece of work there: boards stacked over your head water leaking through, tide surging around it. Makes a hell of a racket. We'll see how you're feeling about it once we get it set up." A metallic clink came from the stern, and Wood saw Mac bang a knife against his tank. He gave Mac the thumbs up and watched as he entered the water.

* * *

Ned followed Mac's bubble trail around to the port side,

where the piers were dug. Standing by the edge, he watched the buoys pop to the surface. Wood grabbed a fresh beer and went to the excavator, stumbling and cursing along the way. He waited for Mac to surface before he set the bucket over the first buoy and lowered the boom until the pipe was under the water. Now that it was out of sight, he was working by feel. The pipe soon met resistance, and he slid the bucket side to side dragging the tubing along the bottom until he felt the hole. Leaning forward in the seat, he lowered the boom until the pipe hit bottom.

Turning in the chair, he gave a thumbs up sign to Ned, who started the pump. It groaned as it sucked sea water through the intake's four-inch hose, the pressure building as it shot a high-pressure stream of water through the one-inch pipe. A silt cloud formed in the clear water as he inched the boom lower, moving side to side with the bucket.

Satisfied with the first attempt, he repeated the same procedure for the remaining three holes, staying six feet outside the buoys for the last two. The bucket streamed water as it met the air and swung to the deck.

Mac was back on the surface. "Need you to go down again and stick a piece of rebar in each hole. Then we'll set the steel. Got to do them one at a time, though, or the current'll get 'em," Wood said.

He watched as Mac strapped a fresh tank on his back and took a giant stride into the water. Ned was in the excavator now, as Wood slid one piece of twenty-foot rebar off the edge of the boat into Mac's gloved hand. He watched as the steel disappeared, only to pop back through the water a minute later, marking the hole.

Ned swung the excavator's bucket to where Wood waited, a chain in his hands, by the pile of steel I-beams. Working a steel shackle through a hole already bored at the top of the beam, he attached the chain to it, then looped a few links over the teeth of the waiting bucket and signaled Ned to swing it over the water.

Back in the excavator, Wood adjusted the boom to align the

beam with the piece of steel, and started to lower it. With three feet showing above the water line, he stopped, lowered the bucket and released the chain.

"Dammit Wood, the boy's still under. Told you to lay off the beer!" Ned climbed up to the cab. "Hold on until he surfaces."

They gathered at the side of the barge, waiting for Mac to come up. With no way to communicate, all they could do was watch his bubbles. Suddenly, the steady stream increased tenfold.

"He's in trouble. Bet he's purging his regulator, trying to get out attention." Wood ran for the container and emerged with a tank and regulator. He strapped the tank to his back, donned fins and mask, and jumped backwards off the barge.

Chapter 9

Mac's arm was pinned between the beam and the coral. He could still feel his fingers — a good sign — but he couldn't dislodge it. After several breaths, his breathing normalized and he checked his gauges. Plenty of air, and at fifteen feet, no chance of decompression sickness. Thankful that Ned was aboard the barge, he wondered furiously what the deal was with Wood and his drinking. The guy was clearly in his prime — somewhere in his 40s — and definitely competent even with a few beers in him. Yet, every day seemed a new struggle for him, and every day he seemed to drink more. And now he'd put his life in danger. A sober equipment operator would never have rushed through that process. He would have double checked that his diver was clear before doing any work. It was as if Wood had forgotten that he was in the water or something.

The barge was visible above him in the clear water, but there was enough of a ripple on the surface to obscure any activity. Not knowing if his absence had been noticed, he used the only method to signal available to him. He took a deep breath, removed the regulator from his mouth, and held the purge button. A violent wave of air bubbles released toward the surface. Checking his watch, he repeated the procedure every thirty seconds.

Several minutes later, the shock wore off, and his arm started to throb. He was about to release another round of bubbles when he saw a splash from above. Wood swam into view, caught sight of him, and approached. Mac pointed to his arm and waited while Wood prodded around and tried to pull on the beam. Mac was getting frustrated, and knew he needed to do something fast. There was no way he was going to move the steel beam by himself. In the short time Mac had been under, he had watched the hole fill halfway with sand, brought in by the tide to embed the beam even further.

They had to find another way.

He grabbed Wood's arm, caught his attention, and gestured for him to surface, and then to lift the beam with the excavator. Wood seemed to understand, and ascended, leaving Mac to again wonder about his new employer.

He relaxed again, breathing regularly until finally he felt the beam lift. His arm was almost free when the steel jerked suddenly upwards, taking a piece of his wetsuit with it. It was just enough, and he yanked his arm out of the hole and started for the surface, swimming diagonally away from the beam.

Ned was at the port side when he emerged from the water. He looked up at the older man, who just nodded. Both men looked at Wood, who sat in the excavator, still manipulating the beam, unaware that Mac was free. Back on the boat, he dropped the tank and weight belt to the deck and went for the excavator. He climbed up to the cab and turned the key off. Wood looked at him, a foggy look in his eyes.

"You need to get off that thing, and we need to talk," Mac snapped as he climbed back to the deck and waited by Ned, his arm limp at his side.

Wood climbed from the cab and went toward the cooler, but Mac raced to it, knowing his intention. He grabbed the handles, and dumped the contents over the side.

"Now what the hell'd you do that for?" Wood shouted.

"It's all good if you want to drink, but not out here. And not while I'm in the water. That could have gotten me killed."

"Ah, stop it. Just an accident."

"It's not an accident when you're drunk." Mac was enraged by his attitude, and went toward Wood, catching him in the gut with his shoulder. His momentum took them both overboard. They struggled in the water, neither gaining advantage, when suddenly Wood stiffened. Mac realized he was in trouble, and quickly switched from aggressor to rescuer. He grabbed the older man and spun him around so that his mouth was out of the water.

Once he had him on his back, he got his arm around Wood's neck and started side stroking for the boat. Ned was waiting, and held Wood in place until Mac could get out of the water and drag him on deck.

Wood spat water and started breathing again. Then he lifted his head up and muttered something under his breath.

Mac turned toward Ned. "I'll take a ride back to shore. I can't work like this. He almost killed me today."

"I understand, just wish you'd give him another chance. He's not normally like this. I'll go talk to him and see if I can straighten him out. He's a stubborn old boy, but he'll come around."

Mac didn't answer. He went toward the container and started pulling his gear out and packing it in his bag.

* * *

Cheqea had a better understanding of the law and business than Pagliano had anticipated. They sat around the table in the sparse hut, exchanging papers.

"You need to sign this agreement before we can continue. It gives my corporation the rights to the casino for ninety-nine years. You or the tribe, if there even is one, gets 10 percent of gaming revenue."

"Ten percent?" She relit the pipe and smoked.

Pagliano was getting annoyed by the smoke and her delays.

He breathed deeply and tried to bring his temper under control. Losing control might mean losing the deal. If the woman wanted to get stoned and kill some time, whatever. As long as the papers got signed.

"How 'bout you just sign? This is the only deal you're going to get, and you can't do it without us. It'll give you enough cash to keep that peace pipe of yours stuffed for the rest of your life."

She blew smoke toward him. "I need to read the fine print, Jersey." She got up and took the papers to the window.

Pagliano was losing his cool again, and looked over at Braken. "Get her to do it, or this is going to get ugly." He got up and started pacing. Opening the cylinder, he spun it several times, and replaced it.

Braken moved toward the chief and spoke in hushed tones. This was going nowhere, and Pagliano needed results. Already in deep water with the bosses in Jersey, his failure here would mean extinction instead of just exile.

He pointed the gun at her. "Let's go. I gotta get out of this mosquito-infested paradise of yours and get this shit done." He yanked her by the hair. "None of that kung fu shit, either, or I'll put a piece of lead in you."

He grabbed the papers and they walked single file through the overgrown brush around the house towards Braken's Cadillac. "Get in and drive," he said to Braken. "Me and the chief here are going to spend some quality time in the back seat."

"I'll put the juju on you so bad your cock'll fall off if you lay your Jersey hands on me," she snapped.

Pagliano pushed her into the car and slid in next to her. "Key West."

Braken pulled out of the driveway and back onto the washboard road. "Key West?"

"Yeah, that's where the federal building is this freakin' paradise. The chief here is going to walk in and sign the damn papers right in front of the clerk."

Braken glanced at the clock in the dashboard. "We'll never make it in time. It's almost 5 now."

"Shit, must've lost track of the time with all the smoke she's been blowing in my face. Go to your place, then. We'll spend the night there, and head to Key West in the morning."

"You ain't gonna want me around without my medicine," Cheqea said. "Life around you white pricks makes me crazy. Just sayin'."

Pagliano looked her in the eyes, and watched her pupils, dilated and dancing. He'd seen crazy eyes before, and this chief or whatever the fuck she was had them. The last thing he needed was her melting down in a federal building. "Take the bitch and get her shit," he ordered Braken.

* * *

Wood had sobered considerably when they reached the dock, but Mac's mind was made up. Despite the work and the lure of the relic, it wasn't worth getting killed over. He jumped out of the skiff and tied the line to the forward cleat, waiting for the stern to drift closer to the dock as Ned reversed the motor. As it closed, he tossed another line to Wood, who grabbed it and wrapped it around the stern cleat. The gear bag landed with a thud on the dock as Wood climbed out of the boat.

"Sorry, I ain't got much to pay you. I'll go up to the house and see what I got." He walked away, brushing past Mel without a word.

She came toward the dock and stopped in front of Mac. "There's some bleach blond-haired girl, kind of crazy maybe, I ran into. Says she's looking for her boyfriend, a diver. Any chance that's you?"

Mac flinched. "Maybe." He sat down in an old lawn chair by the dock, gear bag at his feet, and stared into his hands. What was it about him that made him a shit magnet? First his drunken boss, and now his crazy ex. If Wood didn't do something stupid and kill him - she just might.

Ned looked over at him. "You know, he's still drunk enough that you don't have to go through with it. He'll never remember you quit in the morning."

"What happened?" Mel asked.

"Seems your dad's about to drive another one off," Ned said. "And this one's good help."

Mac thought about it. At least here, provided they could get Wood sober, he had good work, and he could stay under the radar living here. If he had to walk away and look for something else, he was sure she would track him down. That girl had radar. "Maybe, but I'm not diving anymore unless he can get himself sober."

Mel and Ned looked at each other, reaching a silent agreement. "Done," Ned said.

"Now that we're back together, there's something I need to show you guys." Mel went upstairs without waiting for an answer, and the two men followed.

Mel stood over the kitchen table, a large book opened in front of her. They went to the table and stood by her side trying to see what she was looking at. Mac looked over her shoulder he saw that the library book was opened to a page showing an old Indian canoe.

"I know that book," Ned said.

"Well, look at the bow and stern of the canoe. If you look closely, you can see the piece we found looks like it could fit."

"Hmm. *Could* is a vague term in the treasure business," Ned said. He looked at the book. "That's a Mayan canoe. Specifically a Chontal Mayan boat. There's never been any evidence that they stopped here. We know they were up and down the Gulf coast, but no evidence has ever been found that they were here."

"And there are no pre-columbian artifacts here from before the Spanish. That's pretty hard to believe. My history teacher has a theory it is the hurricanes. There was no way anything could have survived one of those storm surges, at least before concrete foundations and stilt houses. How many storms do you think have passed through here, grabbing everything and taking it out to sea?"

Ned rubbed his chin. "Point taken. I've heard that theory, and there's something to it. Suppose the Maya did come through here, though? It's a clear path on their route up the west coast of Florida, and old No Name is one of the only two Keys with oolitic limestone. That was a big deal back then. Fresh water was a huge issue when traveling and this type of formation is the only kind of rock here that can be tapped for water. The rest of these piles of coral are Key Largo limestone; bone dry. Any trade route through here would have known that and used No Name to replenish water supplies."

"See?" Mel said.

"Don't get too excited. The chances of one of those canoes being in that channel when a hurricane came through here are pretty small, and the boat getting wedged in the coral there in such a way as to stick is even less likely. And then no other storms coming through for long enough for coral to grow around it ... that's a stretch."

"Yeah, but it could have happened," she said. "In the right conditions, coral can grow a couple of inches a year. Then it would have been protected."

"Suppose it's worth looking into. Don't have any better theories at the moment," Ned said.

Mac sat back, wondering if they had indeed found a Mayan relic. Maybe they had found all that was there, a piece scattered by a storm and nothing else was down there, but the lure of finding more excited him. "So how do we get Wood to buy into this and take enough time to find it?"

Ned and Mel threw each other a conspiratorial look. "We don't."

Chapter 10

Cody stood in the bow of the boat, cast net draped over his shoulder, waiting for the wake to settle and the mullet to start jumping again. He was drifting with the current through an area known as the grasses, just off the south side of Anette Key. It didn't take long for the fish to forget he was there and start feeding again, breaking the surface to show their location. He wound up and tossed the cast net at a pod of fish, waited for the weighted edges of the nylon mesh to close on the school, and pulled the net in.

A dozen mullet flapped in the net as he hauled it over the gunwale. Carefully, he separated the fish from the mesh and carefully placed them into the live well, trying not to bruise them. The single cast had yielded enough bait for tomorrow's tarpon charter. The big fish were around the bridges this time of year, and live mullet gave the best chance of hooking a hundred pounder for his clients.

He checked his watch, deciding it would be well worth his time to stay out and catch more. With the price of live mullet, he could wholesale it to the bait house and pick up a couple hundred for an hour's work. Then he'd check his pinfish traps and head in for a cold beer or two.

* * *

Mac hopped off the skiff and onto the barge, taking a line tied to the forward cleat with him. He tossed over an old fender,and tied the smaller boat off, went to the stern, and waited for Mel to throw the other line. Ned shut off the engine and held the skiff against the pulling current so Mel could get off. Once she was out of the boat, he used the line to pull the boats together, tossed Mac's gear bag onto the deck and climbed over the side. The consensus was that Wood had passed out again. He had never emerged from his room when they got back earlier.

"OK, what's your plan?" Mac asked Ned.

"You two go dive on that hole where the piling was going to go. It'd be crazy trying to set up the rest of the cofferdam at night. But you can use the Hookah rig and stay down as long as you need. See if there's anything there or not. At least we'll know before Wood shuts us down again."

Mel followed Mac toward the container, waited while he opened the combination lock and started pulling gear out.

"No fins. Just throw on some extra weight," he said to her as he pulled the small air compressor toward the starboard side. He checked the gas and started the compressor. Next, he attached a tether to the float surrounding the unit, and set the rig in the water. "Too bad we don't have the other boat with all the lights. But I see Ned's point about not being so obvious."

"I brought two dive lights from the house," Mel said as she slipped on her booties and added four pounds of lead to the weight belt. Mac did the same, and they walked to the side, with their masks around their necks. They each took a regulator, set their masks in place, and jumped into the dark water, a hose trailing behind them, hooked up to the compressor floating on the surface.

Fish darted in and out of the beams of light as they settled on the bottom and tried to get their bearings. What was so simple in daylight was difficult at night, and Mac realized he should have brought a compass to navigate with. In the dark, with no landmarks, he wasn't sure which way he was moving. He moved the light back and forth on the bottom, cautious not to lead them into one of the holes. With no reference points, he signaled to Mel to surface with him. Not sure he would be able to find her again, their lights only penetrating ten feet in the murky water, he preferred they stay together.

They ascended quickly, and came up on the barge, startling Ned, who quickly ran toward them. "Y'all alright?"

"I need my compass. There's crap for visibility down there. The lights are only good for a couple of feet."

Ned got up and went toward the container while Mac and Mel clung to the side of the barge, fighting to stay above water. Without the buoyancy compensators used when tank diving, their weight worked against them. Ned returned and held a disk with a string attached to Mac.

"Best I could do. Had to pop it out of your gauges. Just loop the string on your wrist and you should be good."

Mac held the compass in front of him and leveled it, allowing the needle to swing freely. He pointed it at the pier closest to the hole and took a bearing, then aligned the lubber line with north. Nodding to Mel, they put their regulators back in their mouths and let go of the barge.

He was quickly on the bottom, alternating the light's beam between the ocean floor and the compass, Mel followed close behind. They reached the pier, and he had to create a mental picture of where the original hole was. Another few steps and a darker spot became visible on the bottom. He shone the light into the darkness, revealing two huge lobsters, their antennas swerving back and forth, trying to make sense of the light and activity.

He ignored the crustaceans and kneeled on the sandy bottom. Mel came up beside him and added her light.

The hole was about three feet in diameter and four feet deep, having partially filled with sand from the changing tide. He leaned into the hole, motioned to her to hold his feet, and went in head first. But the bottom silted up as soon as he set his hand in the sand. Frustrated, he pushed back up, his movements causing a cloud of silt to follow him. He shook his head side to side, and raised his thumb toward the surface. They rose to the surface and swam to the barge where Ned helped them aboard.

"It's no good," Mac said once they were back on the barge. "The hole's partially filled, and the sand is so fine you just look at it and it silts up. We need another way."

"Cofferdam is the only way you're going to see if anything is down there." Wood stepped out of the shadows. "Thought I was crashed out and you could ditch me? Well, you best think again. Old man here was taking a nap and didn't hear the boat come up." Ned shrunk from his scowl. "Riddle me this: What the hell were you going to do if they needed help and you're sleeping?

"And you two. Trying to find treasure with your D-cell flashlights."

Mel was about to answer, but the sound of a motor coming toward them stopped her.

"What're y'all doing out here? Having a party and you didn't invite me?"

"Cody? What in the hell are you doin' out here?" Wood snorted.

"Could ask the same of you. Don't look like there's any work getting done, that's for sure." He swung the searchlight first on the group, causing them to shield their eyes, and then toward the dark water under the bridge. "Seen these same piles before."

"Maybe we're just doing some maintenance. What about you? What brings you out here at night? Don't look good from my side either. Could be you're up to no good, stealing equipment or supplies. I know it was you that cut the excavator hose the other night. Damn Brakens," he muttered under his breath.

"Just catching some mullet for tomorrow. Heading to check

my pinfish traps up in that cove." He pointed towards land. "I got no use for any of your crap."

"Well, be on your way then," Wood said.

Cody looked away, pushed down on the throttle and moved away from the barge. Twenty yards away, too close for them not to feel his wake he accelerated leaving the barge bouncing in the waves. Mac looked at Wood, hands clenched at his side as they watched the white light above the boat's T-top fade into the night.

"Think we ought to head on in. Nothing to be accomplished in the dark. First light, we'll come set up the dam and pump her out." He looked down. "Then, if you want to have a look for whatever you think is down there, go ahead. Travis here is going to weld the rebar cage. As soon as he's done, I'll bring the inspector to have a look. That'll give you a couple of days before we pour concrete and take down the dam. If you can't find anything in forty-eight hours I'm pouring concrete and getting on with it. I need a real paycheck not all this treasure talk."

* * *

Cody was back at the bar smiling into his beer, watching Nicole shake her stuff out of the corner of his eye. He'd already netted two-hundred and fifty dollars for the extra mullet he had caught tonight. And with the live well full, he was bound to have a good charter tomorrow. Feeling cocky, he yelled down the bar for Nicole, proud to be making more than she did for a change.

She moved down the bar, leaving the group drinking at the end laughing. "What's up?"

"How 'bout a shot of Jack for your boy here." He flashed the wad of cash at her.

"Way to go, babe." She returned with a bottle and shot glass.

He downed it and set it on the bar, waiting for her to refill it. "Had a good bait run, and got a charter tomorrow. Seen my dad anywhere? I seen Wood, his daughter, and old man Ned out there, too."

74

"That's interesting." She looked down at the bar, shaking her butt at the group of men calling for her. "I was at the library looking up something for the old man today, and Wood's daughter was there. Had an old-looking thing with her, kind of the same as the one they had in here the other night. Maybe they found something down there."

"Could explain what they were doing sneaking around out there tonight." He watched her saunter down the bar, the hoots of the men getting louder as she approached. Sometimes he enjoyed the show, having all these men leer over his wife, but other times, especially when he had a pocket full of cash, it irked him. He downed the shot in front of him and walked to the end of the bar.

"Y'all need to take it down a notch."

"What's it to you?" One of the men jumped from his stool and hovered in Cody's face. The other three gathered around, ready to follow up.

"Now, boys," Nicole called over to them. "Check this out." She slithered backwards over the bar top, settling her lower back on the bar. In her hand she held a tequila bottle, which she tipped over her belly button. "Who wants to go first?"

They swung around, pushing each other for position, and Cody skulked away, watching her giggle as they sucked tequila from her navel.

He went outside slamming the bar door behind him and went to his car. *Why did she have to go this far?* It was like she was taunting him, walking the fine line between what she knew turned him on and what would set him off. This time she had gone too far. He sat in his car, fuming about Nicole. It didn't take long for his anger, fueled by the alcohol, turned to rage. He got out and started for the door of the bar, but quickly lost his nerve as he was about to pull the handle. Slowly, he wandered back to the car, depression taking the place of his anger.

It was his fault that she needed to work there, after all.

He got into the car and started the engine, trying to gather his wits. Nearly hitting the car next to him, he backed out of the parking space and drove onto the small frontage road. The traffic light just started to turn yellow when he accelerated through it, bounced off the divider, and swung into the middle of the two-lane road. The police car's lights startled him, and he cringed. Hoping it was for someone else, he continued to drive. Two minutes later he was on the ground, handcuffs clamped to his wrists, while the officer read him his rights.

Chapter 11

The only thing that had gone right in the last two days was that her hair was now one color. Kellie looked in the rear view mirror and adjusted her head to check for dark roots. Satisfied with the dye job, she leaned back in the seat and waited for someone to open the club. She was getting desperate, out of drugs and money, she had dyed her hair and driven to Key West, spending her last few dollars on a cheap hotel on Boca Chica Key. Finding Mac had not panned out yet, and she would have to put it on hold until she could earn some money. Her search of the phone book in Marathon for a diving operation that Mac might be working for had proven fruitless. No one she called had heard of him. A couple had said to call this guy named Wood, but when she did, no one answered his phone.

It was getting to be late morning, beads of sweat were forming on her brow and worse, in her cleavage. Frustrated, she called out to a guy walking down the street to find out what time it was. Feeling the tightness around her head, she started to panic. If she had much longer to wait she would have to find a shower. The man said it was almost eleven now; someone should be coming in to open soon, she hoped, as another bead of sweat fell and rolled down her ample breasts. The tourists were starting to cruise Duval Street when a large bald man went up the stairs to the club, followed by three girls. A deep breath and she was out of the car, taking the stairs two at a time. Reaching the landing just as he opened the door, she slid inside.

He turned to her with a scowl on his face. *Great, a hard ass.* This was going to be tougher than she thought. "Hey, hon, I'm no bill collector or nothing." She shoved her chest out, letting him get a good look before she spoke again. "Looking for some work, though. Want a little audition?"

That got the desired response. No one ever turned down a free audition, no matter how hardened they were to watching girls strip every day.

"You go all nude here, or what?"

He shook his head no, then jerked it in the direction of the stage. She went over and set her purse down. The air smelled of stale beer and sweat. Thankfully, the man went to a thermostat, and turned on the air conditioner. The old unit grumbled and started to bring in fresh air.

"Got some music? Van Halen or something works for me." Wondering if he had vocal cords, she watched as he went to the DJ booth and started the music. And then she got to work. He shook his head when she started to peel her G string off, but nodded toward the dressing room when she was finished.

Satisfied, she followed the other girls. Too bad it wasn't all nude, she thought. Always a little more money in that. But then she overheard the girls talking about a cruise ship coming in today, and she was suddenly all smiles.

* * *

Wood stood on the bow of the barge, a beer in hand, watching the building clouds, highlighted by the sun rising behind them. "Red sky, gonna turn to shit soon enough. Nature doesn't lie."

Mac looked over his shoulder, wondering what the other

man saw. His gaze dropped to the beer in his hand, and he lost interest in the prophecy. He had tossed and turned on the couch all night, trying to figure out if it was worth taking whatever paycheck he could get and moving on. Wood's constant state of at least semi-drunkenness bothered him. They were working with heavy equipment underwater. You needed all your senses and then some to do that, and he was worried about putting his life on the line again. But then the old relic they found pushed those thoughts from his mind. He was more intrigued than he wanted to admit.

Then he started to rationalize Wood's drinking with the education he could get from him. Finally, as dawn was about to break, he'd decided to stay put … at least for a while.

Wood interrupted his thoughts. "Best get to work here. Ain't gonna build itself." He went to the container and pulled out some rigging, laying several straps on the deck. "Well?"

Mac went over to help him, unsure of what to do, but sensing the short temper. "What do you want me to do?"

"Build the goddamn thing," he spat. "I'm gonna get in the excavator and you're going to get in the water." He looked over at Ned. "Old fart over there is gonna attach this strap to a panel, and I'm gonna lower it into place. You go under and set the bottom. When you surface, I'll pound her in. Then you gotta drill some holes along the edge and set the bolts to attach the panels. It ain't rocket science. Do that about twenty times, and we can start to pump her out. Then we'll see what's getting y'all so excited."

Mac went for his dive gear with trepidation. It was only yesterday that Wood had forgotten he was under, and almost killed him. He slid into his wetsuit and went over to Ned, promising himself he would keep an eye on Wood. If it got to dangerous he would pull the plug and that would be it.

"Can you keep an eye on him for me? I want to be on the surface before he moves that bucket." He looked around the deck and spotted a float that looked like a kick board with a line attached. "Toss that in the water. When I'm on it, you can give him the green light to pound his heart out."

Ned tossed the line in the water and started to rig the pneumatic drill needed to secure the panels to each other. Once the drill was connected to the air hose, he took a buoy with a small piece of line attached to it and a caribiner on the other end. "I'd drill five holes in each panel. Old boy up there'll be in a rush, but trust me, it'll leak if you don't. When you're done, just clip this to the drill like this." He showed Mac the spot on the drill. "That'll keep it on the surface while you put the bolts in."

"Just keep an eye on him," Mac said again as he went for the BC and turned on the air valve. He checked the gauges and strapped on the tank. Mask and fins in place, he took a giant stride entry into the water, and swam back toward the barge. Ned handed him the drill along with a bag of nuts and bolts, and tossed the float in the water. The weight of the hardware clipped to his weight belt quickly pulled him under, and he shot a burst of air into the BC to compensate for the extra weight, then went for the float. Ned acknowledged the thumbs up signal and went toward Wood.

Mac waited on the surface, holding the float for support and wondering about how many ways this could go wrong. Then the first panel swung into the air and hung above the water next to the farthest pier. Slowly, it disappeared into the water, until only about three feet showed above the surface. Mac grabbed the inflator hose, put his left arm above his head, released the air in his BC, and sank to the bottom. He finned to the panel, which sat in a small cloud of silt. Somehow, Wood had judged correctly; the weight of the steel was still supported by the excavator, making it easy to push into the groove of the I-beam. Satisfied it was in position, he moved back toward the buoy and surfaced.

Ned saw his thumbs up and spoke into a walkie talkie. Seconds later, the bucket of the excavator started its work, pounding the steel panel into the bottom. Only a foot was out of the water when Wood stopped. Mac looked around to check the high tide mark on the adjacent bridge pilings. The panel would easily remain above water at high tide.

He retrieved the drill and went to work, quickly becoming frustrated when the bit seemed to be losing ground on the I-beam; becoming dull before the hole was even bored. Only a foot below the surface, working on the top hole, he heard the dull rhythmic thud of someone pounding against the steel hull. He popped his head above water and noticed Wood standing next to Ned, motioning him over.

When he got there, Wood bent over and handed him another bit. "Sounds back-asswards, but you've got to drill slow as you can in steel. Go too fast and you'll burn the bit. I could hear that drill screaming from up here. Swap the bit out with this one and try again."

Mac took the new bit and swam toward the drill suspended from the buoy. He swapped the bits and went back to work, amazed at how quickly the bit bored through the half-inch-thick steel beam at a slower speed. Holes bored, he went to work bolting the panels together.

Another panel was hanging off the deck, ready to be placed in the water, when he surfaced. It dropped into the water as soon as he reached the float and gave Ned the thumbs up. Their pace increased as they settled into the rhythm of the work, each man working through his job.

The last panel set, Mac looked around for the sun to gauge the time of day, and noticed the thunderhead right on top of them. He swam to the barge and started to climb out of the water.

But Wood put out his hand. "Not so fast. You gotta go in and set the intake hose for the pump." He must have noticed Mac's worried glance at the thunderhead. "Don't worry, that storm's a good twenty minutes from breaking loose," he said reassuringly. "Now, you ain't gonna climb over that metal without tearing yourself a new one, so I'll set you into the enclosure with the bucket, and then send over the hose and weight. Just set it on the bottom so the hose is on its side and not facing straight down."

Mac took a deep breath and slid back in the water. His

confidence, built by the day's work, waned as the bucket approached. Wood hadn't seemed to be drunk, but he had been drinking so much it was often hard to tell. The bucket swung toward him and stopped. Mac grabbed for two teeth, gloved hands tightly gripping the steel. A nod to Ned that he was ready and the bucket lifted him from the water and swung out over the steel plates, raw edges jutting angrily from the water. His grip loosened once he was over the metal, and he dropped into the water.

BC inflated, he waited as Ned loaded the hose and rigging into the bucket. As it came toward him, he swam for the metal side, thinking that Wood might not be able to see him over the wall of steel. The bucket hit the water and dumped its contents. He followed it down and went to work looping the rigging around the hose and securing it to the weights. Suddenly, though, a shadow blocked the light.

He looked up and saw the fish, five feet long, swimming aggressively as it followed the perimeter of the steel, seeking a way out.

* * *

Braken woke on his own couch the minute the sun hit his face. He lay there and listened, hoping that Pagliano and Cheqea were still asleep. Aside from Pagliano taking his bedroom, last night had thankfully been uneventful, Now, the house was quiet, so he lay motionless, thinking about how to handle the mobster. The man's modus operandi was not going to cut it here. Maybe it worked in New Jersey, but this was a small town. Braken had done enough deals to know just about every city or county administrator south of Miami, and he had the experience to say so. Pagliano's plan of hauling Cheqea into the federal building at gun point was not going to work. But how was he going to convince the mobster of that?

The phone rang then, interrupting his thoughts.

He went to the counter in the kitchen and picked up the receiver. "Hello," he said, and then listened. "You got a DUI? Are you an idiot? They set bail yet?" He waited for an answer. "Get comfortable. Maybe Nicole can bail you out; I got some trouble of my own.

"What the hell was that about? Bail can't be good." Pagliano stumbled into the living room.

"Just my son. Idiot. He can rot in jail and think about it for a while. You want to wake the chief up and get this done?"

"Shit, we might have to drag her ass down there on a stretcher. I gave her half a bottle of pills just to shut her up."

"You know, I've been thinking." Braken paused, not sure if it was worth getting Pagliano worked up so early. But the option of marching her into the federal building, risking a scene, would lose any chance of credibility. Building his courage, he decided it would be better to get it out now. "You know she's not real stable, right? We take her into that building with all those government people, and she's bound to start trouble. That might kill our chance at this whole deal."

Pagliano sat on the couch. "Being that she's drugged out of her mind, maybe you should just go deal with that boy of yours. We need his eyes on the construction project. I'll let her sleep it off. Then we'll have a heart-to-pea-brained talk, just me and her. Get going."

Braken took advantage of the respite and grabbed his keys off the table by the door. "I'll get back as soon as I can," he said, and left before Pagliano could change his mind. He made it to his car and pulled out of the driveway. As soon as he was around the corner he breathed a sigh of relief. At least he had a little time to think. And deal with Cody.

The offices of Braken Ventures were located on US 1, above a strip mall that sold discount sandals. Surprised Nicole's car was already there, he pulled into his own space and looked at his watch. Nine fifteen was a little early for her to be in the office. Cody must have called her too, he guessed, and she was upstairs waiting for him with a plea for bail money. He closed the car door and headed up the stairs to his office.

Chapter 12

Wood jumped out of the cab and ran toward Mac. "What'd you see?"

"Scared the crap out of me. I was just setting the last bolt and saw this shadow over me. Then it started moving ..."

"How big?"

Mac wasn't sure where this was going, and was too tired to care. He started to peel out of the wet suit. Once free he extended his arms as wide as they would go.

"Hot damn. Get out of that suit."

Mac stepped out of the suit, pulling the rubbery material off his legs one at a time. Wood moved quickly, showing no sign of his beer consumption, as he went for the fresh tank sitting by the compressor.

"You're going down there?" Mac asked, surprised. "Sure looked like a shark to me."

"Goddam right I am. Where's that old man? Sleeping again, probably. Ned!" he yelled, and waited. Soon enough, Ned came around the corner. "We got a spear gun on this hunk of steel?"

"Naw, don't think so. We could rig that air thing, like last time." He picked up a piece of rebar that sat on the deck and jabbed the air with it.

"It'll do. Boy Wonder here saw something in there. I'm fixin' to go get it."

Mac watched the two men go to work. He could hear Wood digging around in the container, while Ned unwound an air hose and hooked it to the compressor. Wood emerged with a short piece of hose and an air nozzle with a trigger. He connected the fitting to the air line with a hose clamp and squeezed the trigger. Air shot out of the end. With another clamp, he attached a three-foot-long piece of hose to the end of the nozzle.

"You're going to blast it with air?" Mac was confused.

"Just watch. Maybe you'll learn something." Wood took the rebar from Ned and stuck it in the open end of the hose. The smaller diameter steel fit smoothly into the half-inch hose. He pushed the bar in, leaving the last foot exposed.

Mac understood now, and flinched when Wood pointed the gun at him. It looked ominous, as he imagined the pressure with which the sudden burst of air would shoot the steel rod. "Cool. I'd like to try that. But - you're going to freedive?"

Wood laughed. "Yeah boy. Best way to spearfish. All that noise from the tank'll frighten the fish. The only easy way out for whatever's in there is dead. It could get sucked into the pump and bugger up the whole works if we don't get it now." He spit in the mask, and washed it with freshwater from the jug. "You run that thing better than him. Do the same to me as I did with you, and get me in that hole."

"You're not worried about what it is? That's like a shark tank."

"Chances are pretty good it's not a shark. Them beasts need to keep moving. It'd be splashing around like crazy, trying to get out. My bet, if you're right about the size, is it's a jewfish. Now show me what you can do and bring that excavator bucket over here." He pointed to the spot on the water before putting on the long free diving fins and jumping in.

Mac climbed into the cab and started the excavator. A few quick manipulations to get comfortable with the controls, and he manipulated the bucket until it hovered a foot over Wood's head.

He followed the hand signals and slid the bucket, allowing Wood to climb in, the air hose dragging behind, then moved the bucket to hover over the cofferdam.

Wood looked over the edge into the water, but Mac wasn't sure he could see anything. Then, without signaling, he stood in the bucket and jumped in, one hand over his face to keep the mask in place, the other grasping the air gun. Mac couldn't do anything except watch the water for any sign of activity. A small steady stream of bubbles was visible, rising from Wood, who appeared to be stationary.

"What's with the bubbles?" Mac asked.

"He's breathing air from the hose," Ned said.

Suddenly, Wood's head erupted from the water.

"Send over another spear. I got a line on it, but missed the sucker. Boyo here was about right on — it's a helluva big jewfish."

Mac looked over toward Ned, who was scrambling on the deck. He grabbed a twenty-foot-long stick of rebar and dragged it to the cutter, where he quickly cut two lengths, and yelled at Mac to bring the bucket toward him. Shafts loaded in the bucket, Mac manipulated the controls and brought the scoop to rest in the water beside Wood. He waited again as Wood grabbed a shaft, breathed deeply and submerged.

They both stared at the water; Mac from the excavator and Ned from the deck. A long minute passed and Mac started to worry. No movement, no bubbles. Suddenly Mac made a decision and sprung into action, jumping from the cab and running for the container.

"Get in the excavator! There's something wrong!" he yelled at Ned as he emerged with a mask and snorkel.

"I can't run that thing," Ned said.

"Up. Down. Side to side. It's not rocket science." Mac strapped the mask to his face and adjusted the snorkel. Without SCUBA equipment, he could get in the water faster, but he would be limited on search time. Realizing it would be worth the time to gear up, he grabbed the SCUBA tank and BC, and flipped them on his back. No fins were within reach, and he figured the time spent searching and putting them on could be life or death.

"I'm gonna swim to the steel!" he yelled. "Figure it out, you've gotta lift me over the top." He jumped off the edge of the barge, took two strong kicks, and reached the metal wall. Ned was clearly struggling with the bucket, though, and Mac knew he was out of time. He calculated that it had to have been three, maybe four, minutes since the bubbles stopped. Sacrificing his body, he grabbed the steel with both hands and tried to vault over.

But what would have been easy on land was impossible with the friction of the water and the weight of the gear. He took a deep breath and lifted himself slowly this time, his muscles screaming, until his body was over the wall where he landed head first in the water.

Thunder boomed above him, and a gust of wind hit him. It was an ominous sign to start a search. Descending he found the visibility had worsened from the chase. Mac circled the enclosure trying to remember where he had last seen Wood surface. He thought he saw something out of place, but it was hard to tell in the shadow cast by the steel wall. A quick kick and he could see Wood, face down against a pile. He kicked harder, reaching him seconds later and shook him to see if he were alive, but got no response. He took a deep breath and stuffed the regulator into Wood's mouth. Hoping he would breath, Mac hit the purge button, and shot air into the man's lungs, then pressed the inflator button on his BC.

They shot to the surface. Wood still had the regulator in his mouth, but appeared to be unconscious. Out of breath and unwilling to give up, Mac put him in a headlock and dragged him to the wall, gulping air as soon as his head broke the surface.

* * *

Braken considered it a win; Cheqea puked only once on the

hour-long ride. The dashboard clock showed three o'clock, and he worried it was too late to get anything done with the government being a Friday. Especially since they weren't even in the office yet. The whole day had been an expensive waste. Cody was out of jail, but it cost him the charter scheduled for that morning, and another five grand for bail. It was after noon before Cheqea could even stand, and now he feared that Pagliano and the chief might be his house guests for the weekend.

He glanced at the back seat. Pagliano was staring out the window, fascinated by the tourists streaming down Duval Street on foot, bicycles, and pink scooters. Cheqea leaned against the opposite door, snoring quietly.

"Where's the federal building? It's getting late."

Braken braked as several rotund tourists shimmied between the Cadillac and the cab in front of him, red plastic drink cups held above the steaming cars. "It's about a mile, but with this traffic ..."

"Fuck the traffic — look at her. It's hopeless to get this done today." Pagliano was checking out the scenery. "Might as well have some fun while we're here. Ever been to that club?" He stabbed a finger at the closed window toward a sign.

"Hottest place on the strip." Braken thought the day might be saved, but then looked at Cheqea.

The mobster caught his look, glanced at her and shrugged. "Don't worry about her. We can bring her along. They love it when you bring in chicks. Park this beast and let's have us a little fun."

Braken swerved through another crowd of shopping bag-clad tourists, and pulled to the curb. "Valet? That way we don't have to carry her too far." He slung his heavy frame from the car, grunting as he got out into the hot air. "You got her? I'll grease some palms."

He headed up the stairs for the club, reluctantly passed the bouncer a wad of cash, and waited for Pagliano, who followed, Cheqea on his arm. She was now awake, mooning around and trying to get her bearings.

Loud music and cold air greeted them as the door opened.

They entered, and navigated to a table by the stage. Pagliano slid Cheqea into the booth and got in beside side her. Braken sat on the other side, both men tight against her to brace her from falling over.

"Where you white boys take me? I thought we was signing papers so I could get my cash." She looked around. "This ain't no federal building, that's for sure. Nice ass on that one, though."

As if on cue, the girl swung from the pole on the stage and landed on their table. She continued dancing while Braken dug into his wallet for some cash. He pulled out some dollar bills, but Pagliano, seeing the dancer glance elsewhere at the site of the singles, grabbed a handful of twenties from Braken's wallet and tossed them at her. She squatted on the table, allowing him to reach her garter belt to insert the money. With each bill, she inched forward, until her crotch was in his face. Pagliano grabbed the wallet from Braken's hand and showed her the insides.

"What'll you do for that, sweetheart?" Pagliano had to yell over the music.

She leaned over and whispered in his ear. Braken leaned over to hear, but Pagliano swatted him away. By the middle of the next song, the money from his wallet was hers and she was in Pagliano's lap, grinding to the beat.

The chief leaned over to whisper in Braken's ear. "She ain't got shit. Bet I can get you off before she does him."

Braken leaned back and watched as the chief pulled her top over her head and started dancing next to the other girl. A tourists crowded around their table, watching Cheqea and the dancer, each trying to outdo the other. The dancer reached for her G string and, in one move, tore it from her glistening body. Before Cheqea could follow suit, the bouncer was at the table, a hand in each of their hair to escort them to the door.

Braken and Pagliano followed them out, Cheqea's clothes and the discarded G string in their hands. They exchanged a quick grin as the door opened and the hot air blasted them.

It was instantly quiet when the door closed behind them.

90

"Our car's right over there. Come on. I'll go back and get your stuff," Braken said.

Pagliano put his arm around the girl, shielding her from the gaze of the tourists as they made their way to the Cadillac. Before Braken had a chance to go back for her things, a large purse was tossed out of the club onto the street. He quickly retrieved it and ran back to the Cadillac.

"Kellie."

They all turned toward her with questioning looks.

"My name, assholes. You ought to know who the fuck you're hanging out with, duh ..."

Pagliano gave her a cross look, but she sidled toward him before he could act on it. People that talked to him like that usually ended up with a wired jaw. But he decided to give her another chance after she rubbed against him. "Sweetheart. No anger here. We'll take care of you better than that place would. I got a classy joint up in Miami Beach. You don't need the shit down here."

"Totally nude, I hope. These guys are in the stone age. So who are you guys?" She looked at Cheqea. "And babe, me and you got to get together. That was some seriously hot stuff you had going on in there."

"Whatever," Cheqea said and turned toward Braken. "I need my medicinal. You guys blew it today. Probably after 5 now, and the feds are closed up till Monday. Gonna cost you for the weekend."

Pagliano reached past Kellie and grabbed Cheqea's neck. "Bitch. Listen good. It's your own fault for being so freakin' high maintenance. If you would have woken up earlier, we could have had this dog and pony show on the road in time to get it done. As it is, you're staying with us until Monday. So shut the fuck up."

The valet sensing trouble, quickly brought the car. Braken got in, opened the windows and put the AC on high. Pagliano pushed the girls into the back seat and then climbed in between them. "Where to, then?" Braken looked at Pagliano, feeling lonely in the front seat. He was all for a weekend-long party, especially now that they had seen another side of Cheqea.

"Your place is probably the best bet. Be a lot quieter there, if you know what I mean."

Chapter 13

Although Cody was technically a free man, he feared the reprisals that would surely come from his family. From years of experience, he knew that both Nicole and his father would be unrelenting in their criticism. Hoping to dodge both bullets, and maybe garner a little favor, he walked out of the sheriff's office and headed toward the marina. He intended to find out what Wood was really up to.

It was a long two miles to walk in this heat, and he felt the humidity suck the alcohol from the night before through his skin. He knew he stunk, but there was nothing to be done about that now. Head pounding, he trudged along the hot concrete sidewalk until it ended at the asphalt road, where the temperature seemed to increase by another 10 degrees. Fifteen minutes later, when he reached the marina, he ditched his shirt and went straight for the hose behind the tool shed. The tepid water cooled him slightly, and removed the first layer of sweat. Feeling cleaner, he drank from the hose and repeated the process.

There were no towels, so he shook his hair like a dog, left his shirt off, and walked to his boat. After climbing aboard, he started the engines and he let loose the dock lines. Minutes later, he was cruising through the no wake zone, the breeze cooling him. It was evident that the wind was starting to pick up — a sure sign a thunderstorm was near. He looked around the horizon, noticing three separate thunderclouds, their anvil heads reaching high into the sky. Rain was visible, sheeting from the bottom of each cloud.

As if on cue, he heard rumbling in the distance. Something to keep an eye on, he thought. He didn't plan on venturing too far from shore, so he wasn't overly concerned. The boat's course followed the Seven Mile Bridge past Little Duck, Missouri and Ohio Keys before veering to the left of the marker at Bahia Honda. He steered toward the darker water that signified depth as he skirted the Bahia Honda Channel, and went around the top of No Name Key before turning back toward land and coasting up to the bridge. The boat stopped, and he dropped the anchor straight down, tying off the line so it wouldn't swing into the bridge.

He kept his distance, happy to observe without being seen, figuring the massive concrete piers of the bridge would hide him. Another run-in with Wood was not a good idea. Thirsty, he reached into the cooler and pulled out a beer — the only thing available. His head felt better as the warm beer mitigated the hangover, but it also made him groggy. He hadn't gotten much sleep in the jail the night before, so he leaned back against the padding on the gunwale, and was soon out.

* * *

The Cadillac was pulled over on the shoulder of US1, just past Stock Island. They hadn't made it far when the storm hit, and now sat in a line of cars that had also decided to wait out the storm. Often the afternoon thunderstorms put rain down so hard and fast that it made driving impossible, the windshield wipers futile against the onslaught. The air conditioning was working overtime, trying to cut the humidity the storm brought, and the windows were fogged. They were unable to see anything past the sheeting rain. It was loud inside the Cadillac, its vinyl top unable to dampen the sound of the driving rain.

"I'm hungry," Cheqea said.

"We'll get something as soon as this crap lets up. You could chew on your girlfriend here, if you can't wait," Pagliano said.

"And I'm sure you'd love to watch. Too bad, Jersey, show's over."

"You freakin' tease." Pagliano reached his arm out to swat her, but she ducked under it.

"This sucks. If y'all are going to fight, I'm ought'a here," Kellie said.

"Sweetheart, you're not going anywhere." Pagliano reached an arm behind her.

Kellie was getting worried, now. They had been fun in the club, but in the close quarters of the car, things were getting ugly. First the constant bickering, and now he was touching her. Guys didn't get to touch her unless she asked them to — or they paid. It was a double standard, but she was able to compartmentalize her work persona from her personal one; the only way to survive her profession.

She tried to refocus on why she was here — Mac Travis. Getting Mac back was what brought her to this hellhole. The billboards on the way here had called it paradise, but she didn't get it. Paradise was back home, dancing for oil workers just off the rig, their pockets stuffed with cash. But it just didn't work without Mac there.

The rain continued as they sat there in some form of a truce, waiting for it to end. She could tell that Pagliano was getting fidgety. He was playing with her hair, now, and her head felt like a band was tightening around her temples.

And bad things happened when her head hurt. He reached his other hand over and set it between her legs, inching closer to her.

She bit her tongue, restraining the outburst, but with limited options, she finally decided to try to be tactful. "That's for the club, not here." She moved his hand away.

He turned to her, his face crimson. "Don't think you know

the rules here, sweetheart. What Joey wants, he takes. Right Braken?" He looked to the front seat for reassurance.

The tightness around her temples was getting worse, and she knew she would have to make a move. The feeling came and went, often without cause, but she knew stress was bad —very bad. Without thinking of the consequences — that she was covered only in a light jacket and had nowhere to run, especially in the stilettos she wore — she suddenly dragged her pinkie nail across his face. He pulled back in surprise, but quickly recovered, grabbing her wrist with his free hand.

She'd been in close quarters with guys groping her before, but this time there was no bouncer to help. She was on her own. Her head jerked back, and she brought it forward with all the momentum the tight space would allow, head butting Pagliano on the bridge of the nose. This time he screamed and put his hands to his face. It gave her enough time to grab the door handle and jump out of the car.

She slammed the door behind her and ran into the storm, but with her second step, her heel caught the curb, and she fell to her knees. Looking back, she couldn't see the car through the rain. But she was sure that guy would be coming after her. She got up, took off her heels, and started running.

* * *

Mac reached the metal wall of the cofferdam and grabbed the edge, the rough metal cutting through his hand as he strained to keep Wood's head out of the water. The storm was on them now, rain blowing horizontally in the wind. The barge was barely visible, and the noise of the wind and rain made communication with Ned impossible.

Mac knew he was on his own, and had to act fast. Thunder boomed, and a flash of lightning lit Wood's unconscious face. His first challenge was to try and revive him. Unable to position himself for mouth to mouth in the water, he reached up for the regulator still in Wood's mouth trying to find the purge button. A quick hit forced air into Wood's lungs.

Mac waited, but no exhale came. He tried again. This time Wood coughed, and he heard the sound of the regulator cycling air. In better circumstances, he would have waited patiently for Wood to start breathing normally, but lightning flashed again, and he was losing his grip on the metal wall.

He fully inflated the BC and released the button. His hand found the buckles, and he shrugged out of the vest. Wood's head dipped below the water, bubbles slowly breaking the surface. He grabbed him and rolled him on his back. It took several tries, but finally he stuffed Wood into the vest, pausing several times to catch his breath. Wood was finally in the dive gear, breathing through the regulator when he felt a surge causing Mac to lose his grip.

They were off of the wall and floating freely, their weight unbalanced with Mac, Wood, and the dive tank all supported by just the BC. They started to spin as the water formed a vortex, and he found himself underwater, Wood supported in his arms. His lungs were getting tight, and he knew he needed air and would drown if he didn't surface. Forced to trust the equipment, he let go of Wood and broke the surface, gasping for breath.

Just as he was about to grab the wall, something sucked him to the bottom, pounding him against the pier and whipping his body through the swirling water. Disoriented, his training kicked in, allowing his body to float — the only way he could tell where the surface was. As he started to rise, he kicked, and smashed his head against the hull of a boat. Out of breath, he gagged and swallowed water, frantically finning away from the obstruction. Away from the hull, he was able to surface and grab a breath.

The water calmed and the rain had let up enough for him to

see an entire section of wall missing, with a boat sitting where the cofferdam had been. He swam for a small piece of the dam that remained. Supported by the wall, he was able to see the entire scene.

Wood was nowhere to be found.

Chapter 14

The wind howled, and he jumped as lightning struck nearby. Cody was jarred awake when the boat slammed against the bridge piling. The last thing he remembered, he had dropped anchor and had a beer. The anchor must have pulled when the wind picked up, he thought, as he went to the bow and yanked on the line. A set anchor would have pulled back against him, but the line came easily. He quickly pulled in the line and set the anchor on the deck, cursing himself that he hadn't let any extra line out. With only fifteen feet of line out in ten feet of water, the increased wind and waves had yanked the anchor loose.

Before he could get back to the helm to start the engine, the boat was swept past the bridge piling and flung sideways into the steel wall that Wood had been building. Frantic now, he turned the key. The motor turned over, but didn't start. He must have been asleep longer than he thought, allowing the engine to go cold. He depressed the key to open the choke and turned it again, but just as the engine cranked, the boat spun and crashed into the steel wall. The furious flow of incoming water turned the previously contained water into a vortex, flinging the boat against the walls as it spun. Cody saw the figure of a man vault himself over the wall just before the boat hit, but all he could do was hold on until the fury subsided.

The boat spun inside the steel walls, smashing them as it went. After several jarring hits, the cofferdam was open on both ends, allowing the water to flow more naturally. Finally the water spent its energy and the boat sat idle in the ruined enclosure. With a pained look, he surveyed the damage his boat had caused. Then he felt the water pooling at his feet. Seawater was coming in fast from a ragged basketball sized hole in the starboard gunwale. Realizing there was no way the bilge pump could keep up with the incoming water, he started to panic. Sinking the boat in the channel would incur the wrath of his father and Pagliano, and lose him his best source of income. He had to save the vessel.

A cushion strapped to the seat caught his eye. He grabbed it and stuffed it into the hole. It held for a minute, but then the pressure of the water pushed it back in, and the flow resumed. It was past ankle deep in the boat now, and he could feel it sinking. Finally, he got the motor started and turned towards deeper water.

The boat was sluggish as he pushed the throttle down, the water adding enough weight to affect the engine. With one eye ahead and the other on the hole he pushed the boat as hard as it would go. The flow abated slightly as the water was forced past the hole by the speed of the boat, but it wasn't enough. Needing to make landfall before he sunk, he spotted Porpoise Key in the distance, and steered toward it, throttle depressed to its stop. The water became shallower as he steered to the right of the number two marker and then cut a hard left, beaching the boat on the sand.

The hole was out of the water now, and he breathed out in relief, his panic subsiding as he watched the bilge pump strain to pump out the water.

* * *

Mac watched as the panicked man made a makeshift patch and pulled away. He pulled himself as high as he could on the wall and scanned the water, but Wood was nowhere in sight. The water was calm again, as the storm had moved overland and the pressures between the channel and the enclosure equalized. Using one of the missing panels, he skirted the wall and swam to the boat. Ned was standing on one of the excavator tracks searching the water when he climbed on deck.

"Anything?" Mac asked as he climbed the ladder and jumped up on the track, the extra height allowing him a better view.

"Nothing. I can see Cody's boat beached over there on Porpoise Key."

"Keep looking. I'm going to grab the skiff and go over to see if he's seen anything," Mac said.

"No point. Damn fool caused this, and is most likely drunk. He can be a handful when he's been drinking," Ned said as he turned and scanned the water. "First thing we ought to do is figure out the current, and try and make an estimate of where to start looking."

Mac didn't understand what he was talking about, but figured any idea was better than driving around blind. "OK." He hopped down from the track and went over to the skiff.

"In the water. You're a little bigger, but it'll have to do."

Mac looked at him again, but rather than waste time with questions, he jumped in. "Now what?"

"Swim to the mid-point of the barge and float." Ned ran over to the spot and looked at his watch. Once Mac was in position he yelled, "Go!"

"Go where?"

"Just let the current take you. I'm going to time you for a minute. That'll give us bearing and speed. From that, we can figure out when this happened and put it on a chart." He watched Mac move with the current. "OK. Looks to be about 250 feet to the north. Current's running fast." He paused and calculated. "Near three knots."

Mac climbed out of the water. "So, it happened maybe ten minutes ago, which means he should be almost a half-mile north?"

STEVEN BECKER

"You catch on quick," Ned answered. "It's not quite that easy, though; lots of variables can change it, but that's where we start." He got on his knees and slid into the skiff.

Mac hopped in behind him and started the engine. He waited for Ned to release the lines, then headed under the bridge and into the main channel.

"Should be up there." He pointed toward Porpoise Key.

"Nah, it's been a few more minutes, and that'll put him past there. Probably be in the Big Spanish Channel by now. If he gets into that, it's going to be hard to find him."

Mac ignored the no wake zone and sped between the numbers one and two markers just before Porpoise Key. He could see Cody sitting on the gunwale with a distraught look on his face as they passed. Under any other circumstances, Mac would have stopped and given him a piece of his mind, but the search for Wood was urgent. Probably be good for him to spend a couple hours out there for all the damage he caused.

The boat entered the channel and moved north.

"This what you're thinking?"

"It's the best we can do. Old Wood never put a radio on this boat."

"So we either keep looking or go back and call for help, and then he gets even further away."

"Exactly." Ned was scanning the small keys scattered on either side of the channel. "He could be anywhere, and it's getting dark. Cody's boat is closer than the barge. I say we go see if Cody's got a radio on board and call it in. That'll only take a minute, and then we head back out and search until it gets dark."

Mac swung the boat around without responding. "You think he's got one?"

"I can see the antennae. I'm hoping he does."

Mac coasted the boat onto the beach, allowing the bow to just lodge itself in the sand. Cody was still sitting on his boat, watching as the bilge strained and died. "Hey, you got a radio?"

"What of it?"

"Wood's out there somewhere, and we need to call for help." Mac watched him flip his legs into the boat and go to the helm. He lifted the mike and turned on the radio. Silence greeted them.

"Bilge must have run the battery out. You guys give me a ride outta here?"

Mac stared at him and looked over at Ned, who shook his head. "We've gotta go. I'll tell someone you're here." Mac pushed the boat off the sand as Ned moved to take the helm. "What now?"

"Barge is right over there. We can use our radio there, and then go search some more." He looked over at Mac with a worried look. The time was slipping away. "Unless he's grounded, he's pretty far out by now."

* * *

"What's with you lily whites? Scaring the girl off like that," Cheqea said.

Braken turned around to look at her. They were still sitting on the side of the road. The rain had let up slightly, but the cars hadn't started to move yet. Before he could answer, she grabbed the door handle.

"I'm going after her. That girl needs my help. She could seriously use some of my medicine."

Pagliano grabbed the door and yanked it shut, pulling the chief back against him. "Lock the doors. She stays with us."

The sound of the automatic door locks clicked as they stared at each other. "Rain's let up enough, we can start heading back now," Braken said.

"Ain't no heading back. That girl needs my help. We go find her or the deal's off." Cheqea folded her arms over her chest and put her head down.

"What the fuck? Where'd you find this crazy bitch, Braken? And she wants to help the other crazy bitch." Pagliano rubbed the dried blood on his nose. "Pycho meets psycho — if I were in the movie-making business, this would be good shit. But I'm not!" He slammed his fist into the headrest in front of him.

"I'm trained in tribal medicine. Now, You want your casino, we go get the girl." She looked at Pagliano. "You could probably use some of my medicine, too. I know you suffer."

He wound up to hit her, but stopped in mid-swing. "That's it, then. We find the girl for you, and you sign the papers — no more bullshit."

She nodded.

Braken watched them fight, wondering how this had escalated out of control. It seemed every deal he did with Joey Pagliano turned out like this. Someone always got hurt, or worse. If he could just keep the mobster away, get him to go back to Miami, he was sure he could work this out. This was all insanity. Money would take care of Cheqea — it always took care of everything.

"We take her back and get her stoned enough, she'll forget all about the girl," Braken said.

Cheqea leaned forward. "White boy thinks he knows, but he doesn't. This is going to get ugly fast. You saw the girl twist off. Well that's where I'm going if I don't get some stuff soon. You want to see that? I'll tear both of you to shreds. Girl doesn't have her medicine, can do some crazy shit. You know."

Braken had an idea. They had the weekend to kill before the federal office opened on Monday. Why not try and find the girl? It would pacify Cheqea, and maybe he could talk Pagliano into taking the stripper up to Miami to dance in one of his clubs, getting rid of both of them.

"You know," Braken started, "that girl's walking around here in a sport jacket and stilettos. Pretty good chance the police are going to pick her up. She starts babbling about us and the chief here, that could be some attention that we're not looking for. There's no telling what she heard, or if she's crazy enough to file assault charges."

Pagliano had his hand on the door. "First intelligent thing you've said all day." He stepped onto the sidewalk, Cheqea right behind him, smiling. "Either the chief here doctors her up, or I'll take care of it myself." He smiled. "Take the car and head back toward Key West. Check both sides of the road for her. We'll meet you back here in twenty minutes."

Braken pulled out as soon as the door was closed. He thought about just taking off and distancing himself from the situation, but then he thought about the casino and land deal. He'd been in the middle of bad spots before, and landed on his feet. Why should this time be any different? Slowly, he drove back toward Key West.

Chapter 15

Wood opened his eyes and saw nothing. It was dark, the cloud cover hiding the moon and stars. The thunder rumbling in the distance was the first indication that he was still alive. Slowly, he spat the regulator out of his mouth, his jaw sore from clamping the rubber, and tried to sit up. Still disoriented, the tank valve hit him in the head, and he fell back on the sand.

He lay there, trying to piece together what had happened. The last thing he remembered was going in after the fish, but he hadn't had dive gear on. He always free dove to spear fish, believing that no matter how silent a SCUBA diver thought they were, there was always the mechanical sound of the regulator vibrating as the diver inhaled and exhaled. So how was he here with dive gear?

He rolled onto his side and struggled to unbuckle the BC. Whoever had done this had done a sloppy job, he thought, as he uncrossed the buckles. Inching his body forward, he was soon free of the tank, and sat up. It was dark. Very dark. On a clear night, he could tell the time by the moon, but it was invisible, either covered by clouds or having already set. Living in the Keys for thirty years had given him a built-in clock run by the rhythm of the tides and phases of the moon. Wishing he had some water or a beer to moisten his mouth, he tried to bring up some saliva for relief. The moisture-free air from the tank had dried his mouth and throat. Leaning forward, he scooped some water onto his face, brought some to his mouth, rolled it around and spat it out. He knew the saltwater would do him harm in the long run, but the immediate relief was worth it. Thunder rumbled again, and lightning flashed far in the distance as the storm receded.

He got to his feet and arched his back, trying to stretch it out. His body shivered automatically, its natural defense against the cold water. Even though the water temperature was over 80 degrees, you could still get hypothermia if you were submerged long enough, and from the feel of his wrinkled skin, he had been in a long time. Moving on from the state of his body, he surveyed his surroundings. The beach was five feet wide and extended twenty feet in each direction before the mangroves took over. It looked like it was close to high tide, with only the green of the tangled mangrove branches showing above the water.

Knowing the beach would stay above water was some consolation as he peered into the brush trying to see what else the island had to offer. Turning, he put his hands on his hips and scanned the vacant waters. A second look revealed a light blinking to his left. Six seconds, and it blinked again. He sat and studied the light, checking his count. It was every six seconds by his best guess, making it the light on Bullfrog Banks.

He knew approximately where he was, but that did nothing to reassure him of rescue. He tried to orient the area in his head. If he were right about his location, there were two channels leading to the deeper waters of the gulf: East Bahia Honda Channel to the east and Rocky Channel on the other side of the flashing light. This left him in a desolate area ringed with shallow water and shoals. With the exception of a few fishing guides seeking bonefish or permit, the area was generally untravelled.

Taking inventory of the few items available to him. His pockets came up empty, except for a water-soaked wallet. The dive gear yielded a multi-tool knife clipped to a D ring and a whistle.

Out of habit, he checked the pressure gauge and found only a hundred PSI in the tank — almost dry. He removed the knife and whistle, and searched the beach for anything that might make his stay more comfortable. After a few minutes of beach combing yielded nothing but a couple of shells and a piece of driftwood, which he sat on as he blew the whistle intermittently, hoping someone was looking for him.

The only thing he had in his favor was the wind; blowing from the west, it would keep the mosquitos in the mangroves.

* * *

Kellie was dripping wet when she found the cover of the gas station. She held her shoes in her hand, her bare feet easier to walk in than the stilettos. Braken's jacket was draped around her — the only cover she had. Thankfully he was a big guy, and the jacket covered to mid-thigh. Out of habit, she checked the pockets, and came up empty.

The rain had let up enough now that she could see where she was. The gas station was adjacent to a strip mall right on the main road. She was too visible here if the guy who called himself Joey chose to come after her, and she suspected he would want retribution for his injuries. He wasn't the first guy she'd had to hurt, but she usually had the backup of a handful of bouncers or at least some friends. Now she was on her own.

The tight feeling in her head finally dissipated, and she started to smile as she walked down the sidewalk toward the Stock Island Bridge. It was usually like this after one of her episodes. First the maddening feeling that her head was about to implode, then the relief and euphoria that came after. The only problem was that whatever she did to release the pain often had bad consequences — usually very bad.

The rain had stopped and the dispersing storm clouds displayed a vivid color show as the sun set. But her confidence started to wane as the sun dropped below the horizon and twilight took over. She crossed the bridge, shivering in the rain-cooled air, her current predicament again overwhelming her. And she felt the tightness in her head returning.

The bridge behind her, she reached a dead end and was forced to make a decision about whether to go right or left. The street signs were starting to blur — a sure sign that the beast was upon her. She spotted a bench on the corner and went to sit down when a pink golf cart pulled up beside her, and the driver called out. The cart was a Key West limo — a pimped-out stretch version of the standard golf cart. With nothing to lose, she walked toward it.

"Hey, sweetheart. Looks like you could use a ride," a man in the back seat called out, patting the empty seat next to him. All three men had red solo cups in hand — definitely not their first, she thought. "Want to party?"

With no other options, she went toward them, swinging her hips as she went. The sports coat, still wet from the rain, clung to her body. "What d'you boys have in mind?" She had played this game before. The least she could get would be a ride to her car and a meal. A few drinks, to ease the pain building in her head, wouldn't hurt either.

"Just a little party, honey."

She went to the empty seat. "What you drinkin' there, big boy?" She took the cup from his hand and drained the contents. Fire burned in her belly, but the pain in her head started to subside. "Got some more of that? Y'all take care of Kellie, and Kellie will take care of y'all." The man blushed as she put a hand on his thigh. This wasn't her first rodeo, and she knew if she played it right she could empty their pockets later.

"We were heading down to Duval Street. Check out the scenery, but it looks like we got all the scenery we need right here," the driver said.

"Not so fast, boys. You want to play with Kellie, you need to

show her a good time first. Duval Street sounds fun!" She knew
they'd do whatever she wanted now. A quick glance showed that
all three had pot bellies and wedding rings. Perfect. Get a few
drinks and some food, and then grab a wallet if she could. Things
were starting to look up.

"Really could use a refill here." She extended the cup out to
the man in the passenger seat, who gladly dumped the remains of
his into it.

* * *

Mac could see the spotlight from the helicopter hovering
above as it went through its search grid. Darkness was coming fast,
and he knew their search was done for the day. Without a spotlight,
he would have to rely on Ned to get them back to the barge.

"Think this is all we can do until dawn."

"Yeah, Coasties are on it." Ned looked at the sky. "Old boy's
tough, though, he'll make it until morning. Chances are good that
he grounded somewhere. Probably caught him some lobster, and
he's living large about now."

"Let's hope so. You're going to need to get me out of here,"
Mac said, confused by their surroundings.

Ned guided Mac out of the maze they had entered, and back
into the marked channel. It was dark now, the water black, and
Mac finally steered into the channel, the outline of the No Name
Key Bridge barely visible as they passed the number two marker.
As the boat slid under the bridge, they saw lights on the barge and
heard the generator running. "What the hell?"

"That was all off when we left," Ned said. As they got
closer, they saw a small boat tied to the barge. "Crap, it's Mel. She
must have heard about the search from the Coast Guard."

"Where's my dad?" she screamed as they approached,
running toward the skiff with a line in hand. She tossed the line to
Ned, who quickly tied off the boat. "I heard the Coast Guard on the
radio in the house."

"Sorry, girl," Ned started. "They're out there looking for him, but we don't have search lights. He'll be OK until morning."

"What happened here?" She pointed at the remains of the cofferdam.

"Boat crashed into it during the storm this afternoon. Your dad was in the water and got pulled out by the current," Mac started to explain, leaving out the part about him being unconscious. "He had dive gear on," he added, hoping to reassure her.

"Well, I'm not waiting until morning. This boat's got lights. Let's go," Mel said as she hopped into the center console and turned on the lights. "See, plenty of light."

Mac was skeptical as he saw the limited reach of the lights. But he figured it couldn't hurt, so he shut down the generator, grabbed some rope, and joined her. They waited impatiently as Ned sat on the barge, swung his legs over the edge and slid into the boat.

Mel started the engine and spun the boat to face the bridge. She steered underneath the old structure and called out, "Shine those lights ahead."

Mac stood on the cooler in front of the console and adjusted the lights to focus on the path in front of them. Something in the distance reflected back. "That's where the boat that wrecked the dam is." He pointed toward Porpoise Key. "That guy's probably still there."

"Who is it?" Mel asked.

"Cody Braken. It was his boat that did this," Ned responded. "Just drive right past. That boy's not gonna do us any good. Maybe if he's still there when we head back, we can get him."

Mel drove past the small key, the lights illuminating the boat, although no one was in sight. Cody was quickly forgotten as they searched the mangrove islands that passed by on each side.

Once the deep water ended, Mel tilted the engine up slightly and reduced speed. "Ned, you know this area better than me, and my eyes are probably better than yours. Take over I'll go up front and watch the water."

Ned went to the wheel, while Mel went forward. Mac watched her, impressed that a girl of her age could show this much composure as she directed the boat with hand gestures.

The hours passed, the boat slowly zigzagging through the flats, their tired eyes growing tired of searching as the eastern horizon started to lighten. Helicopters had been the only sound throughout the night, reassuring them that they were not alone.

Suddenly they heard a loud whistle.

"What was that? Did you hear it?" Mel jumped down from the gunwale and went to the helm. "Listen, there it is again. Over there!" She pointed to a mangrove covered hump just visible in the pre-dawn light.

Chapter 16

Wood swatted the cloud of mosquitos swarming around his head. The wind that had kept them at bay for most of the night had faded with the dawn. He picked up the whistle again and started blowing the morse code distress signal — short, short, short; long, long, long; short, short, short. But it was no good. He had been at it all night, and was tired and cold, his head nodding every now and then.

Still, the search would intensify with daylight, and he needed to remain vigilant. If only there was some other way to attract attention. Helicopters had been in the sky all night, and one beam had skirted the island, but without a better way to signal, they would never find him. Fire was out of the question, with everything on the island drenched by the storms. A mirror would have worked — if he had one. Noise was the only thing he had, and it wasn't much.

He looked at the small whistle in his hand and once again blew the distress call, this time answered by a flock of birds rising from the mangroves behind him. He needed something louder. Something that could be heard over an engine. He had already heard several outboards, but they sounded far off. As the day progressed, there would be more. He went through his supplies again, his focus on the dive gear. If he could use the air to blow the whistle, maybe it would be the signal he needed.

It was a harder than he expected, but the knife from the multitool finally cut through the regulator hose.Carefully, he slit the end of the hose lengthwise, a tiny cut each time, and dry fitted it onto the mouth of the whistle. It would not stay on itself, but the hose covered the opening. With one hand he held the connection, and with the other he slowly opened the tank valve.

Air shot from the hose and he looked down as the whistle remained silent; the ball pinned against the outlet. Turning the tank off, he tried a different grip on the whistle, this time putting a small bend in the hose to control the air flow. His hand started to cramp from the position, and he realized he hadn't had any water for at least twelve hours; more if you didn't count the beer as water. He shook out his hand and steeled himself for the pain he knew would come.

Again, he turned on the valve. This time, he was greeted by a low sound. Easing the bend brought a little more air, and the tone rose to the high-pitched screech he wanted - much louder than he could blow. He changed hands regularly to relieve the cramping, and held tight as the whistle's screech broke the silence of the dawn.

* * *

Braken woke to banging on the door. After another night on the couch, forced to give up the two bedrooms to Pagliano and Cheqea, his back felt like a truck had driven over it. He rose slowly.

"Hold on. I'll be right there."

The door burst open, though, revealing a distraught Cody. "I need to talk to you," he panted.

Braken looked at his son. He had clearly been up all night, but didn't appear drunk. That was a first, and probably not good news. He shook his head to clear the cobwebs. "What's so important that you have to barge in here?"

"The dam is gone. Something happened in that storm

yesterday, and it's wrecked. I was out there watching and —"

"Slow down and start from the beginning. Last I heard was when I bailed you out of jail. And don't think that's going away, either."

"OK. I got out of jail and went to go have a look at what Wood was up to — you know, be useful, like you said. I got out there just as the storm broke, and the dam was wrecked. Nobody on the barge, either," he lied.

"Good work, boy. Give me a minute and we'll go find old Wood and put the screws to him. If this is negligence and he's delaying the project, I'm going to pull that contract and let Joey have a piece of him," Braken boasted.

"Joey what?" Pagliano stood in the hall.

Cody burst out before Braken could speak. "The dam is gone. Something happened in the storm."

"What freakin' dam. I thought we were fixing the damn bridge. You said that guy you hired was the best." Pagliano was across the room in Braken's face.

"He is. I was about to go find him and see what's going on. I'll take care of this."

"You better, or I *will* be getting involved, and that's never good for your image, is it?" Pagliano backed away. "Go. Find out what happened and get back to me. Then we'll make a plan. I'll stay here with Sleeping Beauty."

* * *

Kellie woke in the gutter, both literally and figuratively. A jail cell would have been more comfortable. The pounding in her head was different now, the hangover replacing the tightness. She looked around at the snoring people around her, and was instantly both awake and disgusted that she had spent the night in an alley with the Key West homeless. Instead of scoring the wallets of the men she had met, she was destitute. She now had a t-shirt and shorts under the sport jacket — the only rewards for a hard night. Either the men were not as naive as she thought, or she had gotten lights-out wasted. From the pain in her head, it was probably the latter, though she hated to admit to herself that they had ditched her when she passed out.

"Dude, you got some water?" she asked the body on the ground next to her.

"Nah, there's a public bathroom over there." He pointed towards something but she couldn't see what it was.

With a desperate need to get the taste of last night out of her mouth, Kellie struggled to her feet and headed in the direction he had indicated. She discovered she had spent the night in an alley three blocks from Duval Street, not in the guy's hotel room as she had planned. Crossing Catherine Street, she headed toward Duval. Once there, she turned right and saw the ocean several blocks in the distance. She walked the early morning streets barefoot, her stilettos long gone. As she reached the end of the street, she looked to the left and saw a small park with a public bathroom by the beach.

Minutes later, safely ensconced in a stall in the women's room, she started crying. It didn't take long for her to taste the mascara running down her cheeks. Knowing action was better than self pity, even if it was usually the wrong action, she left the stall and went to the sink, where she joined another homeless woman in a quick bath.

Outside, she found a drinking fountain and quenched her thirst. Feeling better, she spotted an outside shower set up to wash sand from the beach goers, and didn't hesitate to take advantage of it. Not shy with her body, and with no concern for the consequences, she stripped and let the tepid water run over her body.

Although it was refreshing, she soon realized she was drawing a crowd. She shut the water off and covered herself with the jacket after scowling at the onlookers. Using the foot shower, she rinsed out the t-shirt and shorts, and went to a bench by the beach, where she laid them out to dry. Using the stem from a palm frond, she started combing out her hair. While she waited for her clothes to dry, she felt the euphoria and clearheadedness that usually lasted for a few days after an episode, but dark thoughts soon closed in again. The episodes were becoming more intense and closer together.

Finding another club she could dance at was her only solution for getting some quick cash. She couldn't afford to waste time on another failed scam that might land her in jail. At the least, she needed gas money to get back to Marathon and find Mac. A little makeup and some clothes would be nice too, she thought as her mental shopping list grew. Anxious now, she got up, went back into the bathroom, and changed into the damp clothes. Sport jacket slung over her shoulder, she set off in search of work.

Twice she passed Teasers, the club she had worked at for an hour, looking for her car. On the third pass, she realized that it was gone. The tightness in her head intensified.

* * *

"It's coming from over there!" Mac yelled over the idling engine as Mel put the boat in gear. The sun had just broken the horizon. She pressed the throttle down and watched Ned, who was sitting in the bow giving hand signals to keep her away from the sand bars and shoals. The sound was getting closer, and the mood in the boat changed as they heard it. Ned guided her around two small keys, causing a long but unavoidable detour, and Mac climbed onto the hard t-top over the center console for a better view.

The whistle was the first encouraging sign since the search had started.

He was crouched on top now, with his hands gripping the fiberglass edge as Mel increased speed after clearing the last key. Dead ahead, he saw a small mangrove-covered hump, about a quarter mile away. They were closing fast. He watched Ned, who remained in the bow pointing out the obstacles as Mel drove. A small dot on the beach started to turn into a figure as they approached.

"There!" He jumped down and moved next to Mel. "I saw something on that key." She pushed the throttle forward, ignoring Ned's protest to slow down. Soon a man was visible standing by the water.

The boat coasted to a stop, the bow touching the sand. Before it hit, Mel jumped off and ran to Wood, who embraced her.

"What are you doing out here? Shouldn't you be in school?" he chided her.

"Glad to see you're OK, Dad."

"Never mind girl," he embraced her again then looked at the two men. "What happened out there?"

"You look all right but we ought to get out of here and have someone look at you," Ned said.

"I'm good. Could use a cup of water, though, and maybe a bite to eat." He put his arm around Mel. "Then we're going to have a look at what happened to the dam."

Mac stared at him, not sure that if *he* had gone through the last twelve hours marooned, he would be able to look as unaffected as Wood did. "There's some water in the boat." He went and grabbed a half-gallon jug and handed it to Wood who drank deeply. When he had finished Mac gave him the bad news. "As far as the dam, it's pretty much gone."

Ned interrupted. "It was Cody Braken that ran into it. We saw the boy marooned on Porpoise Key. Left the son of a bitch sitting there."

"Brakens! Goddam Brakens!" Wood muttered as he went to retrieve the dive gear piled on the beach. They loaded it onto the boat and pushed off the beach. Wood and Ned hopped in the boat as Mel pulled back on the throttle and backed off the sand. As soon as the water was knee deep Mac jumped aboard.

"Have to come back and check that place out some time. Got kind of attached to it," Wood said as the small island receded.

Chapter 17

"Where the hell is that fat bastard?" Pagliano was pacing Braken's living room, the white shag carpet showing his path. It was getting close to noon — several hours since Braken had left — and he was not a patient man.

"What?" Cheqea broke his thoughts. She stood in the hallway, half dressed, rubbing the sleep from her eyes. "I need some food. You white boys want me to sign that shit, you got to treat me better than this."

"Aren't you pleasant in the morning. No wonder there is no Mr. Chief. Or do you just like girls? I saw you watching that dancer."

"Whatever. That girl needs my help, and so do you. It's a burden I carry, not that you would know anything about that. You're like my brother — all you can do is break shit." She went to the kitchen and opened the refrigerator door. "I guess he can't cook either." She stuck her head in. "How is that dude so fat when there's nothing in here except styrofoam containers?" She started opening the take-out boxes and smelling them. Finally she settled on something, and set the box on the counter. "Well, what do you have planned for today?"

"I ought to just drug you up and let you sleep until Monday. What a freakin' pain you are." He felt his face flush, and had to control the rage that was sweeping over him. Was everyone south of Dade County a freak or an idiot? If he didn't need her to sign the papers, she'd be feet-up in a dumpster.

She went to the drawer for a fork, and saw the computer screen on the desk. "Got some anger issues, I can see." She went to the computer, chewing on the fork. "Looks like you got some porn issues, too."

He was about to strike her, but turned away, thinking about having to spend a whole weekend with her. Maybe drugging her *was* the best solution. "Maybe we ought to get you some more of that medicine you keep talking about. Got to say you were way more cooperative."

"You know, that's the first good idea that's come out of your mouth." She pointed the fork at him. "Too bad we lost the girl. I could have helped her. She has demons, you know. But I can help you; Cheqea can tell you have demons too." She went to the counter and started eating.

"The only help I need from you is to sign the freakin' papers." It was taking everything he had to control himself.

"Come on, what do you have to lose? You're stuck with me all weekend, might as well relax a little. It might even be fun." She set the fork down and went to him. He started to recoil, but she was behind him with her hands on his temples, hitting a pressure point before he could react. "Settle down and give it a chance." She started rubbing his forehead with one hand and the back of his neck with the other.

Instantly his body relaxed.

"Now, you gonna let old Cheqea fix you up?"

The rage was gone, and he had trouble talking. "What kind of voodoo …"

"You know you want me to help you."

He was past reasoning now, all the rage gone, and a feeling he had never felt before overcame him. The anger and anxiousness that were his constant companions had dissipated, replaced by a calm he had never known. "What do you have in mind?" At least if he had to spend the weekend with her, he could keep feeling like this. Let Braken deal with the contractor and bridge.

"Me and you are gonna take some medicine." She went for the bedroom, and came back with a vial. Inside were six small green chunks. She took two out and put one under her tongue. "Here." She offered one to him, and he took it.

* * *

Braken sat in front of Wood's house, steaming, despite the air conditioning in the Cadillac running on high. *What else could go wrong?* He looked over at Cody, who had just gotten in the passenger door, and wondered how the apple had fallen so far from the tree.

"You checked everywhere?"

"Yeah, they're not here. I checked the house, and dock. Both the center console and skiff are gone."

"Shit," Braken said under his breath. Pagliano was probably getting hotter by the minute. He picked up his cell phone and held the cumbersome device to his ear. It was the newest model, all self-contained instead of the old bag model he used to haul everywhere. But it was still an expensive pain in the ass.

He dialed and waited while it rang, letting it go until his answering machine picked up, hoping Pagliano would answer. Able to say he had tried, at least, he hung up, cursing that the call would be charged now that the machine answered.

"Well, at least he didn't answer. Guess we ought to go out to the site and see if they're working."

It took five minutes to reach the Big Pine side of the bridge. Braken pulled the Cadillac against the barricade blocking access to anyone trying to enter the road leading to No Name Key, and parked. With a grunt, he got out of the car, regretting the loss of air conditioning as soon as the noon sun hit him. Cody was next to him as they walked past the barricade and continued to the middle of the bridge. There, he leaned on the concrete rail and surveyed the damage. Steel I beams poked from the water at odd angles, steel panels dangling off some. Several sections remained intact, but the majority was in ruins.

"It's a total loss. They've lost at least a week's worth of work."

"Yeah," was all that Cody could say.

"And where are they?" He looked at his watch. "Lost half a day already, and it's Saturday. Even with the weather they should be about done." He shook his head. "This is bad. Very bad."

"Look." Cody pointed. There's his boat coming at us."

Braken went toward the seaward side of the bridge and stood on the curb. He started to wave his arms back and forth in an effort to stop them, and the boat slowed as it approached.

"What do you want? That boy of yours has caused enough trouble already!" Wood yelled.

The boat was under the bridge now, and Braken went across to the other rail. "What are you talking about? Whatever happened here is on you, and you better get to work. Double your shifts and get it fixed!"

Wood was looking at the damage, shocked. "Me? That son of a bitch almost got me killed!" He pointed at Cody, who was now running down the bridge, toward the road.

"Cody!" Braken screamed, staring after him. But Cody kept going. He was off the bridge and onto the road now, and it looked like he was just as guilty as Wood said. Braken turned to Wood. "Just get it fixed." Then he went back to the car, and went after Cody.

* * *

"Look at that mess." Wood stood on the barge, staring at what remained of the cofferdam. It was ruined; wide spaces were completely missing where the boat had hit it, and what remained standing was mangled. "That dammed thing was just about ready to be pumped out, and he runs into it. Then doesn't even have the balls to face his old man." Wood looked over the site, shaking his head. "We've got to either put it back together or take it all apart. It's a damn danger like this. Some unsuspecting tourist'll run through here, hole their boat, and wind up dead or in the hospital. Then it's on me, and I've got no insurance right now. Damn Brakens."

"There's no fixing it without pulling it apart first, so I suggest that's where we start," Mac said.

"Got a point there. Let's get you in the water, and I'll run the excavator." He turned to Mel. "You need to go back and get to school."

"It's Saturday, Dad." She put her hands on her hips and glared at him. "Don't you think you've had enough for one day? Or two? You should come back to the house with me and get some rest."

"This won't take too long, and we've got to get it done. It's just a pile of liability sitting here like this. Wait 'til someone wrecks their boat in this mess. I'll be totally out of business. Go on, now. I'll be home as soon as I can."

She frowned and turned to Mac. "Watch him."

Not sure why she was placing her trust in him, Mac shook his head and went to the container to start the compressor and fill the tanks. Out of earshot, he watched them speak for a few minutes. Then they hugged and she turned to leave, casting a concerned look at Wood as she hopped onto the deck of the center console.

The three men stood there and watched the boat move away. Once it was out of site, Wood and Ned came over to Mac.

"All right, that's handled. Now this is what we need to do here," Wood said.

"I thought we were going to pull all this up." Mac looked at him.

"That'd waste too much time. There's more than one way to skin a cat without getting scratched." He stared at the wreckage. "We'll pull those beams there and take those two piers there," — He pointed to the two steel beams from the cofferdam still standing on the No Name Key side of the pier — "Set two more about the same distance, and use them as a form to pour the pier in where she sits. We'll have to get a pump rig to place the concrete, so it will displace the water, but it'll work. Been there, done that."

Mac tried to picture the work in his mind. Wood was right. "The reinforcing cage is no problem. We can build that in two parts up here, then set them and tie it together underwater. For the forms themselves, we can make ties from lumber to hold it all together until the concrete cures."

Wood nodded. "Now that you're seeing things clearly, let's get it done."

* * *

Kellie walked down the sidewalk, skipping between awnings to dodge the sun-baked concrete lining Duval Street that were burning her feet. The tightness in her head had abated slightly with the walk, but as the heat rose, she suspected the tightness would return. The nagging presence was always there. Her feet were dirty and starting to blister from the hot sidewalk, and every bar and restaurant enticed her with the aroma of food.

Not sure if she had eaten last night or just drank her dinner, she thought she probably needed food. Her best bet for survival was to find another club, and quickly. She went toward a phone booth and checked the yellow pages, but the page for clubs had been long torn out.

"Hey, you need some help?" A rickshaw cab pulled to the curb.

Kellie went to the driver. "Hey, I need to get some work,

quick. You know some clubs around here? I tried that one down the street, but it didn't work out so well." She pushed out her chest as she approached him. "I could use some food too."

"Hop in. We'll take care of you. Name's Ian. Been running this route for long enough I can tell when the girls need help."

"Your accent's cute." She didn't know what it was, but whatever. This guy was going to help her, and that was all that mattered at the moment. She got in the back of the rickshaw. "Name's Kellie. Thanks for helping me out."

He handed her half a sandwich, which she greedily took, not speaking until it was finished. A portable phone was to his ear when she looked up, and she wondered what a rickshaw driver was doing with one. But between the shade of the awning and the breeze from the open carriage, she was starting to cool off, and didn't feel like questioning him. She leaned back, and was quickly asleep.

* * *

"Wake up love," Ian called from the bike.

Kellie shook out her head and looked around. Surrounded by dumpsters, she wondered if she hadn't fallen in with a serial killer. The man got out and banged on a large steel door. Several seconds later, the door opened, the shadow of a large man visible inside. Kellie watched as they spoke, both men glancing over at her every few words. The large man handed Ian a wad of cash and he walked toward her.

"Come on sweets, meet your new daddy," he said as he reached into the carriage for her arm.

Her initial reaction was to run. This was no good Samaritan. She didn't know what he'd done, but she *did* know she didn't want any part of it. She pulled against his arm, but the grip strengthened. The other man walked toward her, and Ian moved out of the way. The larger man gripped one of her fingers, targeting a pressure point, and she was forced to submit. He held the grip as she got out of the carriage and walked side by side with him to the door. It slammed behind them, causing her to jump. The man laughed, released her, and locked the door.

"Mac Travis, he's my boyfriend. He'll pay you whatever you want!" she cried, her voice breaking on a sob.

Chapter 18

Mac climbed out of the water, exhausted. It had been four hours of non-stop work since they had started to clean up the wreckage. After being unbolted and hoisted from the water, the twisted steel sheets now lay stacked in a pile on the deck. Two of the I-beams were laying alongside, also ruined. It had been harder to disassemble the mangled metal than to put it together. Many of the nuts and bolts were torqued, and some even bent; the former were a struggle, the latter needed to be cut.

"About time. She should be safe overnight now, and we need to get more materials to finish it," Wood said as he climbed out of the excavator. He cast an eye to the sky. "Ned, maybe we ought to throw a strap over this, in case one of those thunderheads out there comes through here and kicks things up."

Mac was peeling off the wetsuit, his gear laid at his feet when Ned emerged from the container. He carried a strap in one hand and the old piece of wood they had pulled up two nights earlier in his other hand. He handed the piece to Wood. "Might want to look at this. We pulled it up that night you were hurt, so I just tossed it in the bin. Look." He extended it toward Wood, who took it.

"Well would you look at this? The old boy might have been right after all." He turned the relic in his hands, studying it. "Have a look at this, Travis. You pulled it up, after all."

Mac took the piece of wood. It was rounded on the end, the joint where two pieces of wood had been carefully joined visible just below the curve. The whole piece was burnished, not rough like the piece they had found earlier, with the copper on it. As he looked, he could make out a carving of a canoe with four men paddling. "What do you think the carvings about?"

Ned took it from him. "Never seen anything like it, and I've been kicking around here a long time. Seen just about everything salvaged here in twenty-five years, but nothing like this. It's not Spanish, or even European. More like Central or South American Indian. Mayan, maybe. There's a group on Big Pine, call themselves a long-lost tribe of the Mayan. We should take this over there and see if they'll have a look."

"Not so fast." Wood grabbed it. "This stays between us until this pier is fixed and Braken pays up. Then, if you want to go chasing old Indians, have at it. You show this to the wrong person now, they'll have every ABC agency sniffing up my butt. This job will be closed down fast as you can say bullshit."

"You know the historical significance of this?"

"I know the significance of a paycheck, and right now that's my top priority." Wood took the relic with him as he went for the skiff. "Let's go. I could use a beer and a little shut-eye."

Mac closed the container doors, slid the lock in place, and joined the two men in the skiff.

* * *

Cody breathed a short sigh of relief as he took his eye off the gas gauge with its needle well below the empty line, and pulled the old truck into the parking lot. It was Saturday night, and Key West was rocking. He left the truck, and looked back, as he went through the tinted glass doors into the air conditioned club.

It took a few minutes for his eyes to adjust to the dark room.

While he waited, he thought about his latest predicament. The DUI and night in jail were on the back burner; Pagliano and his friends were more efficient at dispensing justice than the locals. After wrecking the cofferdam and lying to his father, he had grabbed a backpack full of clothes, scribbled a sorry apology to Nicole, and run for the only source of redemption he could find. He would need a load of cash to go back and clear this up.

Finally his eyes acclimated, and he could see the bar to the left, and the stage straight ahead. Music blared from stacks of speakers as the girls plied their trade through the club. He went to the large figure at the bar, and stood a respectable five feet away — close enough to be seen, but far enough away to be out of ear shot. All he could do was watch the man and wait while he talked to his two body guards.

"Cody Braken, or by the look of you, the ghost of Cody Braken. Come on over and have a drink. Looks like you could use one," the man said. The stage lights reflected off his freshly shaved bald head and his black tank top showed the hours he spent in the gym. Around his neck, he wore a gold chain with a machine gun. But it was the tattoos on his arms that Cody focussed on, their intricate patterns were rumored to conceal a secret when matched with his sisters. Cody went to the offered bar stool and sat. The bartender brought a bottle of beer and a dirty glass, which Cody pushed aside. He drank from the bottle. "Teqea, my friend," he said respectfully. "I need some work. Things are slow up there, and I could use a big score." He noticed the girl on the other side of the big man shoving a burger in her mouth.

"So, the old Braken clan is out of business? Doesn't ring true to me, not that I care." The man leaned back and noticed Cody looking at the girl. "Say hello to ..." — He turned toward her — "What was your name, honey?"

"Kellie," she said, trying to swallow as she said it.

"She's new down here. We'll get her cleaned up and working in no time. You know, I've got a soft spot for lost girls."

He grabbed her butt. "But back to your situation. You got your boat? I could have you make a run over to the Bahamas."

Cody looked at the floor. "No, it needs some work. That's kinda why I'm here."

"Can I have another burger?" the girl asked, saving Cody the embarrassment of the story.

"Sure, sweetheart." The man nodded to the bartender. "Just know that it's going on your tab. Now back to you — without a boat, you're not much good to me. See, that's your particular talent. I've got plenty of guys with a lot lower profile than you that can do my land work."

Cody put his head down. There was nowhere else to go. Everyone in the lower Keys either knew of or feared his father and his acquaintances, except the man here. If he couldn't pull a rabbit out of his hat, he'd have to go back to Marathon and beg forgiveness. And that was not likely to go well.

"If I got a boat, you'd have work for me?"

The man looked at him. "I don't ask any questions. You got something that can get a couple girls into the Bahamas the back way, we can work something out."

Cody's brain was churning now. "Sure thing. Tomorrow morning, I can be at the Marina early. I'll run the girls." He looked over at Kellie again, hoping she would be one of them. He had made this run before, and once the girls were on his boat, they were at his mercy. "Can you front me a little cash for gas money?"

The man dug in his pockets and pulled out a handful of soiled hundreds. "Here, and it's an advance. Don't screw it up, or your father won't be the only one looking for you."

* * *

"You got to relax, man. Let the magic work," Cheqea said. She sat on the counter, staring at Pagliano in the bathtub. "Never seen a hard case like you. I'd give you another dose, but don't know if you could handle it."

130

Pagliano turned to look at her. "Some crazy witch doctor chick feeds me magic whatever you called it, and I'm supposed to relax? Give me another. I'll show you what I can handle."

"I feel your pain, and it's giving me a headache." She reached into her bag and withdrew the vial again. "I need some more meds, and it doesn't seem to be working for you either - so here." She swallowed one and handed him another.

"Ain't nobody said Joey Pagliano's a lightweight and can't keep up." He popped it in his mouth.

"There you go. I'm going to make us some food, cause once that kicks in, baby, we're gonna be electric." She left the bathroom and went to the kitchen.

The stereo was on, and he could hear her singing. A weird feeling took over his face, and he formed a grotesque smile, the muscles in his face clearly not communicating with each other. Worried now that she had poisoned him, he tried to get up, and almost fell. He grabbed the toilet and got one foot out of the tub, and then the other. His face flushed and he felt a weird kind of energy surge through his body — unlike anything he had ever felt before. Now he had an unusual feeling like he was calm and energized at same time. He had to stop himself when he realized he was laughing uncontrollably, and humming to the music. A towel around his waist, he went into the kitchen and started picking at the potatoes frying in the pan. Cheqea was cutting some frozen meat to add to the mixture already cooking.

"Not much here, but it'll do," she said as she floated toward him and kissed him on the cheek. "See what happens when you're a good boy and listen? You're feelin' it now. I can tell."

"Yeah," was all he could say. He knew the effects of alcohol and cocaine, but this was different, and he was starting to understand what an out-of-body experience felt like. It was almost like he was standing next to himself, watching his alter ego. Most female hostages tried their ploys with him and he would often accept the favor. But he was always in control. This was new for him — she was dealing the cards. It would have been unsettling if he didn't feel so good.

"Sit down, I'll bring you a plate. And stop looking at me like that."

"Like what?" He went to the oven door and looked at his reflection. He jumped back, almost falling to the floor as a caricature of himself stared back and winked at him. "What the fuck?"

"Seriously, sit down and get some food in you. It's gonna be a wild ride."

Chapter 19

The sun was already on his face when Mac rose. He had forgotten to close the blinds on the sliding glass door before falling, exhausted, on the couch last night. His body had been screaming at him after being awake for forty hours, and the work of first building and then removing the cofferdam. *How did Wood still do it?* he wondered. He had to be at least forty. Slowly, he rose from the couch and planted his feet on the floor.

"About time to get moving," Wood called out from the table.

"It's Sunday, I think. Don't you take any time off?" Mac asked.

Wood sat hunched over the library book that Mel had brought home. Reading glasses were perched on his nose, and the relic was by his side. "Damn, son. I'm no slave driver. But you didn't exactly start on a good week here. It's not usually like this. No, I wasn't gonna work today, but I been thinking about that carving." He picked it up. "That piece we pulled up first wasn't worth getting all excited about. I know Ned and Mel did, but he's an old professor and she's a high school kid. Just an old piece of wood with a hunk of metal stuck in it." He rubbed his face. "There was nothing about it to tie it to anything, wreck or otherwise. I've been working on bridges and canals here for almost twenty years. Could fill a warehouse with all the crap I've found out there. They all get excited, and then it doesn't pan out. Used to happen to me, too. What you need is a provenance; a connection to show that what you found actually relates to something. This here is something we could document though I'm not sure what it is yet." He went back to the book, flipping pages. There was a pile of three books that Mel had brought back and he had already been through two. "It's not looking good here. All's that left is this journal by this guy that tried to follow the ancient trade routes in his sailboat."

Mac took the book from his outstretched hand. "You didn't look too excited about it yesterday." He leaned back and flipped through the first pages then leaned forward. "Douglas Peck is the guy's name and this book shows the ancient trade routes of the Chontal Maya through the Caribbean and up the west coast of Florida." He started reading, ignoring Wood's impatient look. "He's got maps here and sketches from something called the Dresden Codex. Is that Codex in one of the other books? I have an idea." He waited as Wood scanned the other books.

"Here it is. I went through it and looked at the pictures trying to match the carving to something, but there is nothing that looks like it."

"Not the whole carving. See if you can find the people, either separately or together."

Wood slowed down and studied each drawing. The codex showed Mayan gods and divinations. "This one is close. So's this." He pointed to two drawings.

Mac took the carving and set it next to the book. The similarities were startling. "Does this give you your provenance?"

"I'm still reading, here, but it ties what we found to the Chontal Mayan. Old Ned'll be happy to dive into this and figure it all out. Probably not a pot of gold, but interesting just the same."

"What do you have in mind?" Mac was excited by this turn of events. The thought of actually finding something like this when he took up commercial diving had never crossed his mind. This was really cool. Even if it wasn't gold and jewels, the history alone was enough to get him excited.

"The whole job is upside down now. I gotta sort it out and get a change order from Braken before we do any work. I doubt he'll be checking on us today. He's probably trying to find that no-good boy of his. I'll bet he's figured out that Cody lied to him by now. I was gonna go back to the site and take a casual dive. Have a look at the area, figure out what it's going to take to make the bridge right before I talk to Braken. We can spend some time looking there. Then I want to dive on the rubble pile out by the reef, and make sure we didn't dig up something important and dump it out there. After we get a better picture of what's going on, I'm going to see Braken about a change order for what his boy did."

Mac was excited now. He had heard about the reef here. As a commercial diver, he spent a lot of time underwater, but the work and surroundings were mundane. "I'm in." He felt the energy come back to him.

"Relax. Like you said, it's Sunday. Slack tides at noon. That'll be the best conditions to dive the reef. Sun overhead, and no current to stir things up. We can have a look at the pier again after that. Conditions will be better there around 2, with the incoming tide. Now let's see about some food." He went to the kitchen, pulled a cast iron skillet off a peg on the wall and started to cook bacon.

Mel came out of her room just as the bacon finished, and Wood turned to her. "Teenagers. Sleep and eat," he said. "The boy and I are going to do some dives today. You interested?"

She nodded and went back to her room.

"Seems like a good kid," Mac said.

"Still half asleep though. Can't complain. For just me and her, we do alright." Wood laid out three plates and dished out bacon, eggs, and toast. "Come and get it. I ain't serving you."

Mac went for a plate and sat at the table across from Wood. They both stared at the relic between them. "Any idea what it is?"

"Ned'll know better than me, but there's been rumors for

years about the Mayans having come through here. No trace has ever been found to confirm it, though. Storm surges would have erased anything on land, and unless it's got some serious mass and ballast, the smaller wrecks disappear with time. Somehow, though, this survived."

"How?"

"Legend has it, No Name Key was a stop for them. Only place before you get to Key West that they could have provisioned. Key Deer from Big Pine and fresh water from the limestone on No Name. That key's got the only reliable fresh water aquifer for miles." He paused while he shoveled several fork loads of food into his mouth. "They could have got caught in a big storm, and whatever this came off got caught in the channel. The right currents and a fresh water seepage would have accelerated the corral growth around it, preserving the wood before it could rot."

"What are you guys talking about?" Mel entered the room again and went for the kitchen. She sat down with a plate in front of her and started to eat.

"Just speculating," Wood said.

"Never thought he had this side did you?" she asked Mac. "Always a hard ass at work, but this stuff lights him up. You think AA straightens people out, this is it for him. Until the mystery's solved, he won't touch alcohol."

Mac nodded and finished his food. He took his and Wood's plate to the kitchen, and started doing the dishes. Still not sure how he fit in here, he was growing increasingly comfortable with these two, and if it took a mystery to stop Wood from drinking, he was all for that.

* * *

Braken woke on the couch again. If he would have looked harder, he could have had a bed. One of the bedroom doors was open, the room unoccupied. And if he'd checked the other room, he would have seen that it was also vacant. But he was too tired by the time he got home last night to do anything except lay down on the couch and pass out.

He'd searched for Cody for hours, checking every spot he knew the boy to hang out. The bridge was hopelessly behind schedule now, and he feared that Cody had more to do with it than he'd said. Relieved that Pagliano was still asleep, he thought about sneaking out and checking on progress. Maybe offer Wood some kind of bonus from his own reserves to get it done and save Cody. Pagliano didn't have to know what happened.

If he could find the kid. He'd been out past midnight, searching the bars from Islamorada to Big Pine, but no one had seen him. He had Nicole asking around, and had checked the house and marina several times through the night. With no sign of Cody, he had been rehearsing in his head what he would tell the mobster. The story came together painfully: how this was all Wood's fault, and he had another contractor lined up to finish it. Maybe if they could get Cheqea down to Key West in the morning and get her to sign the papers, this would all go away.

The front door slammed open, startling him. Pagliano and Cheqea stumbled in, arm in arm. He sat on the couch and stared at the couple.

"What's the matter, never seen two people have a good time?" Pagliano asked as he entered.

"Cheqea gave Joey some medicine, and look at him now," she laughed. "Now you know I got real powers, if I can turn around a head case like him. Almost makes up for losing that girl." They went over and sat on opposite sides of him. They started giggling. "Cheqea can fix you up too."

He got up and went for the door. "You guys have a good time. I'll be back."

Quietly closing the door behind him he went down the stairs and to the car. He sat in the Caddie, motor running to power the AC. It might have been eight am, but it was already eighty five degrees. Whatever was going on with those two, it was clearly in his favor. No mention about business; not the bridge, not the casino. If they could stay on whatever they were on until tomorrow morning, he might have time to fix this after all. He pulled the shifter into reverse and backed out of the driveway. One look around Marathon; see if Wood was working and maybe grease that wheel a bit. Then take another look for Cody. Maybe after that, he deserved a little reward; take a ride down to Key West and have some fun before Pagliano and Cheqea sobered up.

* * *

Cody cruised the docks of the marina at daybreak. He needed a boat — something with a small cabin to hide the girls, and enough range to make the Bahamas and back without refueling. The big sport-fishers lining the docks were too visible for this trip, and the cigarette boats attracted customs agents like honey. What he needed was a nice family boat. He settled on a cuddy cabin about twenty-four feet long, stable enough for the seas that were forecast. It was the right size, and with the two motors, he had backup as well as speed, if he needed it. The twin 250 hp engines were oversized for the boat, and he expected he could get forty knots out of her if the conditions were right.

She would make the run there and back in less than four hours.

He leaned against a railing, studying the scene. Despite the hour, there was activity as fishermen got their boats ready. Many slips were already empty from those wanting to hit the bite as the sun came up. After a half hour of patient surveillance, he made his move. He tossed a duffel bag on the deck and hopped onto the boat. Looking around, he reached into the bag for the bolt cutters and went for the padlock on the cabin. Twice he had to set them down and look like he belonged as people walked by. Finally, though, he had the break he needed and cut the lock. The cabin was dark, but he withdrew a flashlight from his bag and quickly found the battery switch. With the cabin lights on, he could see the screws for the access panel behind the helm. One at a time, he removed the screws and pulled the panel away. Wires were everywhere, but he knew his way around boats, and it only took a few minutes to find the ignition pair. With a pair of wire cutters, he cut the two wires, stripped their ends and wound the bare metal together.

The engine should have started. He knew he had the right ignition wires, but realized he had forgotten the dead man's switch. Carefully, he found the back of the switch, cut the wires from each terminal, and attached them together.

This time the engine cranked and turned over.

He checked his watch and realized it had taken longer than planned to obtain a boat, and he was already late to meet Teqea at the marina entrance. The other outboard started and he replaced the access panel. Back on deck, he started up the electronics and familiarized himself with the chart plotter and depth finder. By the time he had made himself comfortable with the controls, two figures were walking down the dock toward the boat. There was only one girl, which meant only half the money, but he smiled when he saw that it was the girl from the bar last night alongside the heavy set man. They approached, and he offered a hand in welcome.

Teqea pushed the girl on board, but remained on the dock. "Why didn't you meet us? It's not good for my image to be cruising around here. You know where to take her," he said. Without another word, he turned and walked away.

Cody offered the girl his hand. "Cody's my name. Make yourself at home in the cabin, and we'll get underway. Stay down there until I tell you. I don't need anyone seeing us going out together and me returning alone."

She put her head down, went down the narrow stairs, and sat on the V berth, head in hands, crying. He quickly closed and locked the companionway door. She would start screaming soon - they all did. This wasn't his first rodeo running girls across the Gulf Stream to the Bahamas. They were usually like this — realizing the extent of their circumstance as soon as he locked the cabin door. But that wasn't his problem. He was in it for the money, and that was it.

Without a second thought for her well-being, he cast off the lines and pushed down the throttles. The boat pulled out of the slip, and he checked his speed, not wanting to catch the eye of any law enforcement agent, and followed the markers toward open water.

Chapter 20

"Go ahead and toss it!" Wood yelled as he pulled the throttle back to neutral. "About ten feet out."

Mel tossed the empty bleach bottle over and watched it spin on the surface as the weight took the line to the bottom. As soon as it stopped spinning, Wood engaged the engine and started to move in a circle around the bottle. Mac leaned over his shoulder, watching the depth finder. Its screen showed a flat grey line in sixty-five feet of water, indicating flat bottom. Wood widened the circles until he was about forty feet from the buoy.

"See here?" He pointed to the screen as the flat line transformed into humps. "That's our spot. Toss the her!" he yelled to Mel. The anchor splashed, and he waited for the line to slack, before backing away.

Mac watched Mel tie the line off to a cleat and join them in the shadow cast by the t-top over the center console. He looked at the small waves, their glassy crests sparkling in the sun, allowing shafts of sunlight to penetrate the surface revealing depths of blue he had never seen before.

"Don't stand there staring. Let's get wet." Wood went past him toward the gear stashed under the bench seat. "Put the dive flag up and toss that buoy over the transom. Ain't worth taking any chances if the current starts running."

Mac followed his orders, appreciating the buoy floating on a hundred feet of nylon line behind the boat. He had needed the security of the line once before, during his training in the Gulf, when the current was too strong for him to swim to the boat. The red and white dive flag, was hoisted up the outrigger line, showing other boats that there were divers down and increase their safety.

Without further ado, they geared up and sat on the gunwales. A glance around and they back rolled into the water, one hand on their masks, the other gathering the hoses into their bodies. Mac relaxed in the eighty degree water and swam for the anchor line. Mel and Wood were already there, and he gave the OK sign, which they returned.

Mac was stunned by the visibility as he descended next to the line. The bottom, barely visible at the surface, soon came into view, the rock pile in stark relief to the sandy bottom surrounding it. He could already make out schools of bait fish circling above the rocks.

Small fish greeted him as he checked his depth gauge. Now forty feet down and enveloped by the clearest water he could imagine, he couldn't help but smile. After the last few days in the murky bay waters, this was indeed a treat. Piles of corral and rubble came into view as he approached the bottom, the pile they had dumped the other day clearly visible in relation to the older rocks now covered with marine growth. Lobsters waved their antennas from their holes in greeting, as if they knew they were safe until the season opened.

As he approached the bottom, he saw a two-foot line move along the sand. A hand grasped his shoulder and Wood swam past him, Hawaiian sling in hand. He watched as Wood slowed his breathing and coasted above the fish, making as little disturbance as possible. He pulled back on the surgical tubing with his hand, sliding the shaft up his arm as he added tension.

Once the sling was fully cocked, he took one quick fin toward the fish and released the spear. The fish shook violently and took off, but Wood held the tubing and pulled it toward him. With a grin, he swam past Mac toward a sand patch, where he carefully stood on the bottom and threaded the fish onto the steel stringer attached to his weight belt.

The three regrouped and swam together with Wood slightly ahead. Mac checked his gauges and abruptly realized that half the dive was gone already. They had been down for almost thirty minutes, and he showed about 1,500 psi left in his tank. Having memorized much of the dive charts, he calculated this would give him about another half hour at this depth, with a pretty good safety margin before decompression stops were necessary. Ahead of him, Wood moved toward the newer rocks and started searching the crevices, poking into the holes with the tip of the spear. Mac and Mel followed his lead, searching the rubble for any sign of an anomaly.

They were working through a section of broken pieces when Mac saw something unusual. He reached his hand into the crevice created by the rocks' irregular shapes, but couldn't reach far enough in. Wood swam toward him and handed him the pole shaft, then backed away to give Mac room to work. With the pronged end of the six-foot shaft, Mac reached into the crevice and prodded the tip against the object.

It seemed to resist the pressure of the three sharpened tips, but did not feel like the adjacent rocks. He twisted and maneuvered the tip in the hole, hoping to loosen whatever was there. Wood tapped him on the shoulder and waved his gauges at him, indicating that he was low on air. Mac checked his and realized they had been down for fifty-five minutes now, and he only had 250 PSI left in his tank — well into the red zone. Wood motioned again, this time with a thumbs up, indicating that they should surface. Mac jabbed the spear in the hole one last time, gigged the obstruction, and removed it. Then the group circled and swam toward the anchor line, fifty feet away. With only 100 PSI, Mac started up the line to the boat.

Once on the surface, he swam to the ladder, handed the spear to Wood who was still in the water, and tossed his fins over the transom. He struggled up the small ladder, the tank and gear adding weight and making balance difficult. On board, he pulled his mask down around his neck and slid out of his BC, dropping the vest and tank on the deck, he went to help Mel. She moved out of the way and Wood swam to the boat, handing Mac the spear, with a small piece of wood caught between two of the tips. He shook off Mac's aid and climbed into the boat.

"Looks like there's something down there after all. This seems to be the same as the other pieces we found." Wood sat on the gunwale, drinking from a half-gallon of water. He pulled the jagged piece off the spear tip and rolled it around his callused hand. "Both good news and bad. It means we did find something, but the bad news is that it's now scattered to hell and back, and probably got tore up when we dug it out." He passed the water to Mel and the piece of wood to Mac.

"It's still early. Why don't we go and have a look at the work site? We can fill the tanks on the barge and come back for another look."

Wood went to the helm and started the engines. "Go get the anchor then," he called to Mac as he pushed the throttle forward to the idle notch, and slowly drove up on the anchor.

Mac went forward and pulled on the line. "It's stuck hard. You want to drive it off?"

Wood shook his head. "Guess you still have a lot to learn. Driving the anchor off is a sure way to either lose it or wreck it. That's half your paycheck in steel down there between the anchor and chain. Mel. Get the ball."

Mac watched as Mel pulled in the ball drifting behind the boat and unclipped it from the line. She took it forward and clipped it onto the anchor line. "Hold on," she called to Mac.

They grabbed the bow rail as Wood pushed down the throttle and steered a course away from the set of the anchor. Mac watched as the ball floated past the boat and down the line. Wood increased speed slightly and then turned.

"She's free now. Pull it in."

Mac saw the ball floating about two hundred feet behind the boat. The entire anchor line was on the surface, the anchor chain at the ring. He easily retrieved the line and stowed the gear. Back in the cockpit, Wood nodded at him and took off toward shore.

* * *

"Settle down, you can come out in a minute!" Cody yelled over the engines, to Kellie, who was lying on the bunk.

She rolled over, realizing she had cried herself to sleep. Her situation was bleak, and the pain in her head was starting again. At least the man from the club had fed her before locking her in a bedroom overnight. She went to the door and started banging. Finally after what seemed like a half hour she could hear the padlock open and fresh air rushed in.

"We're out of the harbor. You can come out now. Just stop the freakin' screaming or I'll lock you back up."

"Where are we going?" She used her softest voice and climbed the stairs to the deck, brushing against him. This guy was all that stood between her and slavery, and she knew it was her last chance. Once he made the transfer, it would be over for her.

She watched him as he looked up to check his bearing on the compass and then down again.

"Where are we going?" she asked again, as she slid closer to look at the map on the chart plotter.

"Andros Island, Bahamas." There was a computer screen that showed a map of the area with a little boat that she figured represented their position. The plotter showed the boat following an easterly course, running parallel to the Keys. She had seen them on a map and knew what they looked like.

"What's there?"

"Just some guys, who're gonna meet us and take care of you."

"I'm not sure I like the sound of all this. I don't have any ID or a passport or anything."

"Don't worry, it's all good."

"What if I don't want to go?" She started to rub herself against him, hoping to change her odds.

He pulled back from her advance. "Stop it or I'll lock you down there again."

She backed away, trying to think of a way to change his mind. If sex wasn't going to work, she had little else to bank on. Except violence. Her eyes searched the deck for a weapon, but came up empty. Suddenly she sensed her prospects brighten as the boat slowed.

"What are you doing?" She moved next to him again, this time locking a leg around his.

"I told you to stop it." He pushed her away and reached into the storage compartment below the wheel, coming out with binoculars.

She searched the water in the direction he was looking, but all she could see was a smudge on the water far in the distance. "What's so interesting out there? Let me have a look." Maybe if she could see what faced her, she could make a plan.

"We have to get a little closer," he said, handing her the binoculars.

She put them to her eyes and struggled to adjust the focus. Finally the boat came into view. There was a man and a young girl on deck in dive gear, and another man climbing up the ladder and over the transom. He accelerated, causing her to reach for the rail bolted to the console and hold on as they sped toward the boat.

Before he could release the wheel and take the binoculars from her, she put them back to her eyes and scanned the water until she found the boat. And there he was. "It's Mac!" she called out.

"You know the other guy?"

"That's why I'm here. He'll pay you whatever you want to get me back. Take us over there."

"Not so fast." He pulled the throttle back to neutral. "I need to see what they're doing. But you may have just found a way out of your little situation."

She breathed a sigh of relief, but knew that she wasn't in the clear yet. There was a good chance Mac would ignore her, after the way she had treated him. She could probably charm him if they were alone, but with all these strangers around, that wasn't going to work. Focusing on the girl now, it took her a minute for her brain to process where she knew her from.

"The girl. I saw her at the library in Marathon with some old piece of wood." He looked at her, and she knew she had his interest. "So, about my boyfriend there. Seems like you don't want them to see you. Maybe I can help you out here."

He took back the binoculars and watched for what seemed like an eternity. Finally he put them down and looked at her. "Maybe we'll have a change in plans, here. Now, tell me everything you know about the library and this boyfriend of yours."

He sat on the bench and stared at the boat through the binoculars as she told him about Mac, showing their split up as mostly his fault, and her sojourn to Key West, carefully leaving out a few details here and there. Putting down the binoculars he turned and saw the other boat had pulled in their anchor and were heading toward land.

Chapter 21

Kellie looked out the small cabin window as the boat coasted to a stop just short of a small beach. Cody had ordered her back in the cabin after spotting the boat on the reef. She had cooperated, and spent the twenty minutes between stops obsessed with thoughts of Mac. He unlocked the door, hopped out into the water and waded toward shore, where a boat lay beached above the water line.

Having averted disaster and pretty sure she was back on US soil, she sat down in a deck chair, facing the shore. She watched as he walked around the beached boat, surveying the damage. He went over a huge gash in the side and kicked the boat, then climbed over the gunwale and started digging through the compartments. She looked around for any means of escape, but they were alone on a small hump of sand.

"Hey, I need your help over here. Get everything of ours off that boat and bring it here."

She did as he asked, not wanting to upset him when she was so close to freedom — and Mac. She grabbed her small bag and slid over the side and into the calf-deep water. Surprised when the mucky bottom sucked at her feet, she ran toward dry land.

She had just set her bag on the boat when he called out, "Go back and get the life preservers off the other boat. I need about four."

A minute later, she returned with two preservers slung over each shoulder. He took them and started shoving them in the hole.

"That ough'ta get us out of here." He stood back and looked at his work, the hole filled with the orange preservers. "Only got to go a mile or so."

"In that?" she asked.

"That boat there's borrowed. We're gonna take mine back to the dry dock and ditch this one here."

"You sure that's gonna make it?"

He leaned over and picked up a five-gallon bucket. "You know how to use this?" he laughed. "Come on under the top and get in the shade. Be a shame to see that nice little body of yours get sunburned. We've got an hour to kill 'till the tide comes up and floats us off. Maybe we can get to know each other a little better. You know, you haven't thanked me for saving you yet."

"I'll thank you when we're back on real land." She sat in the chair, folded her arms together, and lifted her feet onto the gunwale, out of the ankle-deep water pooled on the deck.

"Well hell, if you're going to be like that we might as well pump her dry and see if we can get out of here." He went back, leaned over the transom, and looked at the engine. "Water's about high enough to cover the intakes. We can start it." He jumped back in the boat and went to the helm. The key turned, but nothing happened. "Shit."

Not knowing what he was rambling about, she sat in the chair, picking at her nails, wishing she had a hot shower and a bed. She sat unmoving and unwilling to help as he scrounged through a tool box, grabbed a wrench, and went for the stolen boat now floating freely in the rising tide. A few minutes later, he was back, carrying a battery. "Thing's dead. Just got to swap it out and we're good to go." He went down into the cabin.

Five minutes later, he hit a switch, and water began pumping out of the side of the boat, the bilge pump whining in the background. He lowered the engine, setting the propeller into the

149

water, turned the key, and started it. The deck was almost dry now as he reversed off the sand bar, lowering the engine as the boat hit deeper water.

"Better get ready to bail. I'm gonna make a run for it." He turned the boat and sped for shore as Kellie watched the water streaming into the boat through the makeshift patch.

* * *

Braken slid into the padded seat at the bar and looked around the empty room as Nicole came toward him.

"Where's Cody?"

"Good to see you too. Want a drink? It's so slow in here I'll even take you for company," she said.

"You seen him or not?"

"What'd he do now? Spent two nights ago in jail, and don't know where he was last night. Figured you had some work for him, so I let it be. You know we're going to need help to pay a lawyer."

"For now, how about we find him?"

"This isn't sounding good. What did he do?"

"How about a Jack and Coke." Braken needed something to soothe his nerves. He'd been driving all day, looking for Cody and checking the bridge - having no luck with either. The last thing he wanted to do was go home and face Pagliano, that crazy woman, and whatever trip they were on.

She turned to make the drink, set a bevnap down on the bar, and set the glass in front of him.

One thing that girl could do was make a drink, he thought, as he inhaled half of the strong mix. "He trashed the work on the bridge. I don't have much for details until I find him, but Wood confronted him and he just ran off." He sucked the balance of the drink through the straw, then pushed the empty glass toward her, indicating that he wanted a refill.

"But you don't know for sure?"

"Sure enough. I've been watching that boy get in and out of trouble for years. I know the signs, and they all say he did it."

She turned, mixed another drink for him, and set it down. The door flew open. Braken squinted into the bright light and saw two figures enter. Once the door closed and his eyes adjusted, he realized it was Cody and a woman. As they came closer, he recognized her as the dancer from Key West.

The world was closing in on him, he thought, and drank deeply.

"You going to explain yourself?" he asked as Cody approached, the two women watching intently.

"I got the boat in dry dock, no worries there," he blurted out. "And this girl and me, we saw Wood diving out on the reef. I think it was his spot out there, where he dumps rubble. This girl's boyfriend was out there with him —"

"Mac Travis," Kellie blurted out. "I've been looking for him."

Braken stood and faced off with Cody, "What does this have to do with anything? You come storming in here with this floozy, like you saved the world. What wrecked boat, and what were you doing out on the reef with her?"

Cody stuttered, moving away from Nicole, who was leaning over the bar. "She says they found something down there. Could be valuable."

Nicole came around the bar and slapped him. "You piece of shit. In the last two days you've been in jail, wrecked your boat, and whatever else they were doing at the bridge. On top of that, you blew off a charter to take this bimbo to the reef?"

"I can explain." He stepped backwards to avoid the next blow, but Braken stepped between them.

"Both of you stop. Nicole, get back there and make me another drink. You two need to separate your domestic problems from business. Now —" He turned to Kellie. "What did they find?"

Nicole interrupted. "I saw it the other night, and it's nothing. An old piece of wood with some copper or something on it. Didn't look valuable to me."

"It's not making sense," Braken sat and took the fresh drink. "Too many coincidences going on here." He rubbed his chin, wondering what to do about this and if there was a way for him to profit from it. Cody was another sore spot. It was one thing to cover up or lie about the damage he'd done to the bridge, it was another to be working for one of his enemies running girls to the Bahamas. He needed to pacify Pagliano as soon as he came off the high he was on, and throwing Cody and the girl at him might be the best way to do that.

"You two come with me."

* * *

"His house is right around the corner," Braken said as they turned onto Wood's street.

Kellie sat on the edge of the seat, looking in the vanity mirror as the wide car took the narrow turn. "Wish I had some makeup."

Her face was a mess, the last few days taking a toll on her. Deep black circles echoed the mascara still over her eyes. The sun exposure was evident in pink spots on her face, and her hair was a tangled mess. Wetting the bottom of her T-shirt with saliva, she tried to clean up her eyes with limited success, then raked her hands through her hair.

The car stopped in front of a house, and she breathed in deeply. Was this the moment of truth, where Mac would take her back and they could go home? Or had she really blown it this time? Pulling the shirt tight around her breasts and tying a knot behind her, she figured she looked as good as the conditions allowed. Chin up, she went up the stairs to the door.

She looked back at the two Braken men waiting in the

running car. One more breath, and she knocked. Tapping her foot, she waited, knocking again after a few minutes of silence. After her third attempt, she put her ear against the door and confirmed that the house was quiet. There was a truck in the driveway, but Cody had said there was a boat missing from the seawall. Determined not to leave empty handed, she went downstairs and quickly took the path around back, waving a finger at Braken to wait for a minute. She went up the stairs leading to the back deck, and peered into the dimly lit room, searching for any sign of Mac.

She tried the sliding glass door, surprised when it opened, letting a small stream of cool air out as she leaned against it. She hadn't intended to break in, but the door slid another few inches, and she couldn't help herself. Inside the house, she looked around, waiting for her eyes to adjust to the dark. She started to wander through the living room, smiling when she saw Mac's duffle bag on the floor.

He was here.

A horn honking brought her back to reality, and she looked around once more. Somehow, she needed something to force Mac to talk to her. She quickly tossed his bag, but there was nothing worth taking. As she was about to leave, she saw the piece of wood sitting on the table. Now *there* was something of value. She went to the table, put it under her arm, and slid back out the door.

Braken looked at her as she got back in the car. "Why not have some leverage. Don't you want to know what they're up to?" she asked.

He took the relic and set in on the seat next to him before shifting into drive. Just as he was about to pull away, two men appeared around the corner, running toward them. She looked over her shoulder and smiled as she saw Mac screaming for the car to stop.

"Shit, they know it's me," Braken said. "Can't hide with this car." He put the shifter in park and waited. "Might as well get this over with now."

Amen, Kellie thought as she opened the door and stood there with her best pose. The intended reaction never happened, though, as Mac stormed up to her and, instead of embracing her, pushed her against the car.

"Easy boyo," Wood said as he placed a hand on his shoulder to pull him back.

Kellie watched Mac as he backed away, and knew from the scowl on his face that he wasn't happy to see her. The tightness squeezed against her temples as she looked at him.

"Babe, I'm so sorry." She cocked her hip. "Why don't we talk in private for a minute?" She hoped if she could get him away from the group, that she could work her charms on him.

"Alone with you?" he mocked.

Harsh words from the other side of the car interrupted her plea, and she turned away from Mac. The other man pulled open the back seat door and reached in for Cody. He grabbed him by the shirt and pulled him out. Mac went to restrain him, but he pulled away.

"Stop it, Wood," Braken screamed as he hauled his bulk from the seat. "This is between us. Leave the boy alone."

"The boy about killed me, and wrecked the dam. What about that?" Wood pushed Cody back into the seat and went toward Braken.

"You touch me and you're going to jail, understand." Braken said.

Wood backed away. "You and me are gonna settle this right now. I want a change order and some cash. You can deal with his reckless behavior, which I guess he's got no control over." He glared at Braken. "He cost me half a week of work."

Braken nodded, waiting for the terms, while Kellie took the distraction and slid closer to Mac, who was so intent on the conversation he didn't notice.

"I'm gonna let the boy off if you get me ten grand for the damage, get off my back, and let me finish the damn job. Any other crap, and I'll pull off the project and turn him in."

Braken nodded. "Guess that's a fair deal." It was a small price to save the job and his son. "Come by my place in a half-hour and I'll get you the cash." He got in the car and set it in drive, anxious to get away.

Kellie got in and rolled down the window. She knew she had to make her move now or lose him. "Mac," she pleaded, "can't we just talk?"

He ignored her, so she played the last card she had. "I might have something you want." She held the relic out the window as the tires screeched and Braken pulled away.

Chapter 22

"Chin up," Wood said as they walked back to the house. "We'll give him his thirty minutes and go settle this."

Mac took another look at the empty street, hoping it had been a dream. "I thought I was done with that one. You have no idea how crazy she can get."

"Can't always choose your fate, especially with women."

Mac needed something to do while they waited, so he walked around the house to the boat, got on, and started unloading the gear on the dock. When the boat was empty, he took the hose and started cleaning the dive gear. The equipment rinsed he sprayed the boat, mesmerized by the refraction of the light through the water, and he started to think.

He'd tried to leave her before, but every time she had managed to bewitch him, and he'd gone back. There was a diagnosis for what she had: some psychotic disease with a handful of smaller disorders. If and when she stayed on her meds, she was stable, but then she would start to think she was better and stop taking them. It was a vicious loop that he had seen many times before, and knew every phase of. From the look on her face — that pained, unfocused look — she was deep in it now, and close to breaking. The fall to the dark side was well underway, and this was where bad things happened.

Wood walked down stairs from the house. "Let's go settle this."

Mac turned off the hose and followed him toward the front of the house.

* * *

Pagliano woke when he heard the door slam, and rolled over to see Cheqea next to him. He jumped out of bed, wondering what had happened, his memory of the last day a blank. He had done his share of experimentation — mostly with coke and quaaludes —but had never felt like this before. Like yesterday never happened.

He dressed, then went to the living room and saw Braken, Cody, and Kellie. He ignored the men and watched as Kellie went to the couch and sat down with a piece of wood in her hands.

"Well look who's back." He smiled wondering what the hell was wrong with his brain. "The chief will be happy about that. She wants to help you, sweetheart, and I can tell you her shit works." He went toward her. "Whatcha got there?"

Kellie flinched as he grabbed the artifact from her. "I don't know. Took it from the diver guy's place. Just hoping my boyfriend would come after it. I really miss him."

Pagliano looked toward Braken for help. The girl was clearly distraught, and as he looked at the piece of wood, he couldn't figure out why anyone would be interested in it.

"We've got trouble," Braken said as he went toward the bedroom. "Forget about her." He entered the room and saw Cheqea in the bed, and turned his eyes to the other side, which had clearly been slept in as well. He looked at Pagliano and went for the closet.

"Just cementing our alliance. You know, keep your friends close and your enemies closer." Pagliano sat on the bed. "What's up with you?"

157

"My damn boy trashed the bridge project. Don't know the details, but everything the contractor did last week is ruined. It's going to cost another ten grand and the better part of a week to get back to where we were." He started to pull things out of the closet, throwing them to the floor.

"Slow down, there. We're not paying shit to the contractor. Where I come from, we don't have change orders. I'll deal with him."

Braken was still working in the closet. "He's threatening to turn Cody in to the police."

"Well, we'll see about that. You just settle down and let Joey take care of this." He smacked Cheqea on the butt, waking her. "Hey. That girl is back."

"You see? You doubted Cheqea's medicine. You watch. I'll fix her like I fixed you."

"You go do your magic. It looks like she needs some help."

Cheqea got out of bed, grabbed her clothes, and went for the living room.

"Be careful with that one," Braken warned him. "I've heard what that medicine of hers can do to people."

"Whatever. Let's deal with your problem." He went back to the living room. Braken followed empty handed.

Cody stood there, staring at the ground. Pagliano went toward him and placed a hand on his shoulder. Before he could speak, there was a knock on the door, and he staggered as Pagliano brushed past him.

"I told you, I'll take care of this." He opened the door and allowed the two men in. "And you are ...?"

"Name's Wood, Bill Woodson. This here's —"

"Mac Travis," Kellie called out from the couch. "My boyfriend," she swooned.

Pagliano glanced back at her, Cheqea massaging her head. "OK Mr. Wood and Mac Travis, what can I do for you?"

Wood pushed past him and went toward Braken. "It's

158

between me and him. You got my money and that piece of wood the girl took?"

Pagliano grabbed him, spinning him around, the mellow feeling from the drugs a distant memory. "Let's be clear here. *I* am in charge. That fat fuck and his family work for me." He paused. "And believe me, if you could find better help in this shit hole, I would."

"Well, I'll deal with you, then. I want the money for what the boy did. I'll fix your damn bridge and we can part ways. I don't care about anything else."

"You want money? You finish the job." Pagliano pushed him in the chest. He didn't allow others to dictate terms.

Wood was about to push back when Cheqea jumped between them. "Stop it, both of you." She turned to Pagliano. "Pay him and get them out of here. You can take it out of my share if you want. Just do it." She turned towards Pagliano and whispered something to him.

Pagliano released Wood and turned to her. She was clutching the relic to her chest, a desperate look in her eye. "You sure? As long as it comes out of your share ..." Amazed that the words had come out of his mouth, he felt bewitched and wondered what kind of hold Cheqea had over him. It was an unusual feeling, and not one he liked.

"Just do it!" She turned to Wood. "You'll get your money, just get out of here and go fix the bridge. Forget about this." She held the relic against her chest. "And I'll take care of the girl. She needs my help anyway. Deal?"

Wood nodded and waited for Braken, who had gone to the bedroom.

Pagliano took Cheqea by the shoulder and steered her into the kitchen, where they spoke. "What the fuck? I had that under control."

"Don't worry, baby. You're going to get your casino." She held out the relic. "This is both our tickets."

159

"Y'all might be happy, but what about me?" Kellie burst out. Tears rolled down her face. "No one cares about me." She started sobbing.

Cheqea went to her bag and pulled out the vial, then went to Kellie and rubbed her temples. "Sweetheart, I got this for you." She reached for the vial and pulled out a piece of seaweed. "Take this, baby." She held it out.

Kellie stuck out her tongue and took the offering.

* * *

"Good to see you have some baggage there, Travis." Wood was driving back toward his house, an envelope full of cash between him and Mac on the seat. "Makes you more like the rest of us."

"You have no idea," Mac answered as he sat facing forward, not daring to look at Wood out of embarrassment. "I came down here to shake that girl, and now she's here."

"No use feeling sorry for yourself. Question now is, what do we do about all this?"

Mac relaxed slightly. He knew he was naturally defensive, and was grateful that Wood appeared not to care about his personal problems or judge him. But the question was more complicated for him than it was for Wood, who only had to repair the bridge, and now had the money to do it. Whether he wanted to pursue the relic and whatever it led to were optional. From everything Mac had pieced together about the man and his business, once he completed this job, he could pay off the insurance premium and start bidding better work. Aside from the shady customers he was currently forced to work for, he would soon be the master of his own fate.

For himself, Kellie loomed large in his thoughts. There was no living with, or even being near, her. Without her meds, she was a danger to herself and everyone around her. He had tried to extricate himself from their relationship since it started. Able to go

160

from a caring person to an angry witch instantly, she had a sixth sense about when he was about to leave, and had been able to shift back. And yes, when she was in play nice mode, he wasn't going anywhere. But the last fight had been bad enough that he had walked out before she could turn him.

Now, somehow, she had found him.

"Don't think too hard on it," Wood said. "She'll get the message and back off."

"You have no idea," Mac repeated the mantra he had recited to himself and others over the course of their relationship. He thought about how he could escape again, and was starting to get an idea about leaving when Wood seemed to read his mind.

"You could stay out on the barge. It's not the Ritz, but I'll cover for you and tell them you headed back up north, to find work in Miami."

Mac thought about his options. Miami was probably his best option. It was close, and there was no lack of work, but he had no doubt that she knew that too. "Maybe. Let me think about it." He glanced at the envelope, wondering if he would get his back pay now. Wood again knew what he was thinking.

"Go ahead, take your pay. That way you've got some cash if you decide you need to go."

Mac took ten hundreds from the envelope and stuck them in his pocket. At least he had the means to run if he needed it, now. "So what are you thinking?"

Wood glanced over at him as he took the money. "That's about right." He looked back at the road. "Gotta finish that bridge. I'll admit that chunk of wood has my interest up, but if we want to go after that, the first thing to do is fix the bridge. Then they'll be off our backs, and we can figure the rest of the puzzle out."

"Makes sense." Mac was still worried about Kellie, but he was starting to feel a tie to Wood, and decided he wasn't going to abandon him before the bridge project was completed. "I'll be around, and make sure the bridge gets fixed. That's what I signed on for, and I won't go back on my word, crazy woman or not. After that's over, I'll let you know."

"Fair enough." Wood looked over at Mac. "Don't find many stand-up guys down here. Place is full of low-life, pot-smoking, burned-out scam artists. I'd be happy to have you around."

Both men sat quietly, satisfied with their decisions. They reached the house and got out, each having his own unspoken work to do. Wood went to the house, and Mac turned the other way and went toward the shed, to see what kind of welding equipment was there.

The next step to repairing the bridge was to weld the rebar cage, drill and embed the steel into the bedrock with hydraulic cement. From here on, this was a simple operation — something he had done many times. Most of the work would be done on the barge — the rebar cut and bent, then tied into two half circles each several inches larger than half the diameter of the pier. After both sections were completed, the real work would start. Mac would have to go under water and drill the bedrock, epoxy pieces of rebar into the holes, and weld the cage to the pieces and then to itself. Once that was done, all that was left was to pour concrete and strip the forms. They would use a concrete truck on shore with a boom truck, brought down from Miami. The truck would extend its arm over the water and pump concrete directly into the hole. Placed in this manner, the weight and mass of the concrete would easily displace the water in the forms. The cofferdam would have made things simpler, the boom truck and its cost not necessary. But now they had no choice.

Sweat started to pour from him the minute he stepped into the shed. The metal roof groaned as it expanded in the heat, giving an eerie feeling to the building. In a far corner, he found the welding rig and pulled the cables into the center of the room.

Although it sounded complicated and dangerous, metal arc welding underwater was the same as above ground. He pulled out the power source — a two-hundred-amp diesel-fired DC generator

— and the two heavy gauge wires. As he checked the cables for defects, he envisioned the operation in his head. He would first take the cable he was examining and clamp it to the steel cage, then take the cable lying on the floor and attach the electrode to it. This, he would take down with him. Then it was simply a matter of holding the electrode the correct distance from the work for an arc to form, melting the electrode into a puddle weld. It took more touch than doing the same work on land, but with his experience it was second nature. Welding rebar wasn't art; as the work was encased in concrete, once cured, the welds would be protected. There was no need to grind and polish them.

The heat was starting to get to him, so he decided to move everything outside to complete his equipment check. The breeze cooled him slightly as he assembled the welder and started the generator. Satisfied it was all in good order, he pulled out a hand truck to move everything to the dock.

Chapter 23

"See that, fat man, you got your bridge fixed." Cheqea sat on the couch next to Kellie, massaging her shoulders.

"It's your ten grand, and tomorrow's Monday. We'll be at the federal building at nine to sign the papers. Then you can take your freak show somewhere else," Braken said.

"You going to let him talk to me like that?" Cheqea asked Pagliano.

"Whatever. What's the deal with the paperweight, that it's so freakin' important you let ten large go for it?" He picked the chunk of wood up from the coffee table and tossed it in the air.

Cheqea jumped up and grabbed it before it could hit his hands. "And I was just getting to like you." She shot him a look and returned to the couch, relic in her lap. "This is from my people. It is the proof that we were here, and it is what you need to get your casino. I've seen the carving before, in some ancient codexes. We show them this and there won't be any doubt that my people explored and lived here before Columbus, the Spanish, or any of you sorry-ass white boys."

"Easy. Didn't know you were such a history buff. If it's like you say, and this thing goes through, we're all going to be raking in the cash." He smiled at her.

"Hold the phone." Braken had been watching the

interchange. "You show that to the feds, and it's gone. It'll take them ten years to determine that it's real, where it came from, and what it means. No way are we just going to walk in there and hand it to them."

He paced the room, glancing over at the women on the couch. If he hadn't just parted with ten grand, Kellie might do something for him, but he was upset about the money and anxious that this bunch of misfits would blow the real estate deal. He had lost faith in the casino ever being built, and had decided the real estate was the only way he was going to make a dime from this. With or without the chunk of wood, Cheqea was — on a good day — not credible enough to pull this off, and on a bad day she was a laughingstock. He had to admit to himself that he had read her wrong.

"Hey, why don't we have a party?" Kellie was on her feet, dancing to some music residing only in her head.

Braken lost his train of thought as he watched her move around the room. She started to take off her top, and he forgot everything. Soon they were in a conga line, snaking their way through his living room. He had seen Cheqea give her something from a vial. Maybe some of that would erase the last few days from his memory.

* * *

Cody had slid out the door when the melee started. He moved over to the window, trying to hear the conversation, but with the air conditioning blasting it was impossible. Downstairs now, he was thinking that this was getting worse by the minute. Bringing the girl to his father instead of finishing the job and taking her to the Bahamas had been a mistake. Any way he turned, he was in trouble. There was no question what Teqea would do to him. The gold necklace in the shape of a machine gun he wore allowed no delusions of what the man's version of justice was.

Losing a prime girl like Kellie would mean he had at least a handful of goons searching for him right now — and they would come here first. Whether Pagliano was more fearsome was an open question, and he was sure he didn't want to know what was behind that curtain.

The piece of wood seemed to be a big deal to them, but he had no idea what it was. Deep in thought, he was startled when the door burst open and Wood walked out, carrying an envelope that looked like it was full of cash, his new boy behind him.

Cody slid around the corner of the house as they went down the stairs. With no other ideas, and wanting to get as far from Pagliano as he could, he decided to follow the two men. If he could steal the cash and somehow get Kellie back to Key West, that might pacify Teqea. He went for his car, looking back at the house, and heard music blaring from the living quarters upstairs. Relieved no one was following he took off after the old truck.

Wood was well ahead of him, but there were only a handful of places he would go, and it wasn't worth being seen. If he missed them at one, it wouldn't take long to find them. With an envelope full of cash, he expected they would be going to Wood's house first, to stash it.

It looked like he was right as the truck turned off US 1 and headed towards Wood's neighborhood. A block away, he pulled up to the curb, left the comfort of the air conditioning, and set out on foot. Slowly he approached the house. Travis was out back, moving equipment around, but Wood was nowhere in sight. He must be upstairs.

Cody snuck around the back of the house. Creeping around the overgrown oleanders and hibiscus, he rounded the back corner, and heard Wood talking on the telephone. Below an open window, he stopped and listened.

From the one-sided conversation he figured that Wood was talking to old Ned, something about that piece of wood they were all excited about. He heard him explain that Braken had paid him and that the artifact was now with Cheqea. Then it was silent.

Cody was about to leave when he heard Wood again. They were making plans to finish the bridge and then look for more evidence. Again it went quiet, and he crept away, wondering what they were all excited about. But now he knew two things. One, that Wood would not be home tomorrow, and he would be free to break in and search for the cash. And two, that there was something near that pier that might be worth a look before they covered it with concrete.

He got ready to leave, the information making the subterfuge worthwhile, but as he peered out from behind the bushes, he saw Mac coming toward him and pressed himself back against the wall. Mac passed by, climbed the stairs, and entered the house. Cody was about to leave when he heard them talking.

"I've got all the welding gear ready to go, but that power supply is going to be too heavy to take on either of the small boats," Mac said.

"We're going to need to bring the barge around and pick it up. If you're wanting to camp out there tonight, I've got nothing against doing it now," Wood responded.

They were quiet for a few minutes as he waited, his chance to grab the cash looking like it was going to come sooner than he thought. Mac walked out onto the back deck with a duffel bag in hand, and went down the stairs, dropping the bag by the pile of gear on the dock. Wood joined him, a beer in each hand, then jumped into the skiff and started the engine. Mac followed his lead. A minute later, the boat pulled away from the seawall.

Cody waited until the boat rounded a corner and was out of sight, then moved away from the wall and started to go for the back stairs. Climbing them two at a time, he stepped onto the back deck, jumping when a heron took off from the neighbor's dock. The house was quiet as he stepped through the unlocked sliding door, and started searching with the desk by the door. But he came up empty. He went down the hall towards the bedroom - a more likely hiding place. Halfway down the hall he heard the front door slam. Quickly he slid into one of the rooms and closed the door.

Footsteps came down the hall and he heard another door close. Must be in the bathroom, he thought as he looked around, realizing that from its decorations, the room obviously belonged to a girl. Shit. It was Mel's room, and he figured it was her in the house. He went for the closet, barely getting the door closed behind him when he heard someone enter the room.

His heart pounded as he peered out a crack in the door. She was changing — in her underwear now, with a swimsuit laid out on the bed. He had never thought twice about her, but now, looking at her teenage body, he had a thought that could save him. Kellie might have slipped from his grasp, but if he could bring a young girl like this to the man in Key West, all his problems, at least on that front, would be over.

He waited while she changed, trying to resist his growing excitement. After an uncomfortable minute, she left the room. Planning his next move, he snuck out of the closet and went for her in the hall. Taken by surprise, she went down underneath him. She thrashed at him, but her teenage strength was not equal to his, especially with the adrenalin pulsing through him. Damage or bruising would decrease her value, so he carefully locked her arm behind her back and got her up, then walked her toward the kitchen, pulling up and tightening the grip whenever she made any noise.

At the kitchen sink he stuffed the dish rag in her mouth and relaxed his grip slightly, knowing that she couldn't scream. Using one large hand, he engulfed both her slender wrists, and was able to restrain her one-handed while he looked through the cabinets with the other. After rifling through several drawers, he found a roll of duct tape in a hardware drawer. With his teeth he pulled the loose end off the roll, kicked behind her with his right leg, and sent her to her knees. He grabbed both arms and pulled them behind her back, ripped two feet off the tape still gripped in his teeth, and started taping her wrists together.

Satisfied that she was restrained, he went to work on her ankles. She caught him with a quick kick to the groin and he smacked her across the face to stun her while he finished the work. Once she was immobile, he left her on the floor and went to search the rest of the house for the money. He was disappointed when he'd gone through all the rooms and still hadn't found it, but felt better for having the girl. It would have been better to wait for dark before taking her out of the house, but he had no time. Wood would be back well before nightfall.

They needed to get out of here before the old man got back. Just as they were about to head down the stairs, though, a car pulled into the driveway and he jumped back into the house, pulling her behind him and slamming the door. The street and car weren't an option, now. He noticed a boat sitting against the seawall. While searching the desk earlier, he had noticed a set of keys to a boat, identified by the floating buoy attached to them. Pushing her in toward the back door, he grabbed the keys from the desk and slid it open.

He knew he had to get out quickly, so he pulled his pocket knife out and cut the tape binding her feet together. She must have regained her senses as she fought him, her toenails raking against his legs as she tried to kick him. Doing his best to ignore her, he forced her down the stairs, half dragging her to the bottom, less concerned now about damaging the merchandise, and then toward the boat. The back door opened, and he looked back to see Ned standing there, staring at them in shock.

With no time to lose, he tossed her onto the boat and smacked her head with a billy club to knock her out. Ned was down the stairs and almost to the dock when Cody started the engine, he ran forward and tossed the bow line, then rushed back to the helm and slammed the throttles. The boat surged forward as the twin outboards bit into the water, throwing a huge wake behind him as he sped out of the canal.

He plowed straight into the Gulf, trying to put as much water between them and the pursuit that was sure to come.

* * *

The barge crossed the large wake as it turned to enter the canal. "Goddamn tourists. This is a no wake zone!" Wood yelled.

Mac looked back at the skiff towed behind the barge and the boats bouncing off the docks as they idled toward Wood's house. They made the last turn and saw Ned on the dock, waving frantically at them. "There's Ned over there." Mac noticed that the center console was missing. "The boat's gone, too."

"Maybe Mel took it out. But what's got the old man's panties in a wad?"

They eased up to the dock and tossed Ned a line. He tied it off and jumped on the barge. "Cody's got Mel. I saw him take off with her in your boat."

"Goddamn Brakens. Must have been his wake we crossed. I saw a boat heading straight out. Could have been mine, but it was too far away to know for sure." Wood jumped onto the dock and ran for the house. "Secure the barge and untie the skiff. I'm calling the sheriff and then we're going after them."

Mac followed the orders and tied off the barge. He jumped back on and went to the stern, where the painter line to the skiff was tied. The small boat came toward him as he pulled. As soon as it was in reach, he let go and jumped on. Wood was out of the house now, a hand-held VHF in one hand and a gun in the other. Mac started the boat and pulled aside the barge.

"Ned, you gotta stay here on the radio upstairs and coordinate things. The boy here and I are going after them. We'll talk on channel 72, but we'll be monitoring channel 16, too." He ran across the barge and jumped on the skiff.

Mac took off at full speed, not caring about the no wake zone. They had only an hour before it was dark — not a lot of time to find a lone boat in the backcountry. A helicopter was the best bet to search the area where Cody was sure to have headed. Riddled with mangrove-covered islands and submerged shoals, it was hard to conduct an effective search from the water. He glanced at a piling next to an adjacent dock. The water was low, revealing several feet of barnacles. At least the tide was in their favor. A tide this low would make searching easier, by restricting the larger boat to areas of deeper water. They had the advantage of the lighter skiff and Wood's knowledge of the backcountry.

Wood had the VHF to his ear, his free hand shielding his eyes from the glare of the setting sun. Mac squinted as he headed out toward deeper water, glancing over at Wood for direction.

Wood set the radio down. "Coasties and the sheriff are in the air. They'll set up a search and try to find them. Only problem is that once it's dark, he can sneak into the mangroves and be out of sight. There's too much territory to hide in out here. Drug and liquor smugglers have been hiding out back here for all eternity, and most have got away with it. Best bet is to let them search out here, where we're just spinning our wheels. Turn this thing around, and let's go pay Braken a visit."

"What good is that going to do?" Mac asked.

"Damn boy. Gotta think ahead. The boy's got enough of a head start on us, we don't have a damn chance of catching him. It'd be like finding a needle in a haystack. Helicopters will have the best chance at finding him."

"What do we do?" Mac asked.

"Find the old man," Wood replied and spun the wheel.

Chapter 24

Wood was out the door before the truck stopped in Braken's driveway. Mac slid the stick into first gear and jumped out to run after him, letting the car stall on its own. He caught him on the second step and grabbed his shoulder.

"Don't go in there half-cocked, with a gun drawn. That guy from Jersey's a mobster, if you didn't notice."

Wood shook him off. "His kid's got my daughter. I'll do whatever I have to."

"Getting killed is not going to get her back." Mac looked up at the door, hoping they hadn't been noticed. He heard music coming from the house, and the drapes were drawn. "Slow down just a second." He grabbed Wood, moving him away from anyone looking out the second-floor windows. "We've got some leverage here. Ten thousand dollars' worth, and he needs that bridge fixed."

Wood looked at him, the craziness fading from his eyes. "You're right." He set the VHF to channel 72. "Let me check in with Ned and see if he's heard anything. I'll at least tell him what we're up to, just in case."

Mac relaxed as Wood talked to Ned on the hand held, thankful that he had gotten control of himself. The radio conversation went back and forth for a minute until Wood signed off and nodded to Mac. "Smack me if I get out of control."

They went back to the front of the house and climbed the stairs. Mac stood close behind Wood as he rang the doorbell, prepared to control him if needed. After about thirty seconds, he tried again.

"Damn music is too loud."

He pounded on the door, with the same result. Mac reached around him and tried the doorknob. It turned, and he slowly moved in front of Wood, pushing the door open.

It took a few seconds for their eyes to adjust to the darkness. Kellie was dancing on the coffee table, totally nude, swaying to the music blasting from the speakers. Braken sat on the couch, stretched out and watching her, his pants around his knees. There was no sign of Pagliano and Cheqea. It would have been preferable to have the two wildcards out in the open.

The couple in the living room didn't notice as they entered and closed the door. Mac signaled to Wood to stay put while he checked the rest of the house. The less he had to look at Kellie the better. Still unnoticed, he stayed close to the wall in a crouch as he moved down the hallway. The doors were all open; one bedroom was empty, while the other had the bodies of Pagliano and Cheqea motionless on the bed.

He crept back toward Wood, held up two fingers, and pointed at the bedrooms. Wood nodded and went toward the stereo. Mac could only watch as he reached behind his back, pulled the gun out of his waistband, and smashed the amplifier. The music stopped, but Kellie kept swaying to whatever was going on in her head, and Braken sat there staring at her, mesmerized.

"What in the seven hells is going on here?" Wood yelled, trying to break their trance.

Mac went through the house and turned on every light he could find. Kellie kept dancing. Braken, unaware of his state of undress, acknowledged them. He rose off the couch and tripped over his pants. Not as embarrassed as Mac expected, he rolled onto his back and hiked his pants up, having to contort his girth into the waistband.

"Shit, Wood. What's the meaning of this? Breaking into my house," he said as he sat up.

Wood was about to strike him, but Mac grabbed his arm and said, "His daughter's gone. Cody took her."

"What's that you say?" He reached for a blanket and covered Kellie. "I'll be right back. Let me get rid of this distraction." He led her down the hall and into a bedroom. The door closed, and a moment later he was back in the living room.

"What are you going to do about it?" Wood asked as he inched closer.

"I got nothing to do with this. All I want is to get the bridge fixed and sell some real estate. The sooner that guy," — he pointed to the bedroom — "is back in Jersey and the chief goes away, the happier I'll be. You gotta believe me."

"He's your boy. Find him and fix this. Now." Wood was close enough that the spittle from his mouth reached Braken's chin. "Anything happens to that girl and I'll sink that bridge with you tied to it."

"Give me a minute and let me think." Braken paced, then sat down and put his head in his hands. "I don't know. He won't have the VHF on, you can count on that. He wanted one of those new phones, but I wouldn't get him one." It looked like he was crying now. "I'm sorry for what my boy's done, you gotta believe me. I never intended for this to happen."

Wood was about to grab him when Mac pulled him back again. He whispered to him: "It'll do no good to push too far. We'll have to do this on our own."

* * *

Cody was covered in mosquito bites. He could see the welts rising on Mel's skin as well, and hoped the disfiguration wouldn't discount her too much in the eyes of the man in Key West. They were backed into the mangroves on one of the Content Keys waiting for day to fade to night. Darkness had finished spreading its blanket over the area as he started the boat, pushed the throttle in reverse, and backed out of the mangroves. Helicopters had been constantly running search patterns until the sun set about an hour ago, the low light making it fruitless to continue searching. And that's when the mosquitos attacked.

He knew he had to stick it out and wait until total darkness, then run with his lights off, if he were going to avoid being caught. There would probably still be search boats out, but their visibility would be limited, making it the best time to make the trip to Key West. By morning, the waters would again be saturated with Coast Guard and local law enforcement boats combing the area. It was now or never.

He spun the wheel, turning the boat toward the west, and pushed down on the throttles. The twin two hundred fifty horsepower engines quickly bringing the boat onto plane. The water showed twenty-two feet on the depth finder as they travelled to the north of the barrier islands. These small keys and shallows extended all the way to Key West, making it too difficult to pass on the inside - especially at night. He calculated that the sixty-mile run would take a little over two hours at his current speed. That would get them in around midnight — plenty of time to take Mel to Teqea and collect his bounty.

Once he had Teqea placated, he would still have to deal with his father and Pagliano. But that was going to be another problem for another day. Maybe the man in Key West would see his value and give him full-time work somewhere out of the mobster's reach. He thought about Nicole and his son Matt, and how he'd have to leave them alone. Then he figured that he could send money from time to time. Better that than dead.

He looked back at Mel, who had curled into a fetal position, her restraints rendering her helpless. She had struggled, but the duct tape was too tight for her to break the bonds. Finally she had collapsed into a heap in the corner by the transom. A light coating of salt water covered her, the spray hitting her every few seconds as they plowed through waves. He put her from his mind and focused on the water in front of him, his confidence growing as the helicopters receded behind them.

As the hours passed, the lights of Key West became visible to port. He had to pass the entire island to find the green flashing light marking the Calda Channel. Finally, he spotted the flashing light and headed toward it.

Navigation at night was always difficult, so despite his urgency, he took it slow, still making the Key West Bight Marina just before 1 am. The city was still alive, lights ablaze and streets crowded as he pulled into the marina entrance and searched for an empty slip. The slip he had stolen the boat from yesterday would still be open. He went past it, then backed the boat in and tied up to the dock with a quick glance back at Mel, who was still in the same position. Even with the nightly freak show, there was no way he could drag her through the streets of Key West unnoticed. Opening the small door in the center console, he looked into the compartment, thinking he could stash her down there while talked to Teqea.

The storage space stunk of mildew. It was mostly empty, except for a half-dozen life jackets, which he pulled out and stashed under the bench seat. She would fit, but it wouldn't be comfortable. He went back and grabbed her by the arm, meeting little resistance. With a quick look around to make sure no one was watching, he forced her into the compartment and locked the door.

* * *

Braken looked up. "My guess is he's gone to Key West. Maybe he's laid up back in the mangroves, but I don't think so. He's too impatient for that. Dammit!" He pounded his fleshy thighs with his fists.

"You got an idea where he's gone down there?" Wood asked.

"Unfortunately, yes. It's all making sense now, him showing up with the dancer."

"Where do we find him?" Mac asked.

"Man's got a club for a front. Deals in some bad stuff — drugs, sex slaves. Something else you need to know ..."

Wood went for him and grabbed him by the throat before Mac could pull him off. He slammed Braken's head against the back of the sofa before he could finish his sentence. Mac grabbed for him, but he was too far gone.

"What the fuck?" Pagliano stood in the hallway, waving a gun in their direction. "I'm trying to get some sleep."

Mac and Wood backed away. "Bastard's son took my girl!" Wood yelled.

They all turned and stared at Braken now. "It's her brother," he muttered. "That's where he must have gone."

Mac looked at Wood for any clue as to what Braken meant.

"Her brother," he repeated as he pointed to Cheqea standing in the hallway.

"What's he got to do with this?" Cheqea asked.

Braken sat up. "Cody's been in and out of business with him forever. Whenever I don't have enough work or he thinks he needs to be independent, that's where he goes. I keep an eye out, although he's too blind to know."

"My brother?" Cheqea was wide awake now.

"Yes. As much as I hate to admit it, that's where Cody's taken her."

"Shit. That man's bad shit. You white boys better get in gear and get down there. Where'd you put blondie?"

Braken motioned toward the closed bedroom door.

"I'll keep an eye on her. Go. He sees that white girl, she'll be on a boat for the Bahamas or Haiti before dawn. That's some bad shit your boy's messed up in." She disappeared, only to come back with the artifact in her hands. "Take this. You're going to have to trade for her." She handed it to Wood. "Tell him you know where the rest of it is. He'll trade her for it. I guarantee it."

"How do you know?" Pagliano asked.

"You white boys think you're the only ones that came up with this casino scam? He's been trying to get one in Key West for years, but has never had the proof he needed about it being our land. That we were here first. This will give him that."

"Where do we find him?" Wood asked, turning the relic in his hands.

"I'll take you," Braken said. "Cody is going to need to be dealt with as well."

The three men turned to go, but found Pagliano blocking the door. "What the fuck? You forgetting about Uncle Joey here?"

"What do you want?" Wood asked as he pushed past him. An arm shot out, blocking the door, but Cheqea stepped in between them and pushed his gun away.

"You, me, and the girl will leave in the morning and go sign the papers. If there's going to be a casino, it's going to be for me, and not that evil seed of my parents."

Wood lifted Pagliano's hand from the door jamb and went out into the night air, with Mac and Braken behind him. They walked down the stairs to Braken's Cadillac, and Wood got in the back, holding the relic in his lap. Mac got in front with Braken and watched him as he maneuvered out of the driveway. He wondered what the man's priorities really were — the casino or his son. In either case, he was crooked. Mac wasn't planning on taking his eyes off the guy.

"Should be there in an hour, maybe less," Braken said as he turned onto southbound US 1. "Figure we might beat him, if he took the boat. It would only make sense for him to hide until dark and then head down. Too much exposure during daylight, running on the outside of the shallows. That'll probably get him into the harbor around the same time we get there."

"And then what?" Mac asked. His mind was swirling, trying to put all the pieces of the puzzle together. There were too many people and too many motivations to present a clear picture, so he tried to settle his thoughts on the most important. Mel had to be saved. After that, they could decide what to do about Cody, the bridge, and the artifact. They hardly spoke until they entered Boca Chica Key a little less than an hour later.

"We'll be there in ten minutes. How are we going to handle this?" Braken asked.

"You're going to sit your fat ass in the car and wait. Damn family of yours has caused enough trouble." Wood was quiet for a minute. "Travis, you up to this?"

Mac knew he would have to make a decision. He'd been thinking about nothing else for most of the drive, and although he'd only known these people for less than a week, they were starting to feel like family. "I'm with you."

The tension built as they passed over the Stock Island Bridge and entered Key West. Braken turned right, drove for several blocks, then made two quick turns and pulled up in front of a club. "This is it."

"How do we find him?"

"Can't miss him. Name's Teqea. Big guy, all tatted up, with a gold machine gun necklace."

Chapter 25

Mel woke, gagged on the towel in her mouth, and panicked. It took her a long minute to realize that she could breath through her nose, and that she wasn't actually choking. Slowly she started to move, exploring the limits of the space. Her hands and feet felt like they'd been numb for hours. It didn't take long for her to ascertain that she was in the hold under the center console, and the boat was still. She listened for Cody, or anyone else on deck, but only heard muted conversations, from which she assumed that they were docked. Alone and alive, her thoughts turned to escape.

She fought the duct tape binding her wrists and was unable to break its hold, but she still had the use of her fingers. Relief was instantaneous as she pulled the rag out of her mouth. The window was slid closed, and she knew the fresh air would do her good. Twisting her body, she was able to press against the bulkhead and use the force of her legs to rise to just short of standing. The ceiling in the compartment was several inches shorter than she was so she remained stooped as she slid open the small window and gulped in the fresh air.

Lights and boats were visible outside now and she strained to figure out their location. Calculating the length of the ride and the size of the marina, she figured they were in Key West.

She quickly discarded the idea of screaming for help as an

option. She didn't know if Cody was close or not, and if he were, screaming out would probably just get her in even more trouble. Light from the marina entered through the open window, allowing her to look around. She felt better after a few breaths and started looking for a way out. But the compartment had no furnishings — only a small, unused head.

Then a tackle box caught her eye, and she slid her body to reach it. Once there, she manipulated the latch and opened the box. The plastic eyes of brightly colored lures stared back at her. Suspecting it would be difficult to cut the tape with a hook, she continued her search. There was nothing else there. All the surfaces were smooth. Demoralized, she sat back against the access panel that covered the wiring.

A small drop of blood caught her eye, and she remembered that her dad had cut his forearm there. They had been out in the Gulf Stream, fishing for dolphin, when they lost power. She had held the flashlight while he worked in the panel, trying to repair the problem. And in doing so, he'd sliced his arm.

The six large phillips head screws reflected the light shining through the window. With her only tool the large hooks embedded in the lures, she went to work. If there was something in there that could cut through his skin, it could surely cut the duct tape, but she had to get the cover off.

The hook slipped and cut her, but did nothing to loosen the screws. She looked around again, her hope fading as her search yielded nothing. She started to cry.

* * *

The bouncer held out his hand for the five dollar cover charge. Wood was about to push past him, but Mac stopped, pulled a hundred dollar bill from his pocket, and handed it to the man. Disinterested in the two men as long as they paid, the bouncer gave Mac ninety dollars back and moved to the side allowing them to pass.

Mac couldn't help but stare at the stage as the black light illuminated everything white on the dancers, including their tan lines. He quickly moved his attention to Wood's white t-shirt, also aglow, as he headed toward the man at the end of the bar. Two men — smaller in girth, but clearly more powerful — stood to block his way. Mac caught up to him, but could not hear what Wood said to the men. They were obviously not impressed with his rhetoric, and started walking toward the door, pushing Wood ahead of them. Turning, he held out the piece of wood and gestured for them to show the man at the bar. One man took the relic while the other man remained.

The heavy set man at the bar took the relic and stared at it. Then he rose slowly from the barstool and went into what looked like a small office behind the bar. The door opened again a minute later, the light an unwanted intrusion into the dark room, and the man went back to his bar stool. He leaned over to speak to one of the bodyguards, who motioned for Wood to approach, and then motioned them to follow him.

Mac and Wood brushed past the body guard and entered the cramped space. They stood side by side in the office. A small desk and chair were surrounded by wooden shelves filled with liquor bottles. The man sitting in the chair took up most of the available floor space. His large hands caressed the carving on the piece of wood sitting on the deck. It was hard not to notice the intricate pattern of tattoos covering his arms.

"Where did you get this?" he asked without an introduction, his voice surprisingly smooth — in stark contrast to his face.

"It comes from a dive spot we were working," Wood responded.

"And why bring it to me?"

"Truth be told, we need your help. Rumor has it you know Cody Braken. Maybe he does some work for you."

"Nah, don't know nobody by that name," the man responded.

182

Mac could tell he had a poker face, but they were holding a royal flush. The man couldn't take his eyes off the piece of wood. They had him, they just had to play it right.

"Maybe you do, maybe you don't," he said, trying to play the same game. He had watched plenty of cop shows in the recreation rooms of the oil rigs.

The guy nodded. "OK. We understand each other — 'maybe' is a good word. So, maybe I know somebody named Braken. What's that got to do with this?"

Suddenly Wood lost patience. "Son of a bitch has my daughter. And we suspect he's bringing her to you. Maybe you know something about the sex trafficking that goes through here?"

The man's dark red complexion started to turn redder, and Mac knew he had to diffuse this fast. "Look. You've got an interest in that," he said, pointing to the relic. "We just want the girl back. Surely a man of your importance has the means to find a young girl."

The redness subsided slightly, but small beads of sweat started to dapple his bald head. "I will help find your girl and make sure no harm comes to her, but I want to know everything about this."

Mac was about to speak, but Wood interrupted. "First you find her. That thing's been down there for hundreds of years. It's not going anywhere."

The man picked up the phone and dialed. He spoke clearly so Wood and Mac would understand he meant to keep up his end of the deal. Three more calls followed, with the same orders. If he had the influence they suspected, Mel would be found quickly.

Finally he turned toward them. "I have done what I can, for now. She will be found. It is just a question of time. Now, tell me everything about this." He picked up the relic and caressed it as he waited.

* * *

Braken was looking out the window of the Cadillac, watching the men entering and leaving the club. Years ago, he had been involved in a deal with Cheqea's brother, and it had not been a pleasant experience — even compared to his current partner. The siblings shared the same crazy gene, but the older brother did nothing to temper it as his sister did. The medicine made her a different kind of crazy, but at least she was not dangerous. He wondered what would happen to Mac and Wood.

On the other hand, Teqea was. He had watched him as a standout defensive end on the high school football team in Marathon and seen his decline into alcohol, drugs and crime — finally being disowned by the family. How he eluded the police was a mystery to Braken, who had heard rumors of his operation. Owning a strip club in Key West was not a crime, but his other business was. Paying bounties for the runaway girls his team on the streets brought him, and then taking them off the island before anyone knew they were there, was probably well into the realm of ICE and the FBI — two agencies he avoided at all costs. Local law enforcement was pretty laid back here, and it had a face to it. One you could bribe. The faceless feds were not forgiving and he wondered how the man eluded them.

His thoughts were interrupted by someone banging on the window. He looked out the tinted glass and saw Cody staring back at him, clearly distraught.

Braken rolled down the window. "What the hell? You look like crap! And where's the girl?"

"About that." Cody put his head in his hands. "Well, I'm in a bit of a bind and giving her to him," — he looked toward the bar — "It's the only way out."

"Wood's daughter? You idiot. We have our differences, but you don't take a man's daughter. You want to take someone, find a damn runaway like that dancer." He paused, thinking. "Oh, I got it now." It was starting to make sense. "Teqea asked you to deliver our little dancer girl for him, and you blew it. Now you think he's going to take Wood's girl in her place."

Cody didn't have to speak.

"And you almost blew my deal in the process. Wood and that boy are in there now, pleading with him to exchange the girl for the artifact. That means he's going to make a claim for the casino, rather than us. Can your pea brain comprehend that?"

Cody flinched when Braken reached over to turn the AC up. "You've still got the island and the real estate," he muttered.

"Well that's some consolation, as soon as I figure out how to get Pagliano off my back." He turned to face Cody. "Where's the girl? You gotta give her back."

"Jeez. It's not like you never step in shit."

Braken reached out and grabbed the front of his shirt. "Listen to the man who pays the bills and tries to keep you out of trouble. And the key word there, if you hadn't noticed — was 'tries.' Now where's the girl?"

"Safe."

"You don't get it, do you? The girls Teqea takes and sells — no one here knows who they are. They're probably on a milk carton in North Dakota, but down here they're invisible. He gets them so fast that no one here even knows they exist. But Wood is a fixture in this area. He was in the service down here, and has worked on or built half the bridges between here and Miami over the last thirty years. And you took his daughter. You're damn lucky he came to me first, or you would have the sheriff, the FBI, and a posse of locals out looking for you."

Cody put his head back in his hands. "She's at the marina."

Braken looked at the door of the club and pulled the shifter down into reverse. "Let's go."

* * *

Mel bit down on her lip to stop the flow of tears. There had to be a way out; she just had to be patient and keep at it. She started searching again. On her hands and knees now, she worked her way around the back of the head, and noticed the exposed threads of the bolt holding the toilet seat. If she could contort herself and get her arms into the small opening, she was sure it would cut through the tape. Carefully, she snaked forward on her belly to extend herself.

An inch short, she exhaled, giving her body the length it needed for the tape to contact the threads. Holding her breath now, she started rubbing the tape back and forth on the rough metal. It was slow work, and became slower as she tired. Having to hold her breath while she worked, then shimmy her body out to breathe, took time, but after fifteen minutes the tape had a slight tear.

Sitting upright, she grabbed the edge of the tape with her teeth and, with a vicious grunt, tore through it. She shook her hands out to get the blood flowing again, and removed the tape from her ankles. Free now, she went to the door and stared at the missing knob, and tried to turn the small spindle, but could not get enough of a grip on the smooth metal. Frustrated and tired, she sat back down and cursed her dad under her breath for not fixing it after it broke.

The contents of the tackle box were the only thing available to her, so she opened it and removed a lure. Its electric colors reflected the light shining into the console, but she couldn't figure out how twelve feet of leader, a shiny plastic body, and a hook were going to get her out of this.

Exhausted from the ordeal, and with no means of escape, she set the lure down, rolled up in a ball, and started to cry again.

Chapter 26

Mac and Wood stood outside the club, staring at the empty space where the Cadillac had been parked.

Wood scanned the rest of the lot and shook his head. "Bastard chickened out and left us."

"Sure looks like it," Mac said. They needed transportation back to Marathon; the man had cut a hard deal, but it was the best and only chance to get Mel back. They were sure Cody had taken her, and this was his likely destination. Trusting a man of Teqea's stature and reputation was not easy, but the stakes were high on both sides, and that made it appear more equitable. Mel for the artifact.

But not just the small piece. He had to give the man credit for his intelligence. Rather than taking just the relic, he insisted that the authorities would immediately discredit the find without some kind of provenance. And their story was not enough. They needed to document the find, and that meant getting back to Marathon, diving the site again, and photographing the process.

But without Braken, or at least his car, they were stuck fifty miles from the site. Wood had his hands on his hips, a look of determination on his face. Mac was sure that he would walk back if they had the time, but the clock was ticking. The man had given them until noon tomorrow to get the evidence he needed and get back here. He looked around the lot and noticed a pink cab pulling away from the curb. He was about to turn away when he stuck his hands in his pockets and felt the wad of cash.

"Hey! Taxi!" he called out. The cabbie didn't hear him with his windows rolled up and the air conditioning blasting. The car started to move away from the curb and pick up speed. Mac jumped in front of it, desperate to stop it, landing on the hood, as he misjudged the increasing speed. Wood came over and knocked on the cabbie's window while Mac slid off the hood and checked himself for damage.

"Says he'll take us for a hundred. Goddam robbery, but I don't see as we have a choice," Wood said after a brief exchange with the driver. Mac reached into his pocket and removed a bill, which he handed to Wood, who held it for the driver to see. "Ain't gettin' it til we get there. Better get a move on."

They hopped in and the cab accelerated out of the lot just as the back doors closed.

"I'll pay you back soon as we sort this out," Wood said.

"No problem. Let's get Mel back." Mac watched the neon lights pass as they exited Stock Island. The gaudy awnings and billboards faded behind them as they approached the chain of smaller keys leading back to Marathon. He started to make a list in his head, wondering if Wood had any photographic equipment or experience.

They both started speaking at the same time and laughed, releasing some of the tension built over the last several hours. Mac deferred to Wood.

"Got a list in my head. Got everything we need, but I'm not sure if there's film for the camera."

"I was just wondering if you had one," Mac said.

"Yeah, got the whole shebang. Inspectors don't like to get wet, and want pictures of the underwater work before we cover anything up. Same thing I was going to do for the pier we're working on. Take a few pictures for anyone interested in seeing

188

that there's really steel inside the concrete. Only problem is getting the film developed and getting back there by noon. I don't expect we can hand him an undeveloped 35mm cartridge and walk away with Mel."

"What if we brought him something else?" Mac asked.

Wood gave him a questioning look. "He needs to document it for the feds. Give them something that proves without a doubt that the tribe has a claim. He's a damn sight smarter than Braken and that mobster, thinking they could just walk that crazy witch doctor into the federal building, fill out a piece of paper, and open a casino."

Wood stared at him, the look on his face desperate for anything that would save Mel.

"I've got my own problem crashed out at Braken's house. We give him Kellie in exchange for Mel. He's got the relic, and we can offer him the location of the find. He can verify it easily enough." Mac couldn't believe the words had come out of his mouth, never mind even thinking about a trade. Kellie was out of his life, but he also felt somewhat responsible for her. Maybe he could help get her a job in Key West. That might keep her happy and ease his conscience. Dancing was the only thing she could do, and the club looked busy enough. With any luck, she could find another guy to torment.

"Pretty ruthless there, Travis," Wood said. "I know he doesn't want Mel. An underage local, especially as feisty as she can get, is gonna be more trouble than he wants. Maybe it'll work."

* * *

The moon had risen and shown through the open window, jerking Mel awake. She had no idea how long she had been asleep, but the light was different. It was brighter in the small compartment. Feeling better for the rest, she checked the cabin again. The only tools at her disposal were still the fishing lures. Staring at the brightly colored baits, the large hooks gave her an idea.

She opened the box, took out the largest lure, and unwound the twelve-foot-long piece of sixty-pound monofilament leader. The large hook on the end would easily grab the handle on the outside of the door, and the weight of the lure itself would help launch the hook toward the door handle. The only problem was that the handle was on the opposite side of the console from the window.

She wound the leader back into several loose loops, went to the window, and pushed out the screen. With her right hand extended out the window, she dropped some line allowing the lure to hit the deck. She flicked her wrist, wound up, and flung the lure back over the console, releasing the remaining line as it travelled toward the door handle.

Her first attempts fell far from the mark, but each one got closer, until finally she felt the hook grab the handle. It slipped off when she pulled, but her confidence rose. Two more attempts landed the hook on the handle again, and she slowly tightened the line, careful to keep the hook in place. Then she started to pull. It felt like it was slipping, but as she turned to watch the inside of the door, she could see the round metal piece start to rotate. The handle had to be close to vertical now and she panicked, knowing that if the hook lost its grip she would have to start over. She held her breath and pulled.

The door opened and she jumped back, startled by the mass of Eli Braken standing in the doorway.

He seemed to ignore the escape attempt. "At least she's alright," he said to someone behind him she had to assume was Cody. "Only thing that's gone right for you all week." He looked at her, then jerked his head backward. "Out of there."

She stepped tentatively into the night, glancing at the two men. The older man pointed to a spot on the gunwale. Trying to control her breath and not panic she sat. The air felt good, and she looked around while the men talked, confirming her guess that they were in Key West. Braken handed her a jug of water. They watched her in silence as she drank, set the bottle down, and then picked it up and drank some more.

"Can you talk?" Braken asked her.

She could feel her heart pounding in her chest from the escape and then their sudden appearance.

As she calmed down, she realized that their reaction wasn't right. She had expected to be pushed back into the console and locked in again. Now she was sitting outside — unrestrained. She thought about escape, but did not want to be locked up again if they caught her. Lights showed in several cabin windows but otherwise the marina was deserted. Screaming would not work. If she were going to get out of this, she had to at least buy some time until her father found her, or find another means of escape.

The latter would be impossible if they confined her again.

"Yeah," she responded.

"We're not going to hurt you. Are we, Cody?" He turned to look at Cody. "In fact, we'd like to get you back home and forget this ever happened."

She nodded, wondering why he was being so nice.

* * *

Mac stood to the side, one eye on the cab sitting in the driveway, the other on Wood, who was beating on the door. He had promised the driver another of his dwindling hundreds if he would remain. Finally, he could see a light go on behind a heavy drape, and Wood stopped banging. More lights went on, leading in the direction of the door. The door opened then, revealing Pagliano standing in front of them.

"What the fuck?"

"We've got to talk. You and I have a mutual interest, now. Needs to be addressed, there's no time to waste," Wood said.

Pagliano stepped back and allowed them to enter. He went to the table and sat. "Better be good. People that disturb Joey's sleep find themselves not waking up," he said in a low voice. "No need to wake the women."

"Never mind the threats. Listen." Wood sat across from him.

Mac remained in the doorway, still watching the cab and hoping the lure of more money would keep him there. The last thing he wanted was a violent showdown with no means of escape, especially with Kellie behind one of those doors. Noon tomorrow was just not enough time to provide the proof Teqea required, but he wouldn't budge. This plan had to work, but he still wasn't happy about it. The best thing for her was to go dance and find another guy. A thousand miles away in Galveston would have been the preferred location, but he would settle for the fifty miles to Key West if it meant getting Mel back.

"So, the man down there — the other chief — he'll get my daughter back if we get him provenance on the relic by noon tomorrow." Pagliano started to fidget. "I know there's a lot of moving parts here, but hear me out," Wood said.

Pagliano nodded with his best Godfather imitation and sat upright, waiting like a corporate CEO evaluating a business plan for Wood to continue.

Wood went on. "You want your casino and I want my daughter back. This treasure nonsense is crap." Pagliano nodded. "That blonde girl. We trade her to Cheqea's brother for my daughter. Then you can take your choice of which crazy Indian you want for a partner."

Pagliano took a nervous glance down the hall. "Blondie don't mean shit to me. Just a headache, is all. As for the casino and the Indians, I'll get a better deal if they fight it out. Turn them against each other — should be good sport."

"So we have a deal?"

"Maybe as far as the blonde girl for your daughter. That's bad for business, any way you look at it."

Mac smiled, thinking the end might be in sight. Wood rose from his chair, but Pagliano put a hand on his shoulder.

"Like I said, that's bad for business, all those freakin' kids and women. But there's the matter of the ten grand, the bridge, and that piece of wood. I want whatever is down there, and whatever the provenance thing you're talking about is."

"That's fine. I just want my daughter back. I'll finish your job for you." He stood again.

Pagliano reached out and touched his chin. "You will, because I'm going to be making the exchange, and I will be holding your daughter until I get what I want from you."

Chapter 27

Mac got in the cab, and was immediately suspicious when the driver cut short a cell phone call. The phones were scarce and expensive. Too expensive for a cab driver who already had a two way radio for communication. Wood got in the other door and gave him the address and quick directions to his house.

Mac looked over at Wood, sitting stoically, as he gave directions to the driver. Not having children, he could only guess what was going through the other man's mind, but he knew it was bad. They had no choice but to accept Pagliano's word that Mel would be recovered and remain unharmed. It was in Teqea's best interest to protect the girl. She was only a liability to him. Kellie, on the other hand, had value.

He tried to push thoughts of the two girls from his mind and focus on the task at hand. They had to come up with something to document the relic. It didn't really matter whether it was for Pagliano or Teqea; the only way to get leverage was to find something else down there. Looking out the window now, he noticed that the palm trees were rustling quietly in the light breeze. Hopefully the wind would subside and not strengthen. It was hard enough to dive in the channel without the added challenges the wind brought.

The driver pulled up to the house and stopped, looking back

at Mac, who pulled the promised hundred out of his pocket and handed it over the seat back. They exited the cab and watched as it pulled away. Wood went up the stairs but Mac remained, watching the pink cab as it pulled out of the driveway and started down the street. He was just about to follow Wood upstairs when he saw the brake lights flash and hold. Still suspicious of the driver after the cell phone call, he moved into the shadows by the side of the road. There were no streetlights, but the moon illuminated the street enough to make him visible if the man looked back.

The car was two blocks down, still parked. Mac could see the driver in the glow of the dashboard lights, talking on the phone again. The man turned to look behind him and Mac quickly slid behind a large trashcan. The driver didn't seem to notice, as he reversed back toward him. The car stopped briefly, then took off again. Mac stayed where he was, hoping the shadows were deep enough to hide him as the car sped past. He rose as the lights disappeared around a corner and started back toward the house.

He could see the light on, and heard noise coming from the shed as he walked toward Wood's. Bypassing the house, he went right to the shed. "Something's up with the cab."

Wood was immersed in a pile of gear quickly accumulating on the floor. He was pulling all size of hoses and pumps from underneath a shelving unit.

"What'd you say?"

"The cab. I followed it down the street and saw the driver talking on one of those portable phones. He was on it when we got in the cab back at Braken's house, too."

"So, what of it?"

"Those things are too expensive for a Key West cab. It's suspicious. That cab was sitting in front of the club when we got there. I think he's reporting back to Teqea about what we are doing."

Wood looked up. "Wouldn't surprise me if he's keeping an eye on us. I'd be surprised if he *didn't*. Kind of unusual how that cab was racing around the parking lot down there like he was on a mission. Bastard got lucky when Braken was gone and we needed a ride."

"It doesn't bother you?"

"I'd say it's good and bad. I don't like being watched, but as long as we're doing what we said and go dive this morning, he'll report that back to Teqea. That'll keep Mel safe. Now give me a hand with this."

Mac went to the pile, wondering what all the gear was for. There were both air and water hoses stacked on the floor. Wood had a small pneumatic jackhammer out now, checking the fitting on it to make sure it would attach to one of the air hoses.

"Isn't that a big risk, using a jackhammer down there?" Mac wondered if the hammer could ruin what they were looking for.

"Don't see a choice. It's not by-the-book archeological procedure, but I was never one to follow the rules anyway." He continued to check the tool. Several pointed chisel bits lay in front of him, and he chose one and inserted it in the tool. "This'll work."

Mac started to haul the hoses to the skiff, their bulk quickly filling the boat. He went back to see if there was anything else, and watched Wood pull down a box with a warning placard he recognized as explosives. Hoping they would be a last resort if nothing else worked, he kept his mouth shut and finished loading. Wood took off up the stairs to the house, leaving Mac alone to finish loading the boat. Once everything was on the skiff, he boarded, waiting for Wood to come down stairs.

A few minutes later, he emerged with a bag and a shotgun. "Got some food."

He handed the shotgun and bag to Mac, then climbed down into the boat, the low tide dropping the vessel below the level of the dock. Once Wood was situated, he started the engine and waited for Mac to cast off the dock lines. The sky was already lightening slightly in its pre-dawn glow. Several lights were on in the houses they passed as they idled through the canal toward open water.

* * *

The phone rang, startling Pagliano. He sat at the table, enjoying Braken's scotch and planning his next move. It rang again, disturbing the silent house, and he got up to answer, hoping that it wouldn't wake the girls. He wasn't ready to face them yet — and there was no telling what kind of condition *they* would be in.

"Hello," he said into the receiver. The signal on the other end was weak and distorted, but he could hear Braken's voice. "Braken, is that you?" He fought the urge to yell into the receiver. "You've got Wood's girl? Is that right?" He smiled and finished the drink. "No, don't take her to the club. Bring her back here, and fast." He hung up, finally feeling like he had something tangible. With both girls in hand and Wood desperate to get his daughter back, he knew he held all the cards. Smiling, he went back to the bar and poured himself another drink.

Leverage was one of his favorite words. The girls were a bit of a wildcard — one clearly crazy and the other a teenager. But better to have them than not. He wanted neither of the twin Indian chiefs, or whatever they were, for a partner, but that was the poison pill of developing casinos. Since the wild west days of early Vegas, you couldn't pick your partners. Legitimacy was a constant concern, and the partner that brought legality was a highly valued asset. Teqea might have more business acumen, but he dealt in sex slaves — something even the mob in Jersey wouldn't touch. Why sell assets when you can rent them? Cheqea was more legit; just crazed. From what he could see, it was more like staying stoned and taking whoever she could with her. It was an easy choice to go with the woman, but her brother would have to be eliminated.

The sun was just coming up now, and he changed his mind and put aside the scotch deciding on coffee instead, hoping that Braken would be here soon. He poured a cup and decided to sweeten it up with a little scotch; the last, he swore, until this was over. The rumble of tires on gravel alerted him to the car pulling into the driveway, and he went to the window and opened the drapes. Braken's Cadillac sat there, its polished chrome reflecting the rising sun. Two doors opened, and Braken got out of the front and stretched. Cody pushed a young girl who he guessed was the contractor's daughter out of the back. Pagliano opened the door and squinted in the light. He went down the stairs and patted Braken on the back.

"Good work. Bring her upstairs and tie her up." He looked at Mel, assessing the threat. "Not too tight."

"Don't we have to take her to Teqea?" Cody stuttered.

"Shut up, you fool. You've caused enough trouble." He went to Cody and smacked the back of his head, driving the younger man to his knees. He stepped back, wound up, and kneed him in the head. Cody fell onto the gravel, grasping his face. Pagliano turned to Braken and saw the fear in his eyes. "Get him out of my sight." Then he went to Mel and took her arm, leading her up the stairs leaving Braken hovering over Cody.

Cheqea stood in the doorway, rubbing the sleep from her eyes. "Baby, you look tense," she said to Pagliano. "Maybe Cheqea should give you some more medicine."

"Help me with her." He pushed Mel toward her. "Clean her up and see if she can get some rest. Keep an eye on her." He paused. "And none of your medicine, you hear me?"

Cheqea put her arm around Mel and led the girl into the house. Pagliano turned his attention back to Braken. "When you get your seed straightened out, take a ride to the bridge and see what that redneck is doing out there."

* * *

With three men loaded into the sedan, their bulk and weaponry pushing the old shock absorbers to their limit, the car bottomed out as it left the parking lot. The men shared the same determined look as they glanced to the rising sun on the right as the driver turned onto US1, heading north. Gun barrel between his knees, Teqea sat in the passenger seat rubbed a knife against a whet stone, sharpening the blade.

"You ready to have some fun?" Teqea asked as he rubbed the knife back and forth. "We've got a white boy to skin and a casino on the horizon." The underling nodded. He had just received a report earlier that Braken's Cadillac had crossed the Stock Island bridge, heading north toward Big Pine.

Teqea's network of cabbies and rickshaw drivers was extensive and loyal. He recruited and used the men to bring him runaways, and the bounty he paid for each girl was almost twice their weekly pay. As soon as the two men had left his office, he had roused a driver drinking at the bar and ordered him to follow the men. It was just good luck that they ran into his cab.

He spat on the stone and rubbed the knife again, checking the edge against his thumb. The blade was for Cody Braken for double crossing him. The fool's decision to abort the transfer of the girl to the Bahamas had cost him a large payday. The miles rolled by in silence as the car headed north. Teqea took the piece of paper from his pocket and read it to the driver. It had the address the cab driver had called him with, his foresight in equipping the man with a portable phone was rewarded by the instant and private communication.

He focused his attention on the artifact, the carving of the men in the canoe staring back at him. Obsessed with finding the answer to his heritage, he glanced down at his tattooed arms. The intricate work was done by his grandfather on both he and his sister. Because they were twins, custom dictated that they only have half of the pattern his grandfather had proudly worn. Legend had it that it was a map of their ancestral trade routes, but unless he cut Cheqea's arm off, he would only have half the puzzle. His grandfather had told them it was some kind of key to where their people's treasure had been hidden, but he had been young and wasted the opportunity.

Every day, he examined his arms for any clue that would establish his tribe's pedigree with the government. His grandfather had shown him pictures of ancient drawings from an old codex that traced their roots to the Chontal Mayans, a seafaring northern Yucatan offshoot of the larger Mayan population. Now that these men had uncovered what looked to be a pre-Columbian artifact, all he had to do was establish that it was found where they claimed, and the casino he had long desired would be built.

On land that he could claim as his own.

Chapter 28

It felt like last week that they had disassembled the cofferdam, rather than yesterday. Mac noticed the state of the tide and current as they approached the barge. After a week in the Keys, he was starting to get an intuitive feel for the factors that affected everyday life on the water. The phase of the moon and tide changes were becoming second nature. He confirmed his feeling that it was high tide by looking at the top of the marker at the entrance to Spanish Harbor. Only dry wood showed on the pressure-treated pile; no barnacles or wet wood, which would indicate a falling or low tide. In theory, this would be the best time of the day to dive, without the tidal current stirring up the bottom and decreasing visibility. Current brought on by tide changes could be swift in the narrow channels and around the bridges. The level of his alertness surprised him after several sleepless nights; the adrenaline was still working on him. He wondered how many sleepless nights he could endure. The barge came into view as they rounded the last bend.

"Tie her off!" Wood yelled, an urgency in his voice that Mac had not heard before. He cut the motor, and the skiff slid parallel to the barge.

Mac reached over, grabbed the line on the steel deck, and tied it to the forward cleat. Wood did the same at the rear, and the men started to unload the gear, spreading it out on the deck. "How do you want to set this up?"

"Gonna do a little recon first, but we need to wait for Ned to bring the camera out. Be better to take pictures before the equipment shuts down the visibility." He looked around. "He should be here anytime. For now, we can clear up this mess. You can start by spreading the hoses out lengthwise on the deck."

The low whine of a small outboard could be heard. Mac looked up as the last of the hoses was untangled.

"That'll be him. Know the sound of that tin can engine of his," Wood said as he went to the stern and watched the water, waiting for Ned to round the corner. Less than a minute passed before the small inflatable came into view. Wood strode over to help as Ned cut the engine and tied the boat off. Mac took the camera before helping him out of the unstable inflatable.

He didn't know much about cameras, but this one had to be expensive. It had a 35mm unit housed in a clear plastic shell, with two strobe lights extending from it. Wood took it from him and went to the workbench, where he started to unbuckle the watertight shell.

"You get the film?"

Ned handed him a canister. "Had to search around. Not much open at 6 in the morning."

"Explains why you're late, then." Wood grumbled as he inserted the new canister in the empty compartment, unwound the film onto the tracks, and closed the back. He moved the winder button several times until the display read one, and inserted the camera back in the case. Satisfied, he went to the container and opened the lock. "You gonna stand there and gawk, or are you gonna help? Get those tanks and fill'em." he ordered Mac.

Mac removed the empties from the container and started the compressor. "Couldn't we use the Hookah rig?" he asked.

Wood paused. "Hmm. That'll save twenty minutes." He went back in the container, emerging a minute later with the small compressor and hoses. "Set this up," he called to Ned.

While Ned readied the rig, both men spat in their masks and rinsed them in the clear placid water. Mac couldn't help but notice that the bottom was visible as he bent over. This was nothing like the conditions they had been working in for the past week. He checked the early morning sky for the telltale clouds that would later form into the anvil-bottomed thunderheads, but saw only small cumulous formations - a good sign that the weather would stay fair.

With a mask and four pounds of weight each, the two men grabbed a regulator from Ned, placed their hands on their masks, and took giant stride steps into the water. Mac let his body sink, watching the fish as they schooled around him. His dive booties touched the bottom, a small cloud of silt rising around his feet. He looked for Wood who was ten feet away, camera in hand, and halfway through the twenty-foot-water depth. Mac waited for him to hit bottom, and then began to swim around the pier. The weight kept him close to the sea floor as he surveyed their work. The flash of the strobes startled him, until he realized that Wood had begun to document their search.

Wood moved into the enclosure they had started to build to encase the concrete, but returned a minute later, shaking his head, indicating that there was nothing there. They worked their way around the old pier base and started searching where it transformed from concrete to the native coral. After circling the base twice, Wood gave a thumbs up and both men surfaced.

Once on top, they swam to the barge and hung on its edge. "Nothing exposed, but I didn't expect it to be that easy," Wood said.

Mac realized he had done most of the diving and was more familiar with the structure. "I think I know about where I was when the dredge sucked up the artifact. It was at night, and it's hard to be certain, but I have a good idea."

"Set up the air rig for the hammer!" Wood called to Ned.

"And then we're going to need the dredge." He turned to Mac. "Take the jackhammer down and start chipping where you remember. I'll follow with the dredge, and suck out whatever breaks apart. That should help with the visibility. We're going to use a long discharge hose, and funnel it onto the deck so Ned can sort through it. Don't be in a rush. You've got to work at the same speed as the dredge can remove the material. Too fast and she'll clog up and start swinging around. We've seen how that turns out already."

Mac took the sixty pound hammer, its weight dragging him quickly to the bottom. His feet touched, and he started walking. As he approached the spot, he braced himself and pushed the trigger. The machine jerked in his hand, throwing him off balance. It took several more attempts before he got the touch and angle needed for the tool to work without throwing him around. Small pieces of coral began to fall away, becoming larger as he got the feel for the angles necessary to efficiently remove the material.

Suddenly he noticed a shadow behind him and froze, worried it could be a shark. Startled, he looked around, but it was only the dredge.

* * *

Pagliano looked over at the three figures sitting on the couch. Mel was leaning against an armrest, half asleep, Cheqea sat in the middle, and Kellie sat on the other end. He knew this was bad. The younger girl he could handle, as long as she knew she was going home soon. Cheqea had to sign the papers. Nothing mattered to her but beating her brother to the prize now. As long as he didn't win, she would do whatever it took. The blonde girl was the issue. He had thought about taking all three of them to Key West, but the vision of walking into the federal building with Cheqea alone was scary enough. Bringing a crazed dancer and a distraught teenager was going to attract attention he didn't want. The alcohol he had consumed earlier was wearing off and a headache was quickly forming from the stress. He discounted Cheqea's remedy and went for the bottle of scotch, figuring a little hair of the dog would settle his head.

As he drank, the girls started to fidget, and he knew his peace was going to be short-lived. "Cheqea, why don't you take our dancer friend in the back and give her some of that medicine? I'm going to take this one here, to her dad." He pointed at Mel, hoping if he played the good guy, it would disarm her skepticism.

Cheqea looked over at Kellie and placed her hands on the girl's temples, massaging them. Kellie immediately put her head back and started moaning quietly.

"Maybe you are smarter than I thought," she said to Pagliano. She took her hands from Kellie's head and led her to the bedroom. Now, with those two out of the way, he could deal with the girl. She had no value to him as a hostage, so he went through his options. He drew the line at killing children, and though the thought of ditching her somewhere crossed his mind, he knew charges would be filed against him if she were found, and talked. What he needed was for

"Get up."

Mel stared at him.

"Relax, you're free."

She looked skeptical.

"Come on. No restraints. Run, do whatever you want. Go find your dad. Just go."

She rose from the couch, hesitating, waiting for him to do something, but he took a step back, allowing her free access to the door. With a quick glance at him she went to the door, turned the knob, and ran down the stairs.

"Where's the girl? You do something to her?" Cheqea asked as she emerged from the bedroom.

"Nah, I let her go."

Cheqea came towards him and kissed him. "See, that

medicine, it works."

"What about blondie?"

"She's lying down. The medicine will fix her, too."

"Good. Get your stuff. We're going to Key West."

* * *

"I don't want to know!" Braken yelled at Cody as they walked down the dock toward his sportfisher. The fifty-two-foot boat stood almost three stories tall, its outriggers and antennas another ten feet above the fly bridge. The stainless steel glistened in the sun as they boarded. "You really wrecked your boat?"

Rather than respond and have another face off with his father, Cody put his head down and prepared the boat.

"You know we're going to have to take the long way around, through the Seven Mile Bridge at Moser Channel. This thing won't clear all those other bridges. If we had your boat we'd be there in minutes. This is going to take some time."

Cody ignored him and started the motor. While the diesel engines warmed up, he released the dock lines and climbed the ladder to the fly bridge, hoping his father wouldn't make the climb to the elevated controls, giving him a much needed respite.

Wondering why he was still outside, he looked down at Braken, settled onto the settee by the sliding glass doors that led to the air conditioned interior. Although it was his father's boat, Braken rarely piloted it himself in tight quarters, making Cody do the harder work. Once they were out in the Gulf Stream, he would run the boat from the deck controls, making Cody rig the baits and rods. He turned and headed out the channel.

Once clear of the last marker, he increased speed and headed for the rise in the bridge. They passed underneath and were quickly into the greener Gulf waters. He navigated through the channels, being careful to stay within the markers; the boat drew too much water to leave their security. They ran a course parallel to the bridge, turning a hard right as they hit the Bahia Honda Channel, which he followed for a half-mile. He hoped the depth finder was correct. After the green number one marker, he was forced to leave the comfort of the channel and cross into the five-foot-deep water between Porpoise and No Name Keys. He knew the boat drew four feet and there was little room for error. Soon, he was able to relax as the water darkened again, indicating depth, and he turned left, the bridge in sight.

He carefully picked a spot behind the bridge, using the pier farthest from Big Pine Key to obstruct the view from the barge. As he cut the engines and tossed the anchor, he noticed that a car was parked at the barricades. He reached into the console for the binoculars, brought them to his eyes, and flinched when he saw Teqea step out of the front seat.

Chapter 29

Mel hesitated at the bottom of the stairs, still expecting something bad to happen, but the closed door stared back at her, and she ran. She reached the end of the block and turned around, not sure what to expect, and still not sure what had happened. The suddenness of her release stunned her, but now that he appeared to be keeping his word, she sprinted until several blocks later, she was breathless and covered in sweat. US 1 was visible in the distance, the traffic giving her a sense of security. She started a slow jog toward the main road, thinking about how to reach her father. The man named Pagliano had told her of the deal the night before, so she figured her dad and Mac would be working on the site, keeping their end of the bargain to get her back. No Name Bridge was several miles away; their house only one. It would be worth it to go home and take one of the boats, she thought. With renewed purpose, she reached the main road, turned left, and started to jog.

Fifteen minutes later, she arrived at their driveway. She ran up the stairs and slowly entered the deserted house. Remembering the last time she had been there, she carefully she checked each room, then looked out at the empty seawall visible from the sliding glass door; the boats were all gone. Out on the deck, she confirmed her sighting, hoping the glass had deceived her. Her only other option was her bicycle. She went back through the house, slamming the front door behind her and started down the steps to the carport, where the site of the rusted Datsun pickup changed her mind. She ran back into the house, grabbed the keys from the hook by the front door and ran back downstairs.

Without a second thought she got in the truck, adjusted the seat and mirrors and turned the key. The truck rumbled as it started, then died. She depressed the clutch and tried again. This time it caught, and she fought the old shifter into what she thought was reverse. Instead, when she released the clutch, the truck jerked forward and stalled. Driving was new to her, as she'd only gotten her learner's permit a few weeks earlier. Wood had been reluctant to teach her on the truck, opting for Ned's car with its automatic transmission instead. Stubbornly she tried again, this time finding reverse, but stalling again as the clutch bucked and she was jerked backwards. Twice more she tried, before she had the truck far enough into the street that she could move forward. First gear was easier than reverse, and the truck crept forward. With a jerk, she found second gear and started moving faster. By the time she reached US 1, she had a feel for the clutch and transmission. She gripped the wheel tightly as she had to face real traffic for only the second time in her life.

Cars and trucks streamed by, but finally an opening appeared, and she hit the gas, the car stuttering before making the turn. A horn blared as a truck towing a boat passed her, but she kept her composure and found second gear. Praying the lights would stay in her favor, she made it into fourth and was able to cruise at the speed of the other traffic.

The turn came up faster than she expected and she braked, the truck stalling as she neglected to downshift. Another car horn blared as she got the car moving again, and turned left on Wilder Street. After a quarter mile, the name changed to Avenue A, and she could see water ahead. Hoping to see if her dad was at the bridge, she continued until the road dead-ended. She looked out, but the view was blocked by a small development just past Doctor's Arm — a small cove in Pine Key Bight. She reversed and backed up to Poinciana, where she turned left. Several blocks later, she turned right onto Watson Boulevard, which wound its way to the bridge.

She braked suddenly, just as she rounded the last turn and the barricade became visible. The outlines of the three large men, guns resting at their sides, standing on the edge of the bridge blocked her view of the barge. One heard the car and turned as she stalled again.

* * *

Kellie started screaming as soon as they left the driveway. She was in the back seat, Cheqea's arm around her, while Pagliano sat alone in front. He had waited a long hour before Cheqea thought the girl was able to travel. They had a heated conversation that ended in Cheqea taking another hit of her medicine.

"I swear to God I am going to tie her up if you can't handle this!" he yelled from the front seat.

"It will only make it worse. You have to pull over," Cheqea pleaded.

"Fuck that. We gotta get this shit done." Pagliano had to figure how to restrain the dancer sooner or later. There was no way in hell he was going to walk into the federal building with both women tripping. Cheqea showed some kind of resistance to the drugs, and maybe he could get her in and out of there without a scene, but the dancer was another matter. He had hoped to take her to Miami and put her to work at one of his clubs, but another glance in the back seat put that plan to rest. He watched the saliva running down her chin and saw her eyes aglow. Maybe the best thing was to dump her in Key West.

She screamed again and he finally pulled over into a small gravel parking area by one of the bridges connecting the keys. He slammed the door as he got out and reached for the back door, grabbed Kellie by the hair despite Cheqea's pleading, and pulled her from the car. "You're gonna stop that shit, or I'm leaving you here."

She was sobbing hysterically now. "I just want my boyfriend. Mac Travis, you know him. Please —"

He smacked her across the face, but she continued.

"Please," she pleaded. "I don't know what's going on. My head is spinning and you look like a —"

"Stop it," Cheqea screamed at him. "You got to go with the flow of the medicine." She looked at the ground. "Maybe I gave her a little too much."

"Shit. Some freakin' witch doctor you turned out to be. Shouldn't you know?"

Kellie started rolling on the ground, giggling now. "You see how fragile she is." Cheqea said as she bent down to help her up.

"Back in the car," Pagliano went to the driver's seat. "Come on, get her in. We're going to find this boyfriend of hers and he can have her. Then you and I are going to sign the papers."

Cheqea pushed Kellie into the car; the girl obviously understood what had been said, and offered little resistance. Pagliano pulled out of the lot and executed a high speed U turn into the northbound lane. It would only cost them a half-hour to go back and dump the girl. Things would be simpler then; just keep Cheqea happy for a little while longer, and the papers would get signed, and he could take some more of that medicine. Crazy as the bitch was, her medicine was good shit — maybe something that could make some money and get him back in the good graces of Mesculine.

* * *

Cody moved the binoculars from Teqea to the small truck that had screamed to a stop and stalled. There was something

211

familiar about it, but he couldn't place it. He tried to focus on the figure behind the steering wheel, barely able to see that it was a girl. As soon as she got out of the car, it hit him. It was Wood's truck. He watched as Mel got out and walked toward Teqea with outstretched hands.

Without thinking he screamed "No!" and all heads turned his way. Teqea pointed to the boat. Fortunately, the sun was behind them and it would be hard for the Indian to identify him.

"What the hell is going on up there?" Braken yelled from the deck.

"That's Wood's girl over there, and Cheqea's brother," Cody called from the fly bridge. Both men leaned over the side for a better look.

All they could do was watch as two of the men went toward her and grabbed her. Suddenly the sound of the small compressor buzzing on the surface stopped, and the scene became still. Cody looked over at the barge and saw Ned stand up after turning off the Hookah. He waited ten long seconds and started it again. The motor started, and he pulled on each of the hoses, signaling the divers to come back. Another thirty seconds and two heads broke the water. They swam to the barge and Cody watched Ned lean over and talk to them. All three turned to the end of the bridge, clearly looking at the boat.

He watched as Mac and Wood pulled themselves onto the barge, not wasting time to swim around to the ladder, and threw their gear to the deck. Wood raced over to the skiff, started the engine, and motored toward the end of the bridge. He stood in the bow, the skiff barely moving in the slack tide. Wood and Teqea were yelling back and forth, but Cody couldn't make out the words. One of the men next to Teqea lifted his gun and fired two shots at the water, one on either side of the skiff — obviously warning shots. Wood didn't back down, though, and the gun barrel moved to point at his body.

Suddenly he heard a splash, followed by another gunshot. He

saw a body disappear beneath the surface of the water. Confused, he looked back toward the group and realized that Mel was gone. There was no sign of her on the surface.

* * *

Mac watched the action across the way. He was close enough to hear, but too far away to help. Wood was screaming at the men to release his daughter, and Teqea, the man from the club, yelling back at him that he would after they produced the evidence he wanted. Wood stood his ground demanding Mel back now. That's when he heard the gunshots. He moved to the right several feet, bumping into Ned, who was also glued to the scene, to get a better look, when he saw Mel dive into the water.

Without thinking, he yelled at Ned to start the compressor and dove in. Grabbing both air hoses, he went for the spot he had seen her enter, hoping she dove of her own accord; he hadn't seen where the last shot was aimed. The hose's hundred-foot lines stopped him abruptly, but Ned must have seen the problem and cut the tether on the compressor, allowing it to be towed freely behind the lines. The extra resistance did little to hinder Mac's progress as he swam to the last spot he had seen her. Ahead of him, a head broke the surface and a gunshot hit the water beside it. Taking a quick bearing, he put the regulators in his mouth and swam toward the spot. The salt water stung as he opened his eyes, struggling to see underwater, the visibility down from earlier, as the tide was coming in. Breast stroking, he covered the fifty feet and saw a body in the water.

Gunshots hit the water again, their path visible as the water slowed their progress. He reached for the body and stuck the regulator in her mouth.

Relieved that she was conscious, he waited while she took a breath, and pointed in the direction away from the gunfire. They crossed under the shadow cast by the bridge, the compressor following behind them. Once they made it back into the sun, he felt they were safe enough and signaled her to ascend. Their heads broke the surface five feet from a white hull, and as he looked up he saw Cody smiling at them from the fly bridge.

Mel looked up, spit her regulator out, and screamed. She gulped seawater and started choking, the action causing her to hyperventilate. Mac moved toward her and grabbed her in a headlock, ensuring her mouth was out of the water, stuck the regulator in, and started swimming away from the boat. Just when he thought he was free something sharp hit his leg. The hook from a long gaff wielded by Braken caught his leg, and he was spun in the water, forcing him to release his grip on Mel. He screamed in pain as Braken pulled back on the hook, then looked down at his leg to see that the sharp point was deep inside him.

He grabbed Mel, who was sinking next to him, hoping she was still breathing, but unable to do anything about it. His other hand grabbed the handle of the gaff and pulled them toward the boat, giving him enough freedom to remove the point from his leg. As he released the gaff, more gunshots hit the boat, and he looked at the shore. The sport-fisher had drifted out of the protection of the pier, and he could clearly see the men at the barricade shooting at them.

Braken swatted once more with the gaff, barely missing Mac's torso as he swam backward, just out of reach. The smell of gas was in the air, and a small slick was approaching them. Mel was fighting his grip now, clearly panicked. He turned to her and paused before he struck her. She settled down after the blow, and he was able to continue swimming away from the boat when a shadow passed behind him.

The skiff brushed against his back, and Wood tossed a line. Grabbing for it, he realized that it was designed to tow a snorkeler surveying the bottom for lobster and found one of the two handholds cut in the board. Wood started towing them. As soon as they were protected by the pier, he yanked Mel toward the boat.

Wood hauled her over the side while Mac climbed over the transom and collapsed on the deck. His leg was bleeding badly, but his initial assessment concluded it was not life threatening. He hauled himself up to a sitting position, his back resting on the gunwale, and watched Wood work on Mel. She was conscious and breathing, but appeared to be disoriented.

"Can you watch her?" Wood asked as he went to the wheel. "I want to get back to the barge. We're sitting ducks out here."

Mac crawled to her and supported her head while Wood drove to the barge. Once there, Ned tied the boat off while Wood helped Mel onto the deck.

Chapter 30

Pagliano heard the gunshots before they reached the bridge. He pulled up behind the Datsun pickup, using the vehicle for cover, and assessed the situation. Now that Kellie's panic attack or whatever it was had subsided, Cheqea was making him nervous The promise to find her boyfriend had instantly settled her. Cheqea had started stressing as if she could sense something as they approached the bridge. She was fidgeting and muttering something about meeting her ancestors. He tried to put her from his mind. His plan was to dump the girl on the edge of the bridge and let her figure it out from there, then take Cheqea to Key West. Whether the girl threw herself into the sea or convinced her boyfriend to take her back was not his concern. His focus was on getting the papers signed. But now the gunshots were making things more complicated.

He got out of the car. "Let's go," he said, opening the back door. "You can see the barge from over there. That's where your boyfriend is."

Kellie looked at him as if she had no idea what he was talking about. Pagliano grabbed her arm and pulled her from the back seat.

"Over there." He pointed. "See?"

As he looked up, he saw Cheqea walking as if pulled by a

magnetic force along the road toward the Datsun in front of them. Kellie took off and ran after her. The two women walked together, oblivious of the danger, toward the men who had their backs toward them, shooting at something on the water. Pagliano ran after them. He had to get Cheqea out of here, or risk losing the casino.

"Teqea," Cheqea screeched loud enough to put some nearby birds to flight. But the gunshots must have stopped her voice from reaching the men. She screamed again, and charged.

Pagliano knew there was nothing he could do; she was out of her mind. He felt naked, unarmed, and went back to the car to retrieve his revolver from the glove compartment. Opening the door, he reached in, but it was empty. Just as he pulled his hand out, he heard the distinct retort of his weapon. Turning toward the end of the bridge, he saw one of the men standing, unsure of what to do, and Cheqea on the back of the other, wildly swinging her fists at his head. Assuming it was her brother she was attacking, he realized that he had to do something before he lost both assets. He ran toward the bridge, but stopped next to Kellie when he saw the revolver in Cheqea's hand swing wildly as her brother spun her around.

He grabbed Kellie turning her towards him. She stared over his shoulder into the distance. "You want to see your boyfriend?" His hands were on her shoulders, and he shook her hard. "If you want to see him again, we need to get these guys out of the way. You go for one, and I'll go for the other." Half hoping that she would sacrifice herself and solve the problem of how to dispose of her, he turned her and pushed her toward the melee.

She went for one of the men, who was standing with his gun raised, watching the siblings fight, and picked up speed as she closed the distance. The fight had moved toward the water, and their backs were turned toward her. Launching her body from five yards away, she went for Teqea, leaving her feet just before she reached him, her momentum knocking all three of them into the water.

With no weapon and the two armed men standing in front of him temporarily distracted, Pagliano slithered back to the car. He knew if either man happened to turn, he was dead. Odds and patience were two things he knew about, and although he was very good at the first, he lacked the second. Years of experience had taught him that when a battle was lost or out of control, you needed to use a tactical retreat. At this point, he could not affect the outcome one way or another without firepower, so he got into the car and pulled backwards down the road. Slamming his hands on the steering wheel, he released his anger, but knew that this was the right thing. Without a weapon and backup he had no other choice than to let them all fight it out, and pick up the pieces when it was over.

He braked and pulled forward, driving slowly to find a vantage point where he could observe the outcome.

* * *

Braken watched as the three bodies hit the water. "Who was that, Cody?"

"Those two Indians and the dancer."

He didn't know what had happened to Pagliano, but he had to save Cheqea. "Head over there. We have to save the chief."

Cody continued to look on. He knew they were leaking gas, but that was nothing compared to his concern over a confrontation with Teqea. "Let them fight it out. Besides, that guy finally stopped shooting at us, and we're leaking gas."

"That's our paycheck in the water there. We've got to get her. If her brother wins, he's going to open his own casino. That'll cut us out of everything." Braken went toward the companionway, entered the cabin, and lifted the cushion off the settee behind the chart table. In a box was a pistol and two clips. He ran back on deck and took a wild shot at the men on the shore. To his surprise one went down clutching his stomach.

"What the hell are you doing? You can't hit the side of a barn from ten feet. You're going to hit those women!" Cody came down the ladder, skipping the last two rungs, and jumped onto the deck. "Just keep that down." He went to the controls on the main deck and swung the boat, bow toward the road. Braken could feel the engine strain as the boat shot forward, covering the distance in seconds.

Braken watched the man on shore stop shooting and run for cover as the boat bore down on him. Cody had stopped just short of the seawall, knocking Braken to the deck when he reversed to stop the progress of the boat. He looked over the port side at the three figures still scrambling in the water. Cheqea still had her legs locked around the man's neck, and Kellie was beating on his back as he tried to scramble over the slick rocks revealed by the low tide. Several times, he fell backwards into the water and had to start again. Braken pulled the gun out of his waistband and tried to aim at the man, but with the two women clinging to him, a clear shot was impossible.

* * *

Mac winced when he saw Kellie take the two figures into the water. He stood on the deck, Ned beside him, watching the action unfold. Wood was trying to get Mel, still distraught and coughing seawater, to drink some fresh water and relax. Glancing backwards, Mac saw that she was calmer now, both arms around her father and sobbing gently.

With Mel in good hands, he turned his attention to Kellie, "I've got to help her. She's gonna get killed," he said under his breath. He wanted nothing to do with her, but watching her in this position and doing nothing to help was not in his genes. "I'm taking the skiff," he said to Ned.

Without waiting for an answer, he grabbed the dock line and pulled the small boat toward him. The skiff bumped against the barge, he untied the dock line and tossed it in the boat with him. Doubting his decision, but unable to override his internal wiring, he knew he needed to get her out of harms way. He started the motor and spun the boat.

As he approached the group, he saw Braken leaning over the edge of his own boat with the same gaff that had snagged his leg, trying to hook Teqea. Mac looked around the boat for a weapon, finding only a fishing pole. He tore the reel from its holder and snapped the rod in half. Grabbing the cork handle like a sword, he vaulted the side of the boat, landing feet first in the four-foot-deep water.

Wading through the current was harder than he anticipated, but as he gained on the shoreline, the water became shallower, and the current less of a drag against him. Knee deep now, he approached the group, reversed the rod in his hand, and backhanded the large man in the back.

The strike caused him to turn and notice Mac for the first time. Teqea came toward him, rage in his eyes, Cheqea still clutched to his shoulders, and Kellie held a death grip around his waist. Mac struck again, then vaulted forward, using the pointed end of the rod as a spear. Before the rod could strike, he tripped on a submerged rock and went down on all fours.

The man would have finished him off under any other circumstance, but two women clinging to him restricted his movements. Mac took advantage of his slow reaction and got back on his feet. The rod whistled as he whipped it back and forth through the air. The man backed up, unaware that the hook from the gaff was behind him. Mac saw the opening and lunged forward like a fencer, the tip of the rod pushing against the man's belly but not penetrating. The parry had the desired effect, and Braken brought the gaff around Teqea and with surprising force, hooked him in the gut. Blood sprayed as he pulled back on the handle.

Both women continued beating on the wounded man, who was now face-down in the water, blood from his wound bubbling up to the surface. Mac went towards them, grabbed Kellie and pushed her away. She tried to grab a hold of him, but he escaped her grasp. Before he could turn to deal with her, the remaining gunman stepped away from the cover of the car and moved toward them. He fired a warning shot into the air and then pointed the riffle barrel at Mac's chest. They all froze.

"Help him up." He motioned at Mac with the rifle.

Mac dropped the rod, bent over, and hauled Teqea to his feet. The blood continued to pour from his stomach.

"Bring him to me."

Mac put the man's arm over his shoulder and struggled the half-dozen feet to shore, where he deposited Teqea on solid ground. Kellie screamed, forcing him to turn away from the gunman, and he saw that Braken had the gaff around her waist and was hauling her toward the boat.

"Let her go!" Mac yelled.

Braken smirked as Cody helped him haul the girl over the side of the boat. "What are you going to do about it?"

Mac thought about his options. Kellie was not in the best of hands, but neither was she in eminent danger. Without a weapon, he knew he had done all he could, and turned toward the skiff. But out of the corner of his eye, he saw Wood in the small inflatable, coasting up to the gas slick around the other side of the pier, a propane torch in his hand.

Struggling through the water, Mac reached the skiff, turning back to see how much time he had. He felt as if he were moving in slow motion, as he watched Wood reach over the edge of the boat and light the slick. It caught with a boom, pushing Mac forward. He struggled to his feet again, frantic to get to his boat and escape.

The car starting caught his attention, and he turned toward shore. Teqea's body lay in a lump on the rocks, abandoned and probably dead, as his remaining soldier drove away. Another scream, this time from Kellie, brought his attention back to the sportfisher. The flames were over the gunwale on the starboard side hungrily seeking more fuel. Cody frantically spent the contents of a fire extinguisher, but it did nothing to abate the fire. Kellie was standing on the deck, lost as to what to do, when Braken and Cody dove off the bow and started swimming to shore.

Before Mac could react, flames had completely engulfed the boat.

* * *

Cheqea released her brother and swam for her life as soon as she saw the gunman confront Mac and Kellie scream. She took a deep breath and swam away from the boat, staying as close to the mangrove-lined shore as she could. The tide helped her progress, pushing her along as she stroked underwater, careful to seek cover when she needed to come up for air. The contractor on the boat was the only one who could have seen her from this angle, but his gaze was fixed, along with everyone else, on the flames spreading over the water.

Mangroves concealed her as she surfaced to catch her breath. Confident she was camouflaged, she turned to watch the scene at the bridge and felt her heart drop when she saw Kellie engulfed in flames, her mouth open in a silent scream. With regret, she submerged and started stroking again, knowing there was nothing she could do for the girl. A large rock pile ahead caught her eye — the first solid land past the mangroves. She took a chance, leaving her cover and starting across the open water.

She grabbed for a rock, took a breath, and got her feet under her. Just as she was about to rise, a giant explosion turned the scene upside down. She turned to watch what was left of the burning boat slip below the surface, when a shadow moved across her.

"Well, look what the water gods have delivered to me," Pagliano said as he leaned over her.

"You! This is all your fault. My brother and the girl are dead, all because of you and that casino."

"Your brother? *Now* you care? Maybe you need some more of that medicine of yours."

She spat at the rocks. "He was still my brother, and tribal custom dictates that I take revenge on his killer. I will avenge his death." Rising quickly, she went toward Pagliano, who shied away. Between her wet clothes and fatigue from the fight with her brother, she was too slow. With practiced grace, he back stepped and let her momentum go past him before he grabbed her arm and spun her. The pressure on her wrist was intense, and he guided her against the car.

"Stop this shit. Just sign the papers and I'll get you some cash. You can buy your medicine — save the world or do whatever your twisted mind wants." The sound of sirens could be heard moving in their direction.

She was against the car when she spotted the antenna. With her free hand, she grabbed it and yanked it from its holder with enough force to tear it from the car. Pagliano was caught off guard, and she slashed the twisted metal, catching him across the face from his hairline to his lip. Blood poured from the wound, and he released her. She was just about to swing again when a police cruiser pulled off the road. Slowly, she regained her composure and backed away, dropping the antenna behind her.

"Help me!" she screamed out. "He was attacking me."

The officers approached, guns drawn, moving toward the man.

* * *

Mac lifted his head from the water to see if it was safe. He had been holding onto the edge of the skiff when the sportfisher had blown, quickly submerging to avoid the debris flying toward him. The blast had torn the fly bridge off the boat and blasted a hole in its side. Water poured through the hole in the hull, and he knew the boat would soon be on the bottom. He swam around the skiff and climbed in, clearing a path through the debris blown onto the boat by the explosion as he tried to reach the helm. The key turned, but nothing happened. Just as he was about to try again, he heard Wood.

"In here. Hurry, we can still catch them."

Mac eased over the side of the skiff and into the small inflatable. As soon as he was seated, Wood opened the throttle and started weaving through the debris, carefully avoiding the patches still on fire. Sirens could be heard in the distance as he pulled past the hull and started to negotiate the water on the Gulf side of the boat.

"What about Mel?" Mac yelled when they were clear of the debris.

"She's OK. Ned's with her and this won't take long."

Mac watched Wood focus on the shoreline, searching the water for the two men. He steered closer to the shore and started running parallel to it. "Don't see the bastards. Damn mangoves - Damn Brakens."

"Let the police pick them up. Look over there," Mac said, pointing to the flashing lights of several firetrucks and police cruisers.

"Yeah." Wood slowed the boat and started to turn back to the bridge. "I would have liked to find them myself and get some payback before the police got them, though. Best go make sure Mel's alright. She's probably taking care of Ned, instead of the other way around." He turned the throttle on the engine handle and sped back toward the destruction.

Chapter 31

"You remember out on the reef where you stuck that spear in the rock pile and came back with the chunk of wood?" Wood asked as they sat at the table eating breakfast.

"Pretty close," Mac said between bites of lobster and eggs. It was late morning, two days after the incident. They had slept most of yesterday, after getting Mel back and filling out the police reports for the deaths of Teqea, the gunman and Kellie. Mac's emotions were as unsettled as the ocean after a storm.

"Stop thinking about it," Wood said as he wiped his mouth and pushed his plate away. "Ain't a damn thing you could'a done, either way. Crazy people do crazy things, and that group was crazy. Best thing I know for getting over stuff is to get to work. Figure if you want to stick around, this would be as good a time as any to see what we dumped out on the reef. Mel's in school — best place for her right now. It's bad enough living with me, and she needs to be around her friends. She's seen too much of the bad side of things in the last few days." He sat back and thought for a minute. "Tomorrow I've got concrete scheduled for the bridge pier, and that'll seal up whatever's left down there. It's time to move on."

"I'd like that, but do you have any other work?" Mac was almost afraid to ask.

"Called the insurance company this morning and they'll reinstate the policy if I can put up the bond. The money from Braken is just going to cover that. It'll be tight for a while, but I know with your help we can put this company back where it needs to be."

Mac looked out the sliding glass door at the tranquil water, the palm trees barely moving. He realized there was nowhere else he would rather be. "You can count me in. Have to get a place of my own, though."

"You can say that again." Wood glanced around at the bedding on the couch and clutter spread over the floor. "There's some good deals around after the hurricane. We didn't take a direct hit, but there are plenty of houses that can be had for a good price." He got up and went out the door.

Mac finished his breakfast, got up, and went to put the dishes in the sink. He started to wash them and thought about living here and working with Wood. For the first time since he had arrived, that rainy night less than a week ago, he felt at peace. If this was what living in the Keys felt like, he was home. Both Wood and the work he did intrigued him, and although the pay was bound to be less than working on oil rigs in Galveston, it was also sure to be more satisfying. The combination of diving and engineering, with a dose of cowboy thrown in, appealed to him. Honestly, he was tired of having a welding inspector hovering over his shoulder, watching him work. Here, he would have more freedom. He turned off the faucet, dried his hands, and smiled. Freedom was what it was all about.

"Daylight's burning." Wood opened the glass door and entered. "Gear's ready to go. I figure we better take the barge if we need to move anything. It's pretty flat out there today, she should be good in these conditions. We're gonna have to move her back to the mooring in Spanish Harbor, anyway. The damn code compliance people will give me a ticket if I leave her at the seawall too long."

They left the house and went down the stairs to the barge. Mac help load the gear and supplies and Wood fired the engines. Mac went towards the skiff. "Follow me to the mooring, and we can leave the skiff there!" Wood yelled over the sound of the motors. The boats pulled away from the seawall, the slack tide and light winds making them easier to maneuver through the canals.

The mooring ball came into view five minutes later, and Wood waited fifty yards away as Mac retrieved the ball and hooked the skiff to it. Once secure, Mac signaled him to come over and pick him up.

Mac sat on the front of the deck as they rode the thirty minutes to reach the reef. This was the first time since he got here that he could sit back and enjoy the scenery. He was like a school boy, peering over the side as they passed over patch reefs, their features and colors easily visible in the clear, calm water. He kept going back to the helm to check the depth finder, amazed at what he could see in twenty feet of water. When he could take his eyes off the water, he noticed frigate birds circling over schools of fish, seagulls underneath them, picking at the bait fish brought to the surface by larger predators below. A few dolphins broke the water and started to swim next to them as they crossed the shallow green water into the deeper blue.

Wood had his head down, watching the screen as he cut the engines to five knots, trying to line up the boat with the pile of rubble, eighty feet below them. He yelled at Mac to throw the buoy and pulled back on the throttle. Waiting for a few seconds until the weight took the line to the bottom, he started to circle, studying the depth finder. After a few minutes, he signaled Mac to drop the anchor. He let the dry line slide through his hands until he felt slack. Turning back to Wood, he nodded and waited for him to put the boat in reverse. As they started to slide backwards, Mac put pressure on the line and tied it to a cleat when he felt the barge stop. "Not much scope?" he confirmed.

"We need to be right on it if we need the equipment." Wood

looked out to sea. "Calm as it is and no thunderstorms yet, we'll be OK. Let's get wet."

The men suited up and were soon in the water, floating freely next to the anchor line. Wood gave a thumbs down sign and both men started their descents. Mac took his time watching the rocks and fish as they slowly fell through the water. Finally at the bottom, he cleared his ears and started to search the rocks for the spot where the spear had gotten stuck. Prodding each hole with the tip of the spear, he soon met resistance, removed his dive knife, and pounded his tank to attract Woods attention.

Both men now hovered over the rock. Mac glanced over at Wood, who was staring at the rough pieces of coral. He took a small float from the pocket of his BC, unhooked the weight attached to it, wedging it into a crack in the rocks. With his regulator, he shot a blast of air into it and watched as it floated to the surface.

Back on the barge, they stripped off their dive gear. Mac took the tanks to the container and started to fill them while Wood went to the anchor line. He started letting out line easing the barge back towards the float. When it was even with the excavator bucket he tied the line off. They were now directly over the site. "How are we going to do this in eighty feet of water? It was hard enough in twenty," Mac said as he followed him into the hot, dark interior of the container.

Wood started grabbing line and chain. "You could give a hand instead of whining." He handed the chain to Mac and dragged the rope outside. "Lay out that chain and I'll show you how this works." He went back into the container and emerged, struggling with a large grappling hook. "Check the anchor again, and make sure it's set."

Mac watched the chain until it disappeared in the water. He turned and looked at Wood, who was putting his dive gear back on. Checking his dive watch he realized the dive had only been twenty minutes. A quick calculation showed that with the half hour surface interval, they still had thirty minutes before he had to worry about decompression.

"Coming? We stay together here, no cowboy shit. First we take the chain and thread it through the cracks in the coral. Then we attach the grappling hook on one end and the rope to the other. We'll come back up, hook the rope to the excavator, and give a yank. She'll pull that whole pile apart."

Mac suited up and followed Wood into the water. As soon as they were back at the pile, he understood what Wood had in mind. After he snaked the half-inch links of the chain through the cracks between the rocks, he attached the shackle on the grappling hook to its end. Wood had already fastened the chain to a braided loop in the end of the rope with another shackle. He rechecked all the connections, and gave Mac the thumbs up sign to ascend. They surfaced, and Wood went back to the excavator and pulled back on a control. The arm moved slightly.

"That's it?" Mac asked as Wood hopped off the excavator track.

"What were you expecting? Doesn't take much with the power of the beast here." He patted the track. "Go on down and check it out. Give a yank on the rope when you're ready for me to pull the rigging up. I'll sort things out on this end."

Mac checked his air, replaced his mask, and took a giant stride entry into the water. The silt cloud on the bottom was evident the minute he hit the water. Slowly, he watched it disperse in the current as he descended. Reaching the bottom, he waited for the visibility to clear and saw the rocks askew, revealing the area where he had found the wood. Silt still hovered stubbornly over the area, so he pulled the hook, chain and rope into the clear and yanked on the rope. A minute later, he felt tension on it as Wood pulled it to the surface.

A large section of rubble lay exposed now, only two boulders high where it had been five or six before. He saw a dark spot near the bottom and moved toward it. Three feet long and partially embedded in the coral were several boards joined together. They pulled apart easily when he touched them, revealing the rot. As he probed further, he was forced to stop, as the wood started to disintegrate in his hands. Dismayed, he moved back from the pile, knowing the remnants of the canoe would require a lot of luck and specialists if they were ever to make it to the surface.

As he moved around the pile, he noticed a small, dark piece extending from the base of a rock. His touch confirmed that this was different from the wood pieces. And in the dim light he saw the glint of metal.

Chapter 32

It took everything he had not to shoot to the surface with the object, but his training took over and he slowed his ascent. From twenty feet, he saw the ladder and finned toward it. Clinging to the steel tubing, he handed it to Wood, and tossing his fins on the steel deck, he climbed out of the water, dumped the BC and tank on the deck and went to Wood.

He already had a brush out and was gently rubbing at the surface. Mac could see the luster of the gold emerge. Wood grabbed a hammer and chisel and kneeled on the deck with the object in front of him. Mac was about to stop him, but before he could, Wood tapped the piece and the coral that had encrusted a large portion of it fell away, revealing a snake like figure.

"Give me some room, boyo," Wood said, setting the chisel into another piece of coral.

Mac backed away, studying the figure that was emerging from the rock. The serpentine shape had the body of a snake with several jewels embedded in it, and the head of what looked like a Mayan god. An intricate pattern emerged as Wood set aside the harsher tools and picked up the brush again. Finally he held it up, but just as he did, a flash from the windshield of another boat caught their eyes. Wood shielded his brow with his hand and scanned the water.

"Son of a bitch, if it ain't the Brakens," he said.

Mac followed his gaze and saw a small flats boat, not a hundred yards away. But there was no windshield for the light to reflect from. He looked closer and caught another flash. "They've got binoculars on us. Think they saw it?"

"With my damn luck they did," Wood said. "Best get gone."

Mac pulled up the ladder and went forward for the anchor. Wood started the engines and signaled he was ready. With no scope, the rode came in quickly, and Wood had the barge heading toward shore just as the chain hit the deck.

"What do you think it is?" Mac asked, rolling the statue in his hands.

"Looks like a god or something to me," Wood replied. "Old Ned'll know. Just hope those damn Brakens didn't see it."

"Do you think they did?" Mac asked.

"You know what they say: if you can see them — they can see you."

Mac looked behind them to see if the other boat was following, but it was gone. "I don't see them," he said.

"More than likely raced in to set up some kind of trap," Wood said.

"What are we going to do with it?" Mac asked.

"Ain't much choice but to turn it in, especially if old Braken's got a whiff of it. I ain't desperate enough to melt it or crazy enough to sell it on the black market."

"But, it would pay off your insurance," Mac said.

"Not my style boyo," Wood said.

Wood made a wide turn around the red marker, and they entered Boot Key Harbor. Cruising past the gas docks, he pulled into a side canal, and docked in front of a small trailer. "Ned's place," he answered Mac's question before it was asked.

They tied off, grabbed the statue and Wood's camera, they stepped up to the dock and quickly followed the crushed coral path to the screen enclosed room on the back of the trailer. Before they entered the small patio, Mac looked back one more time to see if they were followed.

* * *

"What do you think that was?" Cody asked.

"Hell if I know, except it looked like gold," Braken answered.

They were in a small flats boat, its decks stained with fish blood, borrowed from a friend of Cody's. "What are we going to do?" Cody asked.

"You got a lot of questions," Braken dismissed him and thought about that very question. With Teqea dead, Cheqea missing and Paglaiano in custody, he needed to figure a way to salvage something from this. The casino wasn't going to happen. He still had the land to sell, but he needed Wood to finish the bridge.

They cruised through a a span on the Seven Mile Bridge. Even though the water was calm and glassy, every so often the boat hit a small swell, spraying him with water. They entered a small cut on the bay side and entered a marina. Cody backed the borrowed boat into its slip, nimbly hopped onto the deck, and grabbed the lines arresting the boat before it hit the seawall. Braken leaned against the rocket launcher watching Cody work. The boy was good with boats, but that was about all. He was also thinking how he could lever the knowledge that Wood had found something out there, though, as much as he wracked his brain, the answer of how he could benefit from it eluded him.

"I think we need to pay old Wood a visit," he said, and kneeled on the gunwale, using the tower to slowly rise and step onto the dock. He started walking to the parking lot.

"What about me?" Cody asked.

"What about you? How the hell are you going to be any help with this? Wood sees you he's likely to tear your head off — and with good reason. If I were you, I'd consider myself lucky to be alive." He continued to the Cadillac, got in and started the engine. He left the parking lot and turned onto the road, which ended at US 1, where he turned right, toward Big Pine Key where he hoped to make a deal with Wood.

* * *

"Well?" Wood asked.

Ned was hunched over a workbench, using a magnifying light to examine the statue. They had waited patiently while he meticulously cleaned the figure, using the finest grades of steel wool available to remove the residue of two centuries under the sea. Finally, he stepped away from the bench. Wood took it and held it between them. Ned had cleaned it well enough that the intricate carvings were visible. Mac tried to figure what they meant, and couldn't knock the feeling that he had seen something similar before.

"Pre-Columbian. Mayan by the style," Ned said.

"You gonna tell me something I don't know?" Wood scolded him.

"The name is Chac — god of rain and thunder. He was also important to navigators, representing the four cardinal points of a compass," Ned said. "What are you going to do with it?"

"Why does everyone keep asking that?" Wood said, looking at Mac. "It's not going to do me no good. You take it and donate it to whatever museum you think'll want it."

"Don't you think there's more?" Mac asked.

"Boyo, whatever's down there is going to stay there unless someone pays me to get it. Even if that canoe was loaded to the gunwales with gold, it wouldn't pay the cost of bringing it up."

Mac looked down.

"Nothing stopping you from having a look in your free time, though," Wood said. "Come on. Old Ned'll be mooning over this for hours," Wood said. "Borrow your car?" he asked Ned.

Ned was engrossed with the statue, hovering over his workbench. He nodded without looking up. Wood took the keys from the counter and went for the front door. "Be back to pick up the barge later," he said, turning to Mac. "Comin' boyo?"

After a few turns Mac thought the area was familiar. "This looks like the way to Braken's house," he said as they turned off US 1.

"Observant too," Wood replied.

They pulled up in front of the house, left the car and walked up the stairs. There was no answer after several knocks and they turned away. Just as they were about to climb back down, Mac saw the Cadillac pull up. Wood strode down the stairs, looking like he was ready to do battle.

Braken pulled up and drew his bulk from the car. "I was just looking for you. What'd you find out there?"

"Spyin' on me," Wood shook his head.

Braken looked uneasy. "Here's the deal Wood. I need the bridge fixed. That's all I care about. I'll keep it quiet about whatever you found if you fix the damn bridge by this weekend."

Wood took his time. "Your stock is pretty low right now, so you'll have to pay me in advance."

Several minutes later, Wood pulled away with a pile of cash on the seat between him and Mac. 'Why didn't you tell him to screw himself?" Mac asked.

"I still got a reputation. This'll pay the bills and get the insurance reinstated. Then we can get on to some real work."

* * *

"The police were here looking for you, and Braken and Cody came by too, but I hid from them," Mel said.

Wood went and hugged her knowing he shouldn't have left her alone. "What'd the police want?"

"They said you needed to come down and make a statement

about yesterday," she said. "Find anything out there?"

"An old statue. Got some pictures here," he said, setting the camera on the table. "Old Ned's gonna find a home for it," Wood said.

"I don't know about you guys, but I'm pretty hungry. Why don't we go by the police station and grab some food afterward?" Mac asked.

"Hmm. I guess that'd be a plan. Might as well get on with Braken's job in the morning. Sooner that gets done the better. We can run by the insurance companies office and drop off that payment too," Wood said.

"You're still going to work for him? They should be in jail," Mel said.

"Things ain't always right. It's a small town and sometimes it's best just to get along. Their time will come, whether by me or someone else," he said, grabbing the camera. "Might as well get this film developed while we're at it."

They walked down to the truck and crammed into the small front seat of the pickup. The ride across to Marathon took a long forty minutes and it was almost five when they pulled up at the insurance agents office. Wood opened the door, taking a bundle of cash with him and went to the office door. A few minutes later, he emerged with a smile on his face and climbed back in the truck.

"We're good to go. Maybe we can get on with some descent paying work now. No more Braken's that's for sure."

* * *

The lobby to the police station was quiet, and it only took a few minutes before a deputy came out and introduced himself. He took all three statements and was about to let them leave when he stopped suddenly.

"Any chance you can give and ID on the dead guy?" he asked.

Wood nodded and they followed him back to the coroner's

office. Mac shivered when they entered the cold examination room and waited for the deputy to pull out the compartment. Teqea's body was bruised and dirty, still awaiting an autopsy.

"That'd be a fellow named Teqea. Don't know his last name. Has a club down in Key West. Bad character if you ask me," Wood said.

While he was talking Mac stared at the body, focusing on the tattoos. It was then that he remembered where he had seen the pattern carved into the statue: on Cheqea and Teqea. Their body art bore the same patterns as the statue, but had other markings as well.

"Any film left in the camera?" Mac asked,

"Yeah."

Mac asked the deputy if he could take some pictures of the tattoos. He shrugged his shoulders, which Mac took as permission and went out to get the camera. A few minutes later he had used up the remaining film.

* * *

"What was that all about — taking those pictures?" Wood asked.

They were in a booth together waiting for their pizza. Wood and Mac nursed the cold beers in front of them and Mel sipped a coke through a straw.

"Just curious. Cheqea had similar ones. Kind of look like a treasure map or something," Mac said.

Wood took a sip of his beer. "I keep telling you that treasure business'll ain't no way to go," Wood said.

Mac let the comment go. "So, you think they'll be enough work for me now?"

Wood nodded. "Plenty out there. Just needed to get square with the insurance. You thinkin' about staying?"

Both their eyes were on him. "I just might," he said.

Thanks For Reading

If you liked the book please leave a review:
https://www.amazon.com/Woods-Relic-Travis-Adventures-Book-ebook/dp/B00MI4ZRTK

For more information please check out my web page:
https://stevenbeckerauthor.com/

Or follow me on Facebook:
https://www.facebook.com/stevenbecker.books/

Continue the adventure with Wood's Reef
https://www.amazon.com/Woods-Reef-Travis-Adventures-Book-ebook/dp/B00GXKVWOO

Made in the USA
Columbia, SC
25 August 2017